CW01496659

CHRISTOF

THE CASE OF THE
FLOWERY CORPSE

CHRISTOPHER BUSH was born Charlie Christmas Bush in Norfolk in 1885. His father was a farm labourer and his mother a milliner. In the early years of his childhood he lived with his aunt and uncle in London before returning to Norfolk aged seven, later winning a scholarship to Thetford Grammar School.

As an adult, Bush worked as a schoolmaster for 27 years, pausing only to fight in World War One, until retiring aged 46 in 1931 to be a full-time novelist. His first novel featuring the eccentric Ludovic Travers was published in 1926, and was followed by 62 additional Travers mysteries. These are all to be republished by Dean Street Press.

Christopher Bush fought again in World War Two, and was elected a member of the prestigious Detection Club. He died in 1973.

CHRISTOPHER BUSH

THE CASE OF THE FLOWERY CORPSE

With an introduction
by Curtis Evans

DEAN STREET PRESS

INTRODUCTION

RING OUT THE OLD, RING IN THE NEW
CHRISTOPHER BUSH AND MYSTERY FICTION IN THE FIFTIES

"Mr. Bush has an urbane and intelligent way of dealing with mystery which makes his work much more attractive than the stampeding sensationalism of some of his rivals."
—Rupert Crofts-Cooke (acclaimed author of the Leo Bruce detective novels)

NEW fashions in mystery fiction were decidedly afoot in the 1950s, as authors increasingly turned to sensationalistic tales of international espionage, hard-boiled sex and violence, and psychological suspense. Yet there indubitably remained, seemingly imperishable and eternal, what Anthony Boucher, dean of American mystery reviewers, dubbed the "conventional type of British detective story." This more modestly decorous but still intriguing and enticing mystery fare was most famously and lucratively embodied by Crime Queen Agatha Christie, who rang in the new decade and her Golden Jubilee as a published author with the classic detective novel that was promoted as her fiftieth mystery: *A Murder Is Announced* (although this was in fact a misleading claim, as this tally also included her short story collections). Also representing the traditional British detective story during the 1950s were such crime fiction stalwarts (all of them Christie contemporaries and, like the Queen of Crime, longtime members of the Detection Club) as Edith Caroline Rivett (E.C.R Lorac and Carol Carnac), E.R. Punshon, Cecil John Charles Street (John Rhode and Miles Burton) and Christopher Bush. Punshon and Rivett passed away in the Fifties, pens still brandished in their hands, if you will, but Street and Bush, apparently indefatigable, kept at crime throughout the decade, typically publishing in both the United Kingdom and the United States two books a year (Street with both of his pseudonyms).

Not to be outdone even by Agatha Christie, Bush would celebrate his own Golden Jubilee with his fiftieth mystery, *The Case of the Russian Cross*, in 1957—and this was done, in contrast with Christie, without his publishers having to resort to any creative accounting. *Cross* is the fiftieth Christopher Bush Ludovic Travers detective novel reprinted by Dean Street Press in this, the Spring of 2020, the hundredth anniversary of the dawning of the Golden Age of detective fiction, following, in this latest installment, *The Case of the Counterfeit Colonel* (1952), *The Case of the Burnt Bohemian* (1953), *The Case of The Silken Petticoat* (1953), *The Case of the Red Brunette* (1954), *The Case of the Three Lost Letters* (1954), *The Case of the Benevolent Bookie* (1955), *The Case of the Amateur Actor* (1955), *The Case of the Extra Man* (1956) and *The Case of the Flowery Corpse* (1956).

Not surprisingly, given its being the occasion of Christopher Bush's Golden Jubilee, *The Case of the Russian Cross* met with a favorable reception from reviewers, who found the author's wry dedication especially ingratiating: "The author, having discovered that this is his fiftieth novel of detection, dedicates it in sheer astonishment to HIMSELF." Writing as Francis Iles, the name under which he reviewed crime fiction, Bush's Detection Club colleague Anthony Berkeley, himself one of the great Golden Age innovators in the genre, commented, "I share Mr. Bush's own surprise that *The Case of the Russian Cross* should be his fiftieth book; not so much at the fact itself as at the freshness both of plot and writing which is still as notable with fifty up as it was in in his opening overs. There must be many readers who still enjoy a straightforward, honest-to-goodness puzzle, and here it is." The late crime writer Anthony Lejeune, who would be admitted to the Detection Club in 1963, for his part cheered, "Hats off to Christopher Bush....[L]ike his detective, [he] is unostentatious but always absolutely reliable." Alan Hunter, who recently had published his first George Gently mystery and at the time was being lauded as the "British Simenon," offered similarly praiseful words, pronouncing of *The*

Case of the Russian Cross that Bush's sleuth Ludovic Travers "continues to be a wholly satisfying creation, the characters are intriguing and the plot full of virility. . . . the only trace of long-service lies in the maturity of the treatment."

The high praise for Bush's fiftieth detective novel only confirmed (if resoundingly) what had become clear from reviews of earlier novels from the decade: that in Britain Christopher Bush, who had turned sixty-five in 1950, had become a Grand Old Man of Mystery, an Elder Statesman of Murder. Bush's *The Case of the Three Lost Letters*, for example, was praised by Anthony Berkeley as "a model detective story on classical lines: an original central idea, with a complicated plot to clothe it, plenty of sound, straightforward detection by a mellowed Ludovic Travers and never a word that is not strictly relevant to the story"; while reviewer "Christopher Pym" (English journalist and author Cyril Rotenberg) found the same novel a "beautifully quiet, close-knit problem in deduction very fairly presented and impeccably solved." Berkeley also highly praised Bush's *The Case of the Burnt Bohemian*, pronouncing it "yet another sound piece of work . . . in that, alas!, almost extinct genre, the real detective story, with Ludovic Travers in his very best form."

In the United States Bush was especially praised in smaller newspapers across the country, where, one suspects, traditional detection most strongly still held sway. "Bush is one of the soundest of the English craftsmen in this field," declared Ben B. Johnston, an editor at the *Richmond Times Dispatch*, in his review of *The Case of the Burnt Bohemian*, while Lucy Templeton, doyenne of the *Knoxville Sentinel* (the first female staffer at that Tennessee newspaper, Templeton, a freshly minted graduate of the University of Tennessee, had been hired as a proofreader back in 1904), enthusiastically avowed, in her review of *The Case of the Flowery Corpse*, that the novel was "the best mystery novel I have read in the last six months." Bush "has always told a good story with interesting backgrounds and rich characterization," she added admiringly. Another southern reviewer, one "M." of the *Montgomery Advertiser*, deemed *The Case of the Amateur Actor* "another Travers mystery to delight

the most critical of a reader audience," concluding in inimita-
ble American lingo, "it's a swell story." Even Anthony Boucher,
who in the Fifties hardly could be termed an unalloyed admirer
of conventional British detection, from his prestigious post at
the *New York Times Books Review* afforded words of praise
to a number of Christopher Bush mysteries from the decade,
including the cases of the *Benevolent Bookie* ("a provocative
puzzle"), the *Amateur Actor* ("solid detective interest"), the
Flowery Corpse ("many small ingenuities of detection") and,
but naturally, the *Russian Cross* ("a pretty puzzle"). In his
own self-effacing fashion, it seems that Ludovic Travers had
entered the pantheon of Great Detectives, as another American
commentator suggested in a review of Bush's *The Case of The
Silken Petticoat*:

> Although Ludovic Travers does not possess the
> esoteric learning of Van Dine's Philo Vance, the rough
> and ready punch of Mickey Spillane's Mike Hammer, the
> Parisian [sic!] touch of Agatha Christie's Hercule Poirot,
> the appetite and orchids of Rex Stout's Nero Wolfe, the
> suave coolness of The Falcon or the eerie laugh and
> invisibility of The Shadow, he does have good qualities—
> especially the ability to note and interpret clues and a
> dogged persistence in remembering and following up an
> episode he could not understand. These paid off in his
> solution of *The Case of The Silken Petticoat*.

In some ways Christopher Bush, his traditionalism notwith-
standing, attempted with his Fifties Ludovic Travers mysteries
to keep up with the tenor of rapidly changing times. As owner
of the controlling interest in the Broad Street Detective Agency,
Ludovic Travers increasingly comes to resemble an American private investigator rather than the gentleman amateur
detective he had been in the 1930s; and the novels in which
he appears reflect some of the jaded cynicism of post-World
War Two American hard-boiled crime fiction. *The Case of the
Red Brunette*, one of my favorite examples from this batch
of Bushes, looks at civic corruption in provincial England in

a case concerning a town counsellor who dies in an apparent "badger game" or "honey trap" gone fatally wrong ("a web of mystery skillfully spun" noted Pat McDermott of Iowa's *Quad City Times*), while in *The Case of the Three Lost Letters*, Travers finds himself having to explain to his phlegmatic wife Bernice the pink lipstick strains on his collar (incurred strictly in the line of duty, of course). Travers also pays homage to the popular, genre altering Inspector Maigret novels of Georges Simenon in *The Case of Red Brunette*, when he decides that he will "try to get a feel of the city [of Mainford]: make a Maigret-like tour and achieve some kind of background. . . ."

Christopher Bush finally decided that Travers could manage entirely without his longtime partner in crime solving, the wily and calculatingly avuncular Chief Superintendent George Wharton, whom at times Travers, in the tradition of American hard-boiled crime fiction, appears positively to dislike. "I generally admire and respect Wharton, but there are times when he annoys me almost beyond measure," Travers confides in *The Case of the Amateur Actor*. "There are even moments, as when he assumes that cheap and leering superiority, when I can suddenly hate him." George Wharton appropriately makes his final, brief appearance in the Bush oeuvre in *The Case of the Russian Cross*, where Travers allows that despite their differences, the "Old General" is "the man who'd become in most ways my oldest friend."

"Ring out the old, ring in the new" may have been the motto of many when it came to mid-century mystery fiction, but as another saying goes, what once was old eventually becomes sparklingly new again. The truth of the latter adage is proven by this shining new set of Christopher Bush reissues. "Just like old crimes," vintage mystery fans may sigh contentedly, as once again they peruse the pages of a Bush, pursuing murderous malefactors in the ever pleasant company of Ludovic Travers, all the while armed with the happy knowledge that a butcher's dozen of thirteen of Travers' investigations yet remains to be reissued.

Curtis Evans

PART I
THE AMATEURS

1

Death at the Bend

Do you know the roads of rural Suffolk? It may seem a queer question but, believe me, there's a reason for it. I was born in the county but left it when still in my teens. All the same it's my native county and there're times when I boast about it and claim a knowledge of it. That's why I should have known its rural roads, but I didn't. And the reason was, of course, that all those years ago, roads and lanes were never seen through the eyes of a motorist. I merely walked along them or cycled, and that's a vastly different thing.

I don't include the two main roads from London to Norwich on stretches of which you can travel, if necessary, at almost any speed you like. One of those roads leaves Chelmsford for Braintree and on to Bury St. Edmunds and across the heaths beyond Thetford. The other goes on through Colchester and you can by-pass both it and Ipswich, but what I'm talking about is the country between those two main roads. If you look at a map you will be staggered at their eccentricities: if you drive on them and are in anything of a hurry, you will think that you are experiencing some kind of nightmare.

It isn't the actual surfaces of those minor roads, for by and large they're good by any standard. It's the incredibly winding and casual nature of them that bewilders you, unless you're driving with abundant time on your hands. They twist and they turn, and you have to be careful of the fool who may be round any one of the innumerable corners. Sometimes you can see ahead for as far as two or three hundred yards. It makes a sudden lifting of the spirits and you tell yourself that maybe the corkscrew windings have at last ended. Then you get to the end of that short stretch and your foot goes down on the brake again and you twist and circle till another straight stretch deceptively appears.

And, since there are so many villages clustered between those two main roads that bound that biggish area, there are always side roads. Unless you know the country like the palm of your hand, you have to slow at every fork and consult the direction post. By day that's not so bad but at night you have to stop. If you haven't a torch you can't even read the directions and, if you travel on, it's by guess and by God. I hadn't a torch and that's why I was lost. Not irrevocably lost, mind you: I still had some idea of direction. And I definitely knew where I was when that madman went hurtling by me in his car.

It was the early October of 1955. My wife had just gone to Italy for a month to attend an international conference of a society to which she belongs. There was nothing which Norris, my managing director, couldn't handle at the Broad Street Detective Agency, and I was taking a belated holiday myself. Henry Morle and I had been at Cambridge together and in the years that followed he had always contrived to keep in touch. After a brilliant Civil Service career he had recently been axed by the Sudanese. Soon after his retirement we had lunched together at my club and he had asked me where, if I were he, I would settle down. He was a widower, by the way, with an only daughter married and in Kenya.

I plumped for Suffolk, I said it was off most of the tracks and still largely unspoiled, and, if one wanted an occasional trip to town, well, it wasn't so far away. Two months later I heard from him that he had bought a little place in the village of Marstead, about three miles from Edenthorpe. He liked it there. The people were friendly. There was a nine-hole golf-course reasonably near and more than good enough for his declining powers. Edenthorpe was an excellent shopping centre. He also liked his house—it was called Bendacre—and he had a really reliable woman to see to his needs, and a full-time gardener. Everything in the Suffolk garden, according to that letter, was gratifyingly lovely, and he was begging me to spend a week or two there. It was not till that October, nearly two years later, that I was able to accept.

I also tried to kill two birds with the same stone. We had a client at Norwich whom Norris wanted me to see, so I left town early that morning. It was a fine, autumnal day and I took the left main road through Bury St. Edmunds and Thetford, because I knew I should be taking the other direction when I left Norwich for Marstead. As it happened, I was delayed till the late afternoon and it wasn't very far off dusk when I left the city by the Ipswich road. I had taken the precaution of ringing Henry and saying I shouldn't arrive till nearer seven than six. He advised me to take the main Ipswich turnpike and turn off right at Yoxford, and on to Debenham.

It was a clear night with just a touch of frost when I took that right turn and at once I was among the winding lanes. Luckily they were cats-eyed and driving was fairly easy if one kept between thirty and forty. It was at about six o'clock and not long after I'd crossed the main road from Bury St. Edmunds to Ipswich when I knew I was lost. I pulled up at a farm and I was set right again, and then somehow I got muddled with the multiplicity of directions and took a left turn instead of a right. I consulted the map and then struck matches at the next direction post. I was lucky. It said that Bedham was two miles on, and my map showed that Marstead was two and a half miles on from there.

At Bedham village I came to a T-head and turned sharp right and it was only a minute or two later that things began to happen. It was a dark night, as I said, but clear. The road ran between hedges and was narrow; so narrow, in fact, that it was difficult to keep within the grass verges and the winding line of cats-eyes. I met one car and I slowed almost to a halt so that we should pass with no possibility of a graze. A few seconds later the headlights of an overtaking car were at my rear window. There was the furious sounding of a horn. In a flash that oncoming car was there, and something made me jam on my brakes and swerve towards the verge. But that car was by me before I could really see it. It just touched my off front wing and with a squeal of tyres was out of sight round the immediate bend. If its driver had been doing a mile, he'd been doing sixty.

I'm a mild sort of person as a rule and it takes a good deal to ruffle me, but all at once, as that hurtling car disappeared in its squeal of brakes, I was furiously angry. Whoever was driving that car was either drunk or mad. To do anything over forty on such a road, even at night when one could see from a distance any oncoming lights, was sheer lunacy. But for that instinctive swerve of mine, he'd have ripped away the whole off-side of my car and it might even have been the end of both of us. I was feeling pretty shaky as I stopped the old Bentley and got out. The paint had gone in long streaks from that off wing and that was all, and as I drove slowly on again I knew I'd had a lucky escape.

Mine is a mind that's cursed or blest with an insatiable curiosity and, as the car dawdled on, I was thinking about that lunatic in the car. One thing was certain: he must have known that road with its twists and turns like the path to his own front door. And maybe, after all, there had been some kind of method in his madness. Maybe he had been hurrying to fetch a doctor, or some other urgency had driven him to take such a fantastic and callous risk. I didn't know and I didn't have to worry about not knowing. Ahead of me was just the faintest glow and I slowed as I came round yet another corner. Then I braked hard. A curious blackness was partly across the off side of the road and the lights seemed to be coming from beneath it. I drew the Bentley over on the grass verge and got out to investigate, though I knew what must have happened even before I set foot to the ground.

That car, an almost new Ford by the look of it, was piled up against a scrub oak in the hedge and its front was a shambles. I had to crane up to reach through the near window to switch off the ignition. I had caught a glimpse of the driver and in the sudden darkness I felt down where he lay between steering column and door. I found his arm and ran my hand along it till I came to wrist and pulse. There wasn't a sign of a beat.

In the distant sky were the lights of an oncoming car. I nipped across to the Bentley and, when that car came nearer, flashed my lights off and on. The car came cautiously round the far bend and drew to a halt a few yards short of the crash. I got out. In its headlights I saw a youngish woman.

"God, what a mess!" she said. "Did you see it?"

"I didn't even hear it," I said. "He was going too fast and too far off."

"Anyone hurt?"

"The driver. I think he's dead. The car's over so far we can't get him out. You going on to Bedham?"

She said she was. I asked if she'd warn the police there and she said she'd bring someone back. The lights of her little sports car disappeared round the bend and I heard the whine of its engine, and then everything was incredibly quiet and there was nothing to do but wait. I got back into the Bentley, ready to flash my lights again, but nothing came. Ten minutes and there was a light in the sky behind me. The sports car drew up just short of my own. The Bedham constable was with her.

"Hadn't you better draw up on the verge?"

"I'm going on to Marstead," she said. "I'll be bringing the doctor back. And a breakdown outfit if I can, to get the road clear."

She shot the car on. I was left alone with the constable.

Five minutes later he knew as much as I. The driver was dead—he'd verified that—and he'd held me balanced on the tilted wreck till I could feel in the dead man's pocket. The hand that drew out the wallet and a couple of letters was stained with blood. The constable—Porter was his name—had a look at them in the Bentley's headlights.

"An N. Ranger, Esq., The Briary, Marstead," he said. "I suppose you don't know him, sir?"

"Never heard of him," I said.

He had a look at the contents of the wallet.

"Seems in order," he said. "I did have an idea it might've been someone making a getaway with a stolen car, which'd have been why he was going so fast. Which reminds me. While we're waiting I'd better take down your particulars. Name, sir? You'll be wanted at the inquest."

"The name's Travers."

"And the Christian name?"

"Ludovic."

That shook him for a moment. I had to spell it for him. And I told him what I was doing there.

"Sir Henry Morle," he said. "He'd be the gentleman who's just bought Bendacre. Major Somers used to have it."

He broke off and put away his notebook.

"Two cars. Looks as though that young lady's coming with the doctor. Won't be much good unless we can move that wreck."

The sports car drew up just beyond us on our side of the verge. Porter had told me that its driver was a Miss Dupray from a village called Felworth.

"Sorry I've been so long," she said, "but I had to get Doctor Robert. Doctor Frank was out. A breakdown lorry's coming from Edenthorpe."

The doctor was tall and thin and looked about sixty. I'm six foot three and he wasn't much shorter. He had a dry, explosive sort of voice.

"Know who he is, Porter?"

Porter told him. I saw his face clearly in the full lights of the Bentley. The thin lips suddenly parted in a gape.

"Ranger?" he said. "You're sure?"

"We got these letters and this wallet from his pocket," Porter said. "That's who they say he is."

The doctor gave a grunt. He shook his head with a queer sort of reluctance.

"Better have a look at him. If we can get him out."

I had a spare, portable jack in the boot of my car, and the four of us managed to tilt the Ford up the few inches till the jack was slid under. Another five minutes and we could just open the off door. The body slid partly out and Porter caught it beneath the armpits and dragged it just out to the verge. The doctor flashed his torch and got down on one knee. A few seconds and he was getting to his feet again. All I had seen was the dead man's face as the torch rested on it for the merest second. It was the face of a man of about fifty, horribly distorted with pain.

"It's Ranger all right," the doctor said. "He must have come round that corner at the very hell of a pace."

"Almost certainly drunk," Porter said. "Not that we can be certain."

The doctor seemed, curiously enough, to be aware of myself.

"You saw it?" he asked.

I explained again.

"Morle," he said. "A very charming man. A comparative newcomer. If you're staying for a week or more we may be seeing each other again." He let out a breath. "Nothing to keep me here, Porter. Looks as if the lorry might be coming. The body might as well go back in it. The ambulance can pick it up at Edenthorpe."

He'd left his own car on the comparative straight round the bend. The sports car had left. Porter said he'd let me know about the inquest and I left, too. The breakdown lorry had turned the bend and when it had passed me there were no lights ahead in the clear sky. The doctor, I thought, must also be travelling pretty fast. I wondered about his name. That Miss Dupray had said she hadn't been able to get a Doctor Frank so had brought a Doctor Robert instead. It was Henry Morle who explained all that to me.

I had gone up to Cambridge rather early and Henry late, and that accounted for the difference of six years in our ages. Ours had been the association of two opposites: he short and sturdy and I even leaner, and maybe a little longer, than I am today. In those days too, I was more of the studious type and it was he who had the agile body and enquiring mind. I had few outside interests and he many, and, as far as I'd been able to gather, he differed little from what he had always been.

As for that house of his—Bendacre as it had always been called—it was a timbered, pre-Tudor place that had been lovingly and carefully modernised by its previous owner. It lay in the main street of the village, just set back from the road, and cunningly camouflaged by a shrubbery was a double garage, and behind that about half an acre of walled garden. I drew my car in at the side drive to that garage. Henry must have been listening for me.

"Here you are," he said. "I was getting quite worried."

He might be one of the most imperturbable people I've ever known, but I was an hour late, and I guessed he knew those tricky Suffolk lanes. While I was garaging the car I told him what had happened.

"Ranger?" he said, and gave me a quick, peering sort of look. That doctor, I remembered, had looked a bit startled too.

"You know him?" I said.

He temporised.

"Well, just as everybody in a village knows everyone else. He had a bungalow just along the road."

He took the golf bag and I the one big suitcase. I was thinking there must be something queer about the man Ranger. Neither the doctor nor Henry had expressed the slightest regret. Each, unless I was wildly exaggerating, had seemed to accept the tragic accident as something in the nature of the inevitable. Maybe Ranger was a heavy drinker. Maybe he'd had a record as a dangerous driver. And yet that didn't quite explain it.

Dinner was ready to put on and there was no time for more than a quick clean-up in the bathroom. We had short drinks in the lounge. Henry said he was delighted to see me and I that I was delighted to come. But I hoped he wouldn't make any fuss. A few days' rustication would suit me down to the ground.

Dinner was in a smallish dining-room that had its original panelling and some beautifully moulded beams. Mrs. Slack—Edith, as Henry called her—brought in the soup and I was introduced. She was a thinnish woman of about fifty; quiet in manner but pleasant-looking when she smiled. Henry had inherited her from the previous owner. She and her husband—Joe—occupied a small cottage at the far end of the walled garden.

It was a good meal and we had some excellent wine with it, and later a really good port. When we'd installed ourselves comfortably by the lounge fire I thought I might at last get back to Ranger. I asked if he was a heavy drinker.

"Well, not particularly," he said. "I don't say he didn't drink, but I never heard that he couldn't carry it. He was just damned cantankerous by nature. Well, not that, perhaps. Irish and always spoiling for a fight. Putting the local backs up."

"What was he actually?"

"He wasn't anything," Henry said. "I suppose he had private means. None of the local people liked to play golf with him. He'd a genius for making himself unpopular. He got in bad with the Bridge Club at Edenthorpe too. And there was some sort of flare-up with our doctor."

"And how'd you get on with him?"

Henry laughed.

"I didn't. He called on me one morning by way of politeness but I'd been warned. I wasn't rude, of course. I just didn't encourage him. A pity he was such an enemy to himself. He was quite an attractive chap in some ways: good-looking in a rakish sort of way. Quite charming manners, but very much on the surface, if you know what I mean."

"How old?"

"Hard to say. Probably the late forties."

And then he gave me one of those quizzical smiles of his.

"You seem to be taking more than an academic interest. You're not scenting a crime or anything like that?"

"Heavens, no," I said. "Just that insatiable curiosity of mine. After all, I was somewhat involved in the poor devil's death."

"A pity", he said, and then chuckled at my look of surprise. "I don't mean about the death and your being involved. I mean about the possibility of a crime. I'd rather have liked to see you at work."

I told him that if I'd known, I'd have brought my deer-stalker, fingerprint set and a magnifying glass—just in case. "But tell me something," I said, "and still just to satisfy my curiosity. Both you and the doctor seemed—what shall I say—just a bit intrigued to learn that it was this chap Ranger who'd been killed. Was it because quite a few people wouldn't have minded seeing him dead?"

"Callous—and blunt," Henry said amusedly. "Now I come to think it over, I have an idea you're right. I won't say, mind you, that any of us ever thought in terms of *wanting* him dead. I will say I can't think of many who'll be upset about his death."

"Well, that much is ferreted out," I told him. "But where do you collect your gossip, Henry?"

"Collect it, my dear fellow? I thought you were a country-man."

"Only by birth," I said. "I'm a townsman by adoption and grace."

"You disappoint me," he said. "I'm only a countryman by adoption, so to speak, but I don't have to hunt for village gossip. I sit here and it comes to me."

"Your married couple?"

"Exactly. What Edith doesn't tell me, Joe does. A few more weeks and I might even be able to make quite a respectable income from blackmail." He gave me that quizzical smile again. "If anything did go wrong in Marstead, you and I could make quite a team. Me with my knowledge and you with the technique."

"You lay yourself out to be the perfect host," I said, "and maybe I'll do something about it. Any particular person you'd like murdered?"

"Don't hurry me," he said. "It's something that requires thought. There is Joe, perhaps. He seems to have taken posses-sion of the garden. I'm not allowed to have even a say in it."

"Fine," I said. "I'll run my eye over him in the morning."

It was after midnight when we went up to bed. We'd yarned about old times and grown a bit melancholy over too much whisky. Under the influence of the same whisky he'd put me pontifically wise to the set-up in the Soudan and I was just as pontifical over Scotland Yard and the present state of crime. But, at the bottom of it all, we were really delighted to be in each other's company and with a week to which to look forward.

He looked into my room to see I had everything I wanted. I was just about to draw the blinds but a young moon was rising and I could see clearly the open rise of land. Slightly to the left there was a light in what looked like a downstairs window.

"Someone else seems to be keeping late hours," I said.

Henry had a look.

"That'll be Colonel Sterne," he said. "He's secretary of the Bridge Club at Edenthorpe and he'll just have got in. You're playing golf with him tomorrow, by the way. The afternoon. Better then than the morning. If there's a frost, the bite'll be out of the ground. I wanted the doctor for the fourth but he's got some meeting or other, so I fixed up with the rector."

I envied Henry as I lay the few moments waiting for sleep. It wasn't the whisky that told me that a life in the country was the only one. Friendly people and everyone knowing everyone else. Idyllic compared with town, where one's friends were little more than acquaintances, and then within the walls of one's club. Henry, just a short time in Marstead, and already with a finger well on the village pulse. The thoughts wandered finally in that hazy romance and then I dropped off to sleep. But when I woke in the morning I was not harking back to envious thoughts of Henry: I was thinking of that poor devil Ranger. I wondered if the doctor had done a post-mortem and if I could contrive somehow to ring him and to learn what alcohol there had been in the stomach content. Then I remembered that I'd have to attend the inquest, and suddenly Ranger was a kind of jarring intrusion in what ought to be a superb holiday, and I tried to put him out of my mind.

2

BURGLARY ON THE SIDE

JUST before eight o'clock Edith Slack brought me tea. Breakfast was at half-past so I got out of bed. When I drew back the curtains I saw that the fields beyond the walled garden were rimed with frost. There was the movement of a car away to my left and I could discern a side road and that largish house from one of whose downstairs windows I had seen a light the previous night. In front of me and stretching away to the right was a wood and, altogether, the view was of pleasant, homely sort of country, with oaks still green, and here and there a distant roof towards the rise of ground. There was the yellow of stacks: fields still with their stubbles and fields ploughed, and others with the bright green of sugar-beet, so that the whole lay spread like a gay counterpane. Over all was a faint autumnal mist and the sun was almost through the clouds.

By the time breakfast was over, the sun was definitely through and Henry said the forecast had been of fine weather for the next few days. He proposed an exploratory walk through the village, but first I wanted to have a good look at the house itself. Then we went into the walled garden. Joe Slack, the gardener, was rough-digging some ground against the winter. He was a short, thickly built man of about sixty and he was lifting those spade-fuls of solid soil and turning them over as if they weighed ounces instead of pounds. He paused to give a respectful touch of the cap as we came up. Henry introduced me as a Suffolk man and Joe's head went sideways like a blackbird listening on a lawn.

"What part, sir?"

I told him. He allowed that it wasn't too bad a part.

"Suppose you hain't heerd about the burglary, sir?" he said to Henry. "They tell me there was someone in there yesterday evenin' and Alice disturbed 'em."

"News to me," Henry said. "You knew Mr. Ranger got killed in an accident?"

Joe grunted as if that news had on it the dust of ages.

"That's the funny thing," he said. "Here's him go and get hisself killed while someone's tryin' to burgle his house. Not that he ever had a lot in it, so they tell me—not worth burglarin'." A sort of private smile went across his weather-beaten face. "Unless it was some o' that Irish whisky what he allust drink."

Henry said it was certainly queer. Joe bent again to his digging and we moved back towards the house.

"Amazing," Henry said. "Talk about the bush-telegraph and African drums and smoke signals—these Marstead fellows have got them all beaten. How they get hold of the news bewilders me."

"Who was the 'Alice' he mentioned?"

"That'd be Alice Gantle. She's a widow who lives in the nearest cottage and looks after Ranger—more or less."

He stopped for a moment.

"As Joe said, it's queer. There haven't been any burglaries since I've been here. Must have been some kind of sneak thief."

I had to laugh.

"I suppose there's nothing to stop us walking round that way and getting the details on the spot?"

Henry laughed too. It was probably shameless, he said, but townsmen like me didn't appreciate the fact that in a village anyone's news was everyone's news.

"Then we'll both be shameless," I said. "Which way do we start off for this walk?"

We went along the Pinfold Road, past a farm and a couple of cottages. The small Georgian house on our right, he said, belonged to some people named Black. He suffered from wife trouble and from too much elbow-lifting.

We took a stile just short of Colonel Sterne's house. His looked a nice, medium-sized property and well kept.

"I thought we'd go across the fields," Henry said, "because of the frost. The path'll be pretty sticky when this sun gets at it."

"No scandal about Sterne?" I said.

Henry chuckled.

"Not so far as I know. He's a bachelor—a Canadian, though he's lost most of his accent. A quiet sort of chap. Had a bad time in Korea. A prisoner for two years. That's why he's retired. He isn't all that old. But if you really want scandal, then the Blacks are your people. He's a Major—retired. Probably axed."

He broke off to give me one of those looks of his.

"It's very refreshing, you know, to be able to pass on village scandal. I'm usually strictly a receiver, never a transmitter."

"I love it," I said. "It's refreshing for me too. A sort of Lord-I-thank-Thee-I'm-not-as-this-publican."

"Then we're both happy," he said. "But about Black: to put it charitably, he drinks like a fish. A tragedy, really. Once or twice when he was reasonably sober I found him quite a decent, well-bred sort of chap. His wife's much younger—a good-looking woman, and, they say, a regular fly-by-night. A tail-swisher they used to call it in my young days. But here's a curious thing: who do you think the present man in favour happened to be?"

"Ranger?"

He stared.

"How'd you guess that?"

"He's the only man here about whom I know anything at all," I said. "The only man about whom you could speak as something being curious."

"Of course," he said. "I ought to have thought of that. And your logical mind. But about Mrs. Black and Ranger. They've been seen pretty far afield—at Ipswich, for instance. The trouble about discretion of that kind is that it isn't discretion at all. There're regular buses from here and people are always going to Ipswich."

We were practically through the wood and I could see the stile ahead.

"On the left, there," Henry said. "That's Ranger's bungalow. I believe it's called The Briary."

His hand gripped my arm.

"There's Warner, our local constable. Looks as though he's waiting for somebody."

"He may be there to keep the curious away."

"Don't think so," he said. "Villagers don't have that open kind of curiosity."

"Suppose we ask him," I said maliciously.

"You're right," he said. "I think we will."

Warner—tall, burly, red-faced—flicked a hand to his helmet as we came up. Henry was certainly right in that matter of curiosity. There wasn't another soul in sight; there was only a tractor that was emerging from a farm track that lay just ahead on the Edenthorpe Road.

"Bad news about Mr. Ranger," was Henry's opening gambit.

"Yes, sir. A nasty business," Warner said. "They tell me he wasn't a pretty sight."

He'd been casting a sideways look or two at me. Henry introduced me.

"You're the gentleman who's staying with Sir Henry here," Warner told me, and gave me a huge hand. "The one that reported the accident. Must have been a bit of a shock for you, sir."

"Lucky he happened to be there," cut in Henry. "You just having a walk round, Warner, or what?"

"The fact is, sir, I'm waiting for my Inspector from Edenthorpe. Keep it under your hat, but Alice reported a burglary last night and I had to notify it. I couldn't see any signs of entry myself but—" He broke off. "Here the Inspector is now."

He straightened himself. Henry and I shamelessly stood our ground. The police car drew to a halt just in front of us, and Warner again flicked a finger to his helmet and opened the door. A tall, well-built man got out. He had a back like a ramrod and "copper" was written all over him. A plain-clothes man got out too.

"Morning, Warner. What's all this—"

He broke off and his eyes narrowed as he gave me a look. A tentative smile appeared.

"Excuse me, sir, but isn't your name Travers?"

"It is, Inspector. Do we know each other?"

"I certainly know you, sir," he said, and explained why. It's often like that with me. The Yard has employed me for so many years as what might be hyperbolically called "an unofficial expert", and since that so often involves giving evidence at the Old Bailey and elsewhere, I'm always running across police officers who know me. There was a definite warmth in our handshake.

"Come to think of it, sir, aren't you the one who reported the accident to Mr. Ranger?"

I went over it all again and I introduced Henry. Inspector Tagg, or that was my guess, knew all about him.

"And what're you here for?" I asked Tagg. "An enquiry into the accident?"

"As a matter of fact, yes and no," he said. "There's a question of burglary as well."

"Curious?" I said. "I suppose it's too much to ask if we might go along?"

"Why not?" he said. "Pity it isn't something more serious, then I might pick your brains."

It was a brick-built bungalow of the usual four rooms: not a bad property, though the garden was in poor shape. The wooden garage, built as a lean-to, had its door wide open.

"About Ranger," I said. "Was there much alcohol in the stomach?"

"To tell the truth," he said, and gave a look back at Henry who was tagging along behind, "I don't really know. The Doc's being a bit secretive. I don't think he's satisfied. Don't say a word, but I believe the organs have gone to the county analyst."

He gave a tap at the front door and we went through to a tiny hall. A woman appeared at once, wiping her hands on an apron. She was well over sixty but upright and rosy-cheeked. Her grey hair straggled in damp wisps across her forehead. As soon as she began speaking, it was obvious she was Suffolk born and bred. Tagg introduced himself.

"Better come in here, in the lounge," she said. "I was just tidyin' up the kitchen. I hate dirt, even if there ain't no one to see it, as you might say."

It was quite a large lounge, and plenty of room for the six of us, even if we couldn't all sit. The furnishings looked comfortable but there was nothing in that room I'd have had as a gift, except a very nice oak farmhouse bureau with rare Sheraton shell decoration on its outside flap.

Tagg had an excellent bedside manner. I'm sure he wasn't spreading himself for my benefit, but he soon had Alice Gantle at ease. What he'd like to get, he said, was a picture of the whole of the previous day, so that the evening burglary could fit into its proper place and time.

"Just tell us in your own words anything you did here yesterday," he told her.

"Well, sir," she said, "as you may know or not know, I've been workin' for Mr. Ranger ever since he've been here, and that's the last eighteen months. He gets his own breakfast and I come in about ten and clean up and get his lunch if he's goin' to be in, only when I got here yesterday he was out and he hadn't left no message."

"You knew he was out because the garage was empty?"

"Well, yes," she said. "And I did what I allust do and when it was gettin' on for twelve and he hadn't come, I put out some cold meat and tomatoes and cheese and so on, and then, just as I was goin', who should come to the front door but Major Black."

"Just a moment." Tagg turned to Warner. "Who's Major Black?"

Warner explained, but he made no mention of a wife. Mrs. Gantle went on with her story.

"He wanted to see Mr. Ranger so I told him he was out and I didn't know when he'd be back and he said he'd wait. Well, sir, I didn't know what to do. Then I thought that Major Black was a gentleman who might be left, and I told him if Mr. Ranger didn't come in, he was to go out by the back way. That'd be his way home across the path."

"I see. And when did you come back here?"

"The same time I allust do," she said. "Just before six. I make Mr. Ranger his meal and wash up after it, and then I go home. Only as soon as I opened the front door I thought I heard a noise here in the lounge and my heart went clean into my mouth. I come over all of a tremble. 'Who's there?' I say, and then I heard like as if someone was movin' and another noise like someone shuttin' a window. I nearly ran out o' the house myself and then I plucked up courage, thinkin' perhaps it might be Mr. Ranger hisself, and I switched on the light and there wasn't no one here. And there wasn't no one in the other rooms neither."

"And yet you thought there'd been a burglar?"

"Yes," she said, "and I'll tell you for why. I went out to the garage and the car wasn't there, so it couldn't have been Mr. Ranger. And then I saw that someone had been interferin' with that bureau there. One of the drawers was open and there was things on the floor. Then, when Mr. Warner come, he found that window off the catch. I'm sure it wasn't like that when I left in the mornin'. I'd dusted this room, and when I dust, I dust, though I say it."

"You think Major Black might have opened it for some reason or other?"

She looked surprised.

"What should he open a window for, sir? It wasn't as though it was stuffy or anything. The fire weren't lit. It was only laid."

"Of course," Tagg said. "But about Mr. Ranger: do you think he came back here during the day?"

"I know he did," she said. "He allust have his meals in the kitchen. It's warmer there with the stove, and save work, and he don't have to light the fire if he's goin' out again. I know he'd been in and gone again because he'd best part of cleaned up his lunch."

Tagg looked a bit flummoxed. He harked back to the burglary. Had anyone been in the other rooms? Mrs. Gantle said there hadn't—not that she could see.

"I put everything back in that bureau and soon had everything straight again."

I saw Tagg's frown. He was thinking in terms of fingerprints.

"Anything else unusual in the room, was there?"

"Well—no. Not really."

Tagg knew there was something. The hesitation had told him that.

"You're sure?" he said. "Everything you're telling us is strictly confidential. It won't go any further."

"Well then," she said, "there was the whisky."

"Whisky?"

"Well, yes," she said. "I know you won't mention this but they do say in the village that Major Black drinks."

Tagg nodded knowingly.

"And when I left in the mornin' I knew I'd left the decanter half full. It's in the kitchen now because I've been washin' it. But when I come back last night it was empty."

"Where was the decanter when you left at midday?"

She pointed to the small reproduction Sheraton sideboard.

"It allust stood on there and any bottles was kept in the cupboard underneath. Mr. Ranger allust emptied the bottles into the decanter and there was glasses in the cupboard and fresh water. He didn't like his whisky except with water and he didn't have to worry about me 'cause he knew I hated the stuff. Even if I hadn't I wouldn't have took it. He knew that."

Tagg slipped on his gloves and went across to the sideboard. He opened one of its cupboards and took out an empty whisky bottle. I knew it was empty because he tip-tilted it against the light.

"Irish whisky," he said.

"That's right, sir. He was Irish hisself as he allust said. He never drunk nothin' else but that Irish whisky. Never had beer nor nothin'."

"Right," Tagg said. "What about relations? Ever hear him mention any?"

"Never, sir. I think he was alone, as they say."

"And you haven't the faintest idea where he might have gone to yesterday morning?"

She knew nothing. Tagg said he'd trouble her no further—for the moment, but she'd better let Warner have all the keys. The fingerprint man was to get to work and check for footprints outside that window. A shake of Mrs. Gantle's hand and he went out, the three of us at his heels. He didn't say another word till we were out on the road.

"Where's this Major Black live, Warner?"

Warner told him.

"Right," Tagg said. "I'll have a word with him straight away. You have a general look round."

"We'll get on with our walk," I told him. "Thanks for letting us sit in."

"Nothing to it," he said. "How long're you going to be here?"

"If I don't make myself too objectionable to Sir Henry, here, somewhere about a week."

"Then I might be seeing you again," he said, and held out his hand.

We were going round by the church, according to Henry: more interesting than straight back by the village street. We crossed the road and from the land up there by the north, we had a view of a rather spacious meadow, the lower half of which was the sports ground. The goalposts were up and, nearer, hurdles enclosed the cricket pitch.

My eye caught all that as we turned into the lane. Henry was giving a kind of furtive look back and then he held me by the arm. That's a trick of his, due, I suppose, to a sedentary life. He's given judgments and argued points from a sitting position for so long that he has to come to a halt when he knows himself approaching some mental climax.

"What'd you think of that business in there?" he asked me.

"Don't know," I said. "It does seem a bit of a coincidence that someone should be burgling Ranger's bungalow while he was getting himself killed."

"I know," he said, and just a trifle impatiently. "But that chap Black. What was he calling on Ranger for? They weren't on speaking terms."

What could I do but shrug my shoulders?

"And who drank that whisky?"

"Ranger did," I said. "He had a belated lunch, didn't he?" And that brought an idea. "That whisky contributed to the way he was driving."

"You think he drank over half a decanter?"

I had to laugh.

"Henry, what about the beam in your eye? Much as I regret to remind you, you and I made a sad example of a whole decanter last night. I'm perfectly horrified when I think of it."

"But you and I weren't tight, or anything resembling it," he told me indignantly.

"Admitted. Our reasoning powers were superb. But what should we have been like if we'd tried to drive a car?"

He hadn't an answer to that, and somehow or other we had begun walking slowly on. Then he stopped again. He waved a vague hand towards that farm beyond Ranger's bungalow.

"Everywhere one goes this morning one runs up against Ranger," he told me. "That's Culver's farm and old Culver's quite a tough specimen. He told Ranger that if he caught him setting foot on his land he'd kick him off, or words to that effect, as they say. And he could have done it."

I wanted to know what Ranger had done.

"Helped himself to some straw for his strawberry bed," Henry said. "It was some unbaled stuff that was lying about and Ranger said he didn't think it even worth the asking about. Then Ranger got his own back. There's a law, largely disregarded, about tractors and trailers leaving mud from their wheels all over the highway. Culver's a pretty careless old devil and he'd made a sad mess of the road just out of the farm there, and Ranger reported it and Culver was fined."

"And me thinking how peaceful things were down here," I said.

"Just little ripples on the surface," Henry said as we passed the Green Man. "A very well conducted pub, so I'm told. Much patronised by Ranger. And by old Culver. In fact, that's where, according to Joe, they had their stand-up row. You'd like a quick look in the church? Afraid those iconoclasts in Cromwell's time made a sad mess of it."

We spent a few minutes in the church—a fourteenth-century building that must have been exquisite before that wanton destruction of much of its carved stone and woodwork. I could have stayed longer, but lunch was at half-past twelve and already the children were out of school. Then by almost the last cottage that faced the green, Henry stopped again. A car was drawn up by the gate and a man was coming down the short path. I recognised him. Henry called as he came to the car.

"Morning, doctor. How are you?"

"Rather too busy. Sorry about this afternoon. I'd have liked a round."

"Some other time," Henry said. "You don't know my friend Travers, do you? Ludo, this is Doctor Laving."

"We've met," I said. "Last night."

The doctor frowned.

"I think you must be wrong."

"Good lord, no," I said, and very patiently. "Last night on the road from Bedham. The accident to a man named Ranger."

He shook his head.

"I'm still afraid you're wrong."

It was incredible. Why the devil he had to deny it I couldn't for the life of me think. And perhaps I was just a bit too touchy, thinking I was in some queer way being made a fool.

"But I did see you," I said.

The thin lips stretched to a smile.

"Like to bet me a pound?"

I began hauling out my wallet. Henry laughed.

"You're not the first one who's made that mistake," he said. "This is Frank Laving. It was his brother Robert you met last night."

All I could do was look the fool I'd actually been. Or had I? The doctor gave a dry smile.

"You've swindled me out of a pound," he told Henry. "You staying here long, Mr. Travers?"

He went up towards the church, and we in the direction of the school.

"I saw you were getting into deep water," Henry said, "but I didn't step in till I thought you were out of your depth. Identical twins, those two doctors. I wasn't too sure till I'd been here some time which one I was talking to myself."

"They're in partnership?"

"Yes," he said. "Frank is here and his brother's at Edenthorpe. Pretty dry sticks, both of them. Frank's rather the more peppery. He's the one who had a flare-up with Ranger. I'll tell you about it at lunch."

3

A QUESTION OF MURDER

BY THE time we reached the house I'd seen practically all the village except the stretch of the main road between Bendacre and The Briary, and, of course, outlying cottages and farms. The guide-book had already told me that the population was about a thousand.

Lunch was on as soon as we were in. We were just tackling some excellent Stilton when Edith announced that Inspector Tagg wanted to see me. He was in the hall. Henry looked at me rather longingly as I went out.

"Sorry to trouble you, sir," Tagg said, "but there's been an unusual development. You heard me say I was going along to see that Major Black? Well, he wasn't there. His wife says he hasn't been home all night."

"Really?" I said. "And it's the first time it's happened?"

"According to her—yes. He's been brought home from Edenthorpe and elsewhere in the early hours—she didn't make any bones about telling me that—but this is the first time he's been out all night. And the funny thing is, his car's still in the garage."

"Couldn't he have gone somewhere by bus?"

"Yes," he said doubtfully, "but look, sir: I've picked up quite a lot since I saw you and I'll put my cards on the table. Mrs. Black admitted she and her husband had had more than one row over her and Ranger, though she says there was nothing in it and Black was the jealous type. Apparently the Blacks are living together just on sufferance, so to speak. But there was another row yesterday morning and her husband said he was going to settle with Ranger once and for all. She told him if he wanted to make a fool of himself he was to go ahead and do it. Then at about half-past ten she took the car to Edenthorpe and did one or two things, and got back just about twelve o'clock. Her husband was then at Ranger's place, as we know. And that was the last seen of him."

"It's still all capable of explanation," I said. "You'll admit that?"

"It is and it isn't," he told me doggedly. "Too many things happening at the same time."

"There's just one thing: has Mrs. Black reported officially now about her husband's disappearance?"

"The way we left it was that if he hadn't turned up by tomorrow morning, then he might be regarded as officially missing. I promised to ring her."

That was all there was to say. I had nothing to suggest and, as he admitted, Black was entitled to be absent if he so wished. We said we'd probably be seeing each other again, and then I went back to the dining-room. I was practically sure that Henry had listened to every word. In fact, I challenged him and he admitted he'd heard quite a lot.

"My own idea is that he's left her," he told me. "They've been on cat-and-dog terms for quite a time now, according to one of Joe's numerous friends. He lives in the far cottage, almost on their doorstep."

"Surely *she* should have left *him*?"

"He has the money, or so I'm told. She's the second wife, by the way. The other died just before he came here, about three years ago. The village has it that this one was a mannequin or something in one of the big London stores. My own idea is that she's a most attractive woman in a hard, modern way—and not exactly off the top shelf."

Ranger's death had certainly stirred up a peaceful village. As I told Henry, it was as if someone had poked a stick into a wasps' nest.

"That reminds me: what was that about a flare-up between Ranger and your doctor?"

Henry smiled.

"Amusing in rather an odd way. Alice—Mrs. Gantle—had been to the doctor for something or other, it appears, and Ranger enquired about her. He got her to bring him the medicine and sniffed at it and took a sip and so on, and told her to pour it down the drain. He advised her to buy something else—I don't know what it was—from the chemist at Edenthorpe, but the funny part is that the fool of a woman did everything he told her and when the doctor met her soon afterwards and asked why she hadn't been to see him again as arranged, damned if she didn't tell him what Ranger had said and done and all about it. He was absolutely furious. According to the village, he went straight to Ranger and talked about having the law on him. Ranger's supposed to have called him an incompetent fool. That's just gossip, of course."

"But with a basis of truth?"

"Most certainly. Undoubtedly there was a pretty heated interview—Frank Laving doesn't mince his words. And when Ranger was flinging epithets about he wasn't very discriminate either. Oh, and something else: after that episode, Ranger was nicknamed 'the Doctor'. It was quite a village joke."

Maybe Henry saw something more subtle in it, or perhaps the whole thing had certain nuances which I had failed to catch, but he gave me an apologetic smile. "You must pardon our *naïveté*; it doesn't take much to raise a laugh down here in the long grass."

Henry was taking the four of us to golf in his practically new car. It was a high-class job, but then he's a fairly wealthy man for these times, though one would never guess it from his quiet friendliness of manner and his unostentatious way of life. The rector—Andover—had walked down to join Colonel Sterne and it was at Sterne's house that we picked them up. Sterne was about six feet and thin almost to emaciation, though that emaciated look came partly from his hollow jaws and deep-set brown eyes. A bullet had gone clean through both jaws—he had been captured almost immediately afterwards—and lack of proper treatment had accentuated the scars. Henry had warned me about all that, not that those badly scarred cheeks were in any way repulsive. Sterne, he thought, was somewhat sensitive about them. He was a quiet, modest sort of chap, Henry said, and added that in his own experience, bachelors generally were.

Andover was a huge man: six feet of him and shoulders like the end of a barn. Sterne was wearing grey corduroy bags and a brown sports coat: Andover's garments could only be called highly unecclesiastical—old, reddish plus-fours, a canary pull-over, a green tie and a coat on the checks of which one might at a pinch have played chess. He had a hearty, booming laugh and was said to be a great one for a joke.

I was playing with him, which was why Henry had made me sit with him in the back.

"The last time I saw him play," Henry said, referring to me, "he was pretty devastating."

"The sort of partner I want," Andover said. "I think this afternoon it'll be a case of the church triumphant."

"Don't know about that," Henry said. "It may be the church militant. I've got half-a-crown that says it won't be anything more. What d'you say, Colonel?"

Sterne gave a dry smile.

"A half-crown, by all means, but—well, I guess I'm a bit scared about unknown quantities. We might regard this as a try-out and come to the real stuff later in the week."

Henry had told me he was Canadian born but there wasn't all that accent. It was a pleasant, cultured voice with just a touch of accent to give it individuality. But the car was already slowing. The lane wound towards the north and we were now equidistant from Marstead and Edenthorpe. It was Edenthorpe that largely kept that nine-hole course going. There was no club-house except a large shed, but the funds were enough for a working pro.

It was a grand afternoon. Henry and the Colonel were short but deadly straight: the sort of opponents that nag at you till you hit too hard and begin making mistakes. Andover, like myself, hit the very devil of a long ball: the direction it took was quite another matter. Details don't matter, either, but they beat us five and three and it might easily have been more. What was to matter was what I learned about Ranger. Henry hadn't a monopoly of village gossip.

If you're anything of a golfer you'll know that in a four-ball match you're as likely to be walking with one of your opponents as with your partner. When my ball happened to have gone in the direction of the Colonel's, I tried straight away to get to the subject of Ranger. I won't say he was reticent: it was rather as if he preferred to speak little, since he couldn't speak well, of the dead. He did admit that he knew no one, except possibly Mrs. Gantle, who'd regret his going.

"I saw practically nothing of him, except at our Duplicate Bridge Club," he said. "I think there was a kink in him somewhere. He was always trailing his coat. Perhaps what they call an inferiority complex, if that isn't too old-fashioned a term."

Andover was much more outspoken. He didn't say the village was well rid of him: only that he was the sort of person who'd never fitted.

"Why did he come here?"

"Why do people come?" he said. "He played golf and bridge and that may have attracted him. But he was out of place, and I don't mean because he was virtually the stage type of Irishman." He shrugged his huge shoulders. "The man was a mystery. He never let out a single thing that I ever heard about himself—where his money came from or what he'd done. Not a thing. Mind you, I was deceived about him at first. I think everyone was. He struck us as genial and interesting and obviously a man of the world. He was quite accepted and then he suddenly changed." He smiled. "It reminds me of some of those things my wife will get led away into buying at auctions. Wonderful when she gets 'em home. After that you often never see 'em again. Not a good analogy, I fear, but perhaps you follow what I mean."

"He set out deliberately to ingratiate himself?"

"Exactly. Or that's how it seemed to me later on."

While we were looking for a ball of mine temporarily lost in the gorse—the enemy were doing the same on the other side of the fairway—I managed to bring in what I had heard about Ranger's being not too popular at the Bridge Club. I wondered why he hadn't been quietly asked to resign.

"He had the hide of a rhinoceros," Andover told me, "besides, the Colonel's too easy-going. He's the secretary, you know."

"Wasn't there some big row or other?"

"Yes," he said. "It's confidential, in a way."

It concerned the doctor—the Marstead partner, Frank Laving—who was an active member of the Club. I heard again the affair of Alice Gantle and the medicine she poured down the sink, and because it was the natural preliminary to the other affair. Ranger, it appeared, had been playing with Laving on a certain night—a reshuffle of partners owing to absences—and Ranger had accused Laving of grossly undercalling a hand. He said it had been deliberate and that Laving had been playing the fool, as he called it, all night. Ranger's final retort in the heated argument was understood by most of those present.

"As a bridge player, Laving, you're a damn good doctor. Maybe it's the other way about, too."

It appeared we were all having tea with Sterne. His was a comfortable modern house built between the wars, and from its front windows one had a grand view along the valley through which ran the Bedham road. His woman and part-time man lived in a nearby cottage. He wasn't much interested in gardens, he told me; bridge was his hobby, and he also did quite a lot of reading. His tastes seemed catholic enough, judging by the numerous paperbacks on the overflowing shelves that filled the fireside embrasures of the lounge. Some argument or other between him and Henry brought up the question of ages, and it turned out that Sterne was as near fifty as makes no difference. The badger-grey hair and the thinness made him look older. Andover, on the other hand, also owned up to fifty and I'd have put him much younger. But he was easily the oldest inhabitant among Henry's set: fifteen years as incumbent against Sterne's mere two years of residence and Frank Laving's ten.

We didn't as much as mention Ranger. Henry had told me that Sterne was rather shy of mentioning his war experiences but we did get him to tell us about his life as a prisoner of the Chinese. It was Andover who broke up the party—he had a meeting at six. More golf was fixed for the Thursday and Sterne promised to come to dinner and bridge. Andover didn't play. Frank Laving, I gathered, would be asked to make a fourth.

Henry was looking forward to chess. Apparently he thought that I'd kept up my playing and he put me down as cunning when I said I hadn't played for years and wouldn't even give him the beginnings of a game. But mine isn't the chess kind of brain. Somehow I've got to the stage when anything is abhorrent that makes too great demands on concentrative powers. Mine's more of a crossword brain. Give me quick changes of problems and as quick results.

As it happened, we didn't play. We had almost finished the meal when I was called to the telephone. I thought it might be Norris, ringing in connection with something urgent that had cropped up at the Agency, but it was Inspector Tagg.

"Sorry to trouble you, sir, especially at this time o' night, but could you possibly run over to Edenthorpe for a few minutes? The Chiefs here and something's turned up about which he'd like a word with you."

I said it was rather sudden. Could he tell me what it was that had turned up? He said he couldn't over the telephone, but it was urgent. And apparently he was taking it for granted that I'd be coming at once. Henry seemed almost pleased about it all.

"They've found something out," he said. "What do you think it is? About Major Black? Or that burglary?"

I hadn't a notion. But Tagg's Chief Constable couldn't be bringing me to Edenthorpe just for the sake of whatever I had in the way of *beaux yeux*. I didn't tell Henry so, but it looked to me as if there'd been something remarkably unusual about the death of Norman Ranger.

I didn't wait for coffee. Edenthorpe was only ten minutes away and the police-station easy enough to find. The man on duty took me upstairs to Tagg's room. Robert Laving was there too. I couldn't have told him from his brother if he hadn't been introduced by his Christian name.

Bestable, the Chief Constable, was the kind I like: not a figure-headed title, but a man who'd evidently come up the hard way. It was quite embarrassingly that he thanked me for coming. And he was sure I'd realise that I hadn't been dragged away from Marstead without an excellent reason.

"We're having coffee and something to eat in a minute, but perhaps you'll give Mr. Travers an idea what it's all about, Doctor."

Laving smiled dryly. It was curious, I thought, how perfectly these twin brothers had been cast in the same acidulous mould.

"We've got either a case of accidental death on our hands," he told me, "or a case of murder."

I'm afraid I stared. How could Ranger have been murdered? Or was I to hear about Black?

"You didn't actually see the man Ranger at close quarters," he went on. "Would you care to see him now?"

I almost said hastily that morgues were not in my line. What I did say was that I'd see him later if he thought it necessary and meanwhile I'd take his opinion for granted.

"The cause of death was multiple injuries. Simplify it and say a broken neck. It was the contributory cause that's the problem. You can even say that what actually killed him was poisoning by atropine."

"Good lord!" I said. Something was telling me I should have had at least a possible idea why Ranger had hurtled so uncontrollably by me in the dark. "Taken in alcohol, was it?"

"That's right," Laving said. "But not what you'd call an inordinate quantity."

"I expect you've had experience of atropine poisoning," Bestable told me. "Was his driving last night consistent with it?"

I said it was absolutely consistent. I could remember at least three such cases in which George—Chief Superintendent—Wharton and I had been concerned. The first symptoms were constriction and dryness of the throat, and then a gradual loss of control: what might be called an increase of irresponsibility almost similar to that which comes from too much alcohol. That was why Ranger had driven so recklessly.

"If I might suggest something else, isn't there almost the certainty that he knew something was badly wrong with him and what was in his mind was to get to a doctor?"

"A good idea," Bestable said. "You agree, Doctor?"

"Why not?" Laving said. What he added might have been almost rudeness in another man. "Not that it matters. What we're concerned with is the atropine."

"You mentioned the possibility of an accident," I said. "You really think that's feasible?"

"You don't think I mentioned it purely academically?" he asked me bluntly. "There're many cases on record of atropine being taken in error. Belladonna's a constituent of a good many liniments and eye-drops."

"You should know," I told him. I had the idea that he'd taken a dislike to me and it was beginning to irritate. That's why I said what I did.

"Did the analysis show any others of those ingredients?"

"Well, no," he said. "What was found was alcohol with an atropine content. To get down to brass tacks, there's at least the possibility that the atropine was in the alcohol he took with that late lunch."

The tray came up—coffee and sandwiches. After a Bendacre dinner I could tackle only the coffee, but I was glad that at last we were sitting down. It's informality, in my experience, that makes for the better in argument. The last thing I wanted was to do much talking: not that there weren't some obvious problems to face. It was Bestable who brought one up.

"The trouble is we don't know when Ranger had his meal," he said. "Stomach contents puts it as late as four o'clock but no one saw his car draw in at his garage."

"That would make it about two and a half hours till his death," I said. "That'd be consistent: I don't know if Doctor Laving agrees. Naturally it depends on the amount of atropine taken."

"And on the particular person," Laving said. "And on temperature and the state of mind. I'll go no further than to say it's quite possible he drank the whisky at about four o'clock and had arrived at that lack of control which caused the crash at the time it did."

"In other words," Bestable told him, and with just a touch of impatience, "we've got to find just how that poison got into the whisky."

The tray had been cleared. Pipes and cigarettes were lighted and we settled down in earnest. Tagg stirred the dull fire to something of a blaze.

"The more simple we keep this, the better," Bestable said, "so let's begin with the assumption that Ranger was murdered."

"You can't rule out entirely the accident question," Laving told him testily. "That fool of a woman of his—Mrs. Gantle—is capable of anything. You know her, Tagg?"

Tagg smiled.

"Even so, sir, I don't see how she could have put liniment or anything into the whisky decanter. Besides, there wasn't a sign of a liniment bottle anywhere about the place."

"Let's stick to the starting point," Bestable told them. "You've got that local case last summer on your mind, Doctor." He explained to me. An Edenthorpe boy had drunk liniment by mistake but had been rushed to the hospital in time.

"Would you say that everyone in the district knows all about atropine?" I said.

"The whole district's had it as a topic of conversation for weeks," he said. "Only about a month ago two girls ate some deadly nightshade berries and one of them died. The local papers were full of it, and all the schools issued warnings. Everyone must have known you could take an infusion of the berries. Any part of the plant for that matter. It's all highly poisonous."

"And everyone knew that Ranger drank nothing but Irish whisky?"

"Everyone," Tagg said. "You think the kind of whisky made a difference?"

"That's for the doctor to say," I told him. "I think myself the slight bitterness would have been less noticeable in Irish than Scotch."

"Ranger wasn't all that particular," Laving said with a sneer. "That Irish whisky stuff was affectation, if you ask me. Ranger wouldn't linger over a drink. He'd pour a drink and down it would go."

"And that," cut in Bestable, and with a perfect case of *non sequitur*, "brings us to motive."

I don't know why, but it was at me that he looked. I begged the question.

"The fellow had made himself objectionable to practically everybody," Laving said. "Unprofessionally, and strictly between ourselves, it wasn't so much murder as a necessary surgical operation."

Bestable frowned. It had been a remarkably queer remark.

"Murder is murder," he said. "You could kill Judas Iscariot and it'd still be murder. And a murderer knows what he's in for. Murders aren't committed without motives—not those of the kind that killed Ranger. I'd like to know who had that kind of motive."

"Old Arthur Culver's the only one I can think of," Tagg said. "He told Ranger he wasn't going to get away with it after that case was brought."

"If I might suggest something," I said, "it's that poisonings are a peculiar kind of murder. Stab a man or shoot him or strangle him, and that's murder with an element of force or brutality. The murderer accepts it as murder. But poisoning is different. You drop something in and your enemy dies. When it happens you're not there. You've dissociated yourself, as it were, from the murder. You might even convince yourself that it isn't murder at all."

"Yes," Bestable said. "Anyone might have done it. He or she didn't need to be all that callous. One man, of course, stands out: Major Black. He had the perfect opportunity."

"He hasn't turned up yet?"

"No," Tagg said. "I rang his wife a couple of hours ago. To my way of thinking, he's our man. And he's bolted."

"That presupposes," I said, "that he came to the bungalow that morning prepared to kill Ranger, and by atropine poisoning. Which means he had the poison on him. Is that feasible? He went there expecting to meet Ranger, not to be left alone in the place."

"Black could have found a way to slip the poison into the whisky, even if Ranger had been there," Laving said.

"True enough. But what about the man whom Mrs. Gantle surprised in the house? Surely Black wasn't in the house all that time? He couldn't have been. After all, Ranger did come home that afternoon."

"I know," Bestable said dubiously. "That burglary or whatever you call it, worries me. If it was a chance thief, then everything was highly convenient."

"No sign of a forcible entry?"

"No need for it, sir," Tagg said. "Ranger didn't seem to care a damn about that bungalow of his. Half the time the back door was left open. You remember this morning, sir. Mrs. Gantle said she told Major Black if Ranger didn't come, to go out the back way. There *was* a key, but it was handy for anyone, under a mat outside the back door."

We did a lot more talking, and it was getting late. When I asked Bestable what would be his line of action, he said that the cause of Ranger's death would be kept a secret for a day or two and in the meanwhile, a discreet hue and cry would be out for Black. Even if he'd had nothing to do with the atropine, he ought to fill in a time gap.

I said that had rather worried me. If Black *had* done the poisoning, where had he been from the time Mrs. Gantle had left till the time he'd learned of Ranger's death? He definitely hadn't been home. And, if he'd planned what he might regard as a perfect murder, why bolt when everything had apparently played into his hands? Ranger had died from a car accident. That's what everyone was saying.

I shook hands all round and left. Bestable said he'd keep me informed of any developments. And, before I left, did I have any suggestions? I suppose, as a very minor representative in an obscure way of Scotland Yard, I ought to have had plenty of ideas, but I chose the safe way and risked letting down the side. I couldn't mention all the people with motives, for instance, without branding Henry as a gossip. Also, the whole business seemed to me to be in a state far too nebulous and involved.

By beginning at Black, however—that's what I told myself as I was driving back to Marstead—Bestable was taking the obviously easy way. About Black I'd already said far too much, but there were plenty of other things I hadn't even mentioned. Was it so certain, for instance, that it was from his own decanter that Ranger had drunk? Mightn't he have been given the poison elsewhere? Why, for instance, had he come back to the bunga-low pretty late and then taken his car out again? And where had he been all that day till his return?

There was one other thing that puzzled me, and it was some-thing far less tangible. Why had Laving been so insistent that the possibility of an accident couldn't be ruled out? Did he dislike me—if it wasn't my imagination—because I'd been brought in to poke a finger into a certain pie? Could he know far more than anybody about Ranger's death? That his brother, for instance, had somehow been concerned? After all, that brother certainly had motives. And it would have been ease itself for him to have found the atropine.

I didn't know. What I did know was that I'd definitely like to find out.

4

THE PLOT THICKENS

I HAD to give Henry an idea of why I'd been asked to attend that conference at Edenthorpe, so I made up my mind to be perfectly frank with him about the whole thing, and let him know as much as I knew myself. I had every confidence in his discretion. He might have been joking at the time but he had been sincere enough in claiming that he was a receiver of information, not a transmitter.

As for myself in that matter of Ranger's murder, I was neither fish, fowl nor red-herring. Naturally I'd been a bit flattered at having been consulted at all, even if I'd been able to contribute virtually nothing. Also good manners, or one's natural dislike of putting one's self forward, had kept me from presenting all the ideas I'd had. In short, that murder case was no affair of mine. I was at the disposal of Bestable if he thought I still had anything to contribute, but for me to start a private enquiry was professionally unthinkable, however much I longed to know the answers to a considerable number of things.

I was a private citizen, so to speak, and on holiday with a duty towards my host. But the amusing or disconcerting thing about it all was that it was Henry himself who was eager to have me poke a finger more deeply into the pie. He thought we ought to do something, and he brushed aside my talk of unprofessional conduct.

"Very well," I said, and at breakfast the following morning, "Just what do you think we ought to do?"

"No, no," he said, hedging at once. "You'd have to be in charge. I'd just carry out orders. But tell me something: just suppose you were in absolute charge of this enquiry—what would you be doing now?"

"Don't know," I said, "but probably putting cold compresses on a swollen head. After that I'd sneak up on this case from the rear. None of you people knows a thing about Ranger—where he came from to here and what money he had and so on. I'd try to get the answers."

"You mean, it's not so sure that it was a purely local job?"

"I don't know," I said. "But Ranger's a mystery within a mystery. Something tells me that if you knew more about Ranger, then you'd have a better idea of who killed him."

Henry took refuge in deprecation. He didn't know this and he didn't know that: all of which was a stalking horse for the putting forward of his own ideas. Wouldn't it be better to take the short cut? Exhaust local possibilities first and then, if necessary, dig up the past? And didn't it look as if Black was a reasonably obvious suspect?

"There's something I didn't tell you," I said. "It arose out of a question I put just before I left last night. Black's supposed to have put the atropine in Ranger's whisky and then bolted. But Tagg had a long interview with Mrs. Black and he elicited this: if Black had bolted, then it was in the clothes he stood up in. He didn't even take a suit-case, or his cheque-book. Only Mrs. Gantle knows he actually went to the bungalow. When he left no one knows. Or where he went. Or why."

"There we are then," he told me triumphantly. "There's something we could try to find out."

"Oh, no," I said firmly. "This village seems to hold the blue ribbon of the gossip championship. What would Bestable think if he or Tagg were told we'd been trotting round asking questions? Oh, no, Henry. Let's just sit and wait politely till we're asked. Besides, I've been looking forward to that drive round the countryside you'd planned for this morning."

Hospitality won the day. We had our tour in Henry's car. We went to my old home where I recognised scarcely a thing. We had an hour in the Museum at Ipswich and lunch at the White Horse. Then we went round by Bury St. Edmunds and it was about half-past three when we left it. The first dusk was not far away as we came towards the village by the Edenthorpe Road. Just as we were almost level with Culver's Farm, Henry trod on the brake.

"That's Culver," he said. "We can have a word with him if you like."

I was horrified, but I didn't know what was in Henry's mind.

"Perfectly simple," he said. "Just an idea I've got."

I had time for a quick look round. A long open building ran endways almost to the road. The farmhouse and the other buildings that I could see were at right angles to it and in the open space right up to the road was an untidy mass of baled and unbaled straw which was being built into a shelter for cattle or early lambing. Culver was standing with his back to us, talking to one of his men. As we got out of the car, the man must have mentioned us, for he went off and Culver turned. He came towards us.

Old Culver, as he'd been consistently called, was about eighty, but he had a back as straight as my own. Beneath his huge and straggling eyebrows the rheumy eyes betrayed his age, but he walked assuredly, head slightly sideways as if pondering the reason for our call. His cheeks were red but the lips thin and blue, and his jowl was grey and stubbly with a day or two's growth of beard. His voice was firm with never a quaver. His hand went courteously to his battered felt hat as he neared.

"Afternoon, gentlemen."

Henry went forward with hand out.

"My name's Morle, Mr. Culver. Glad to have the pleasure of meeting you."

"Glad to meet you, sir. I've heard a lot about ye."

"I hope it was all to my good," Henry said, and introduced me as a Suffolk chicken come temporarily home to perk. Culver laughed heartily at the good Suffolk phrase.

"I've really come to ask a favour," Henry said. Most local farmers, he'd noticed, burnt their hedge tops after cutting down, which accounted for the high price of pea-sticks.

"What I'd be grateful for, Mr. Culver, is if you'd let me or Joe Slack know when you're cutting a likely hedge and then we can come along and salvage what we want. Naturally we'd be prepared to pay."

"Don't talk about that, sir. I'll let ye know. Come and help yourselves. Won't be afore the spring, though."

"Nothing like being in time," Henry said. "A nice big place you've got here."

"Like to have a look round, sir?"

"It's good of you but we have to get home," Henry said. "A bit muddy, too, at the moment. But I would like to come some time."

Culver laughed.

"You don't call this muddy, sir? You owt've sin it last week after all that rain. What with the frost it've practically dried up. Still, glad to see you any time, sir, you care to come along."

We shook hands. Henry got in a last word.

"You've lost your neighbour then, Mr. Culver."

"Him!" Culver said. "What I say about him, sir, and I don't mind who hear me, is good riddance to bad rubbidge. He weren't no good to nobody, not even hisself."

"A pity," Henry said solemnly. "It's a tragedy when a man's his own enemy."

Culver's thin lips widened to an ironic smile. Or was it one of satisfaction? I didn't know, for I was getting into the car. As we moved off we just heard Culver calling again that we were to come down when we liked. I waved an answering hand but I doubt whether he saw it. And then I was asking Henry to slow to a crawl as we went by the bungalow.

He did more. He drew the car to a halt again.

"What's worrying you?" he asked after a moment or two.

"Nothing," I said. "I was just trying to visualise Black in there that morning. Something just struck me. When Black was in that lounge he had only to look out of the window and he could see Ranger coming either way in his car."

I had to smile at myself, and the way the thoughts had run on. That fertility in theorising is one of the things that can infuriate George Wharton.

Henry didn't get that point about the window and I had to explain. Black, waiting in that room, would have become aware that he would have ample warning of Ranger's approach. That was when the poison scheme might have come to him: that and the sight of the half-filled decanter. His wife was out and he might have slipped home and fetched the liniment, say, that contained belladonna. After putting it in the whisky he might have walked on past the farm and taken an Edenthorpe bus further along. There was one at half-past twelve.

"What was Black like to look at?" I asked as the car moved on.

"Well, I think I'd call him dapper," Henry said. "A neat little man of about five foot six. Hair quite brown, though now I come to think, he couldn't have been more than forty-eight or so. He had a little turned-up moustache. Complexion rather pale, and a very shaky hand."

"And Culver," I said. "A fine upstanding old boy. What's the village think of him?"

"Well, let's call it grudging respect," he said. "He's supposed to be the warmest man in the village, so they say. Naturally we didn't see the pernickety side of him. He's had quite a bit of trouble, by the way, and they say it changed him a lot. His only son insisted on joining up during the war and was killed. They say it killed his mother."

When we went into the house I found that Tagg had left a message for me. There was to be a formal inquest—identification of the body followed by adjournment—at eleven in the morning. Tagg didn't know if I'd be wanted but he thought I'd better be there in case. Perhaps I might see him at half-past ten.

Henry said there were one or two things he wanted in Edenthorpe and he'd drive me in. He didn't bat an eyelid at my rather cynical look.

It was soon after ten when we set off and we'd hardly turned into the main street when he was drawing the car in at the kerb.

"Something wrong?"

"Just along there," he said, waving his free hand ahead. "That red sports car. That's Black's. Mrs. Black's probably in the grocer's. I'll draw up a bit closer and we might catch a glimpse of her as she comes out."

He got a map from his locker and had it ready to use as a screen. We didn't have more than a minute to wait. One of the girls in the shop came to the door and Mrs. Black, full-faced to me, stood for a couple of minutes talking to her. She was a tall-ish woman with a remarkably fine figure. My distance sight is exceedingly good and from where I sat I could see the colour on her nails as she held the lighter to the cigarette she had taken from her bag. She carried herself well. Henry's description—an attractive woman in a hard, modern way—had been singularly apt. There was a competence and a confidence about her. You could see it in the way she moved that car across the road and past us.

"A smart-looking woman," Henry said, putting the map back in the locker. "A kind of ruthlessness about her, don't you think?"

I couldn't help smiling: Henry was just loving his role of conspirator.

"Maybe, yes," I said. "And she'd probably shriek the house down at the sight of a mouse."

He's a placid person, as I've said, and he didn't bridle. He smiled to himself, and it was so complacently that I couldn't help wondering if he knew more about the lady than he'd said. At Edenthorpe he gave me the spare keys of the car and we made in any case a tentative rendezvous for half-past eleven.

When I got to the police station I was told that Tagg was in the mortuary and a constable directed me there. I have an allergy to bodies, especially the messy kind, and there have been times when they have haunted me for days. But Ranger was looking peaceful enough on his tray. Only the staring, almost protruding eyes, and the flush on the cheeks which even death had not been able to erase told of that drug that had caused his death. Even then I could see that he'd been, if in a showy way, a remarkably good-looking man.

"Have a look at his hair, sir," Tagg said. "That's what I wanted you to see."

I had a close look at the black hair: the slight curls in it and the wave that went back behind the ears. Then I saw something else.

"His hair was dyed!" I said. "Got a glass on you?"

He had. I moved the hair aside and looked at the roots.

"His natural hair was greying. What colour do you make it? A reddish brown?"

"That's it," he said. "We'd put him in the forties. Wouldn't you say now he was older?"

"It's hard to say," I said. "If I were you I'd have photographs taken, with him as he is and then with the hair lightened up. A good photographer could do that for you."

Maybe I was misjudging him, but he didn't seem to be catching the point of it.

"Please don't think I'm butting in," I said, "but I heard a very apt remark about Ranger the other day—that he was a mystery within a mystery. No one knows a single thing about his origins. This dyeing of his hair reinforces that, don't you think?"

"Might have been just pure vanity," he said. "After all, he was a bit of a lady-killer."

"Yes, but what's so unattractive about reddish-brown hair that's slightly greying? I was slightly greying before forty. Heaps of people are. Now I come to look at you, you are: and what are you? Thirty-eight?"

"A year younger," he said. "Not a bad guess, though. And your idea, sir, is that the dyeing was a kind of disguise. If so, it wasn't because of any police record. His prints have been at the Yard and they've nothing on him."

"That was good work," I told him. "All the same, I don't think it'd be time wasted if you tried to unearth more about him. He seems to have been remarkably secretive about himself. He had to admit to being Irish because of his accent. He had the accent?"

"He certainly had. A regular blarney, if you know what I mean. I came across him on that case he brought against Mr. Culver. I had the idea he'd lived in Ireland till he settled here."

"Then he was a mighty long way from home," I said. "In fact, he couldn't have got much further."

We left it at that. He told me I shouldn't be wanted at the inquest after all, so we parted outside the morgue and I went in search of Henry. As he had been treating himself to a haircut, he didn't turn up till the time we'd agreed on. He'd also done his shopping and, as I'd none to do, we set off back. He was vastly intrigued when I told him about Ranger's dyed hair. He, too, was inclined to put it down to sheer vanity. I tried to convince him otherwise and I could be more free than I'd had to be with Tagg.

"In fact," I said, when I'd told him what I thought about things, "there's one question that Tagg ought to be asking himself. Can you guess what it is?"

He shook his head.

"Well, my idea is that it all adds up to this: that hair was dyed as a disguise. In other words, *was his name really Ranger*?"

He was so surprised that he slowed the car to think it out.

"You're probably right," he said, and gave that complacent smile. "Didn't I tell you, you ought to be taking a bigger hand in things?"

Allow me to make something perfectly clear. You are in the process—too slow a one you may think—of getting acquainted with people and things. It is a process I was going through myself, and, of course, there were things of which I didn't see the significance till very much later. You are having precisely the same chance. There is no padding. Everything you are told is relevant to the Case: even the golf we played as arranged on the Thursday afternoon.

Henry and I were reasonably subdued in our dress. Colonel Sterne was looking what I'd call chaste in pale green corduroys and a long-sleeved fawn pullover, but the rector was the same walking kaleidoscope. A brown polka-dot tie took the place of the green one, but otherwise he was as hectically colourful as when we had played before. I didn't blink so much and as a pair we did a bit better. We didn't win but we certainly gave the enemy a bad scare. We might have won if I hadn't let the side badly down. There were a couple of ponds over which you drive at the roadside holes—the fifth and the ninth—and I put my ball plop into each.

I liked Andover. He had his own brand of humour and nothing could ruffle him. He confided to me that those garish garments of his were deliberate strategy, and I couldn't tell for a moment whether or not he was being serious.

"Look at Sterne," he said, "colourless, like his game. That's why I can beat his head off in a single. When I turn up in my full regalia at the first tee, he just can't believe it. He fluffs his first shot and there I am—one up. He rarely recovers."

He certainly must have been a bit startling. But there was nothing startling about Frank Laving, who came that evening to dinner and bridge. He and I cut together for the evening and I had plenty of chances of summing him up. I decided he reminded me of a famous French abbé I'd once met in the Pyrenees. There was an astringent, ascetic quality about him and what with his leanness and the slightly stooping shoulders, he should have been wearing a *soutane* instead of the formal black suit. Even the bald patch on his head kept reminding me of a tonsure.

He did have, however, a certain dry humour, even if he took his bridge uncommonly seriously. When we pulled off a hand his thin lips would extend in a smile and he actually gave an audible chuckle when Henry related the old story of Charles Lamb's friend with the always dirty hands and nails who'd have won every whist hand if only dirt had been trumps. But the best discovery I made that evening was the difference between the twin brothers. Frank's cheekbones were slightly rounder and had some colour: Robert's were flatter and had the general sallowness of his face. Frank, in fact, looked slightly the younger and I was sure that from then on I could tell the brothers apart.

Henry and I sat on talking after Sterne and the doctor had gone. Henry had put a question to Laving after a rubber.

"What sort of bridge did that chap Ranger play, doctor?"

Laving had given a quick look.

"Flashy," he said tersely. "Claimed to have intuitions. All he ever had was the devil's own luck."

Henry and I were talking about that and how it had been a pity we couldn't have discussed Ranger at length. The trouble was we didn't know for certain if Laving had been told about the atropine. Sterne might have pricked up his ears if any indication of that had been let fall.

"The funny thing is," I said, "that I rather like Laving—this Laving. I can't say I like his brother. What sort of doctors are they?"

"Excellent, I believe," Henry said. "And strange to say, quite popular. Still, I rather gather that the village people would rather be bullied than cajoled. Marstead takes its illnesses pretty seriously."

We agreed that the Ranger affair had struck a dull patch as far as we were concerned. I promised that if we had no news during the morning, I'd ring up and ask how things were coming along. As a matter of fact I didn't have to. In the morning after we'd browsed through the newspapers, we took a walk and as we were coming home past Ranger's bungalow, we saw Tagg's police car. While we were debating whether or not to go in, he came out. And he made straight for us. I think he would have preferred to talk to me alone, but Henry was sticking closer than a brother.

"Keep this under your hat, Sir Henry, but something extraordinary has turned up. We've discovered where Ranger spent last Monday."

It *was* extraordinary. Tagg had taken my tip and had had the photographs taken. Copies had been sent to neighbouring counties and boroughs. It was Norwich that rang up with the strange news.

On that Monday morning, Ranger had enquired at police headquarters, Norwich, for an Inspector Chadwick who had wanted to see him on confidential business at half-past ten. He was told there wasn't an Inspector Chadwick. Ranger appeared bewildered. He said he'd been rung that morning at eight o'clock by the Inspector, who'd asked him to see him in his Norwich office on an urgent but highly confidential matter. In case the name had been incorrectly heard, Ranger was shown a list of inspectors on the city force, but he persisted that he'd checked the name with the inspector himself. And that was that. All Norwich could conclude was that someone had been pulling Ranger's leg.

At Tagg's request, and with the additional clue of Irish whisky, Ranger's movements had been partly traced. He had had a couple of whiskies at the Bell—some three minutes away— and had returned to that hotel for lunch. He didn't leave till after two o'clock but it hadn't been possible to find where he had parked his car. If he had left the city at, say, half-past two, then the sixty-five miles should have been done in two hours at the most. That gave a rough idea of the time of his return home.

It looked to us as if Ranger had been lured away from Marstead that morning.

"You've checked his calls?" I said.

"Nothing from Norwich," Tagg said. "All the calls round here for miles are now automatic, so all we know is the call didn't come from Norwich. It might have come from here, or Edenthorpe or anywhere within the automatic system."

"No possibility of Ranger himself having been spinning a yarn to the Norwich police?"

"Why should he?" Tagg said. "According to them, he was either a magnificent actor or everything was open and above-board."

"What's your own idea?" I said.

"Black," he said. "He rang Ranger under an assumed voice, and faked a row with his wife to give an excuse to see Ranger. Only he knew he'd be out, and that Mrs. Gantle'd be going too.

That left him with all the time in the world to dope the whisky. That's our theory, sir, and if you've a better one, we'd like to hear it."

I said hypocritically that it sounded all right to me, and the sooner they had their hands on Black the better. And that was all. Tagg promised once more that he'd keep me informed and with that we left him and went on towards home.

"You really think Black's their man?" Henry asked me as soon as we were out of earshot.

I didn't know. What I did know was that if Black had done the poisoning, then he was two things at the same time—highly cunning and an absolute fool. He was supposed to have lured Ranger away and to have given himself a reason for calling at the bungalow. If he had been prepared with atropine and had slipped it into the whisky when Mrs. Gantle was still there, then that would have been in keeping. But to stay on alone and then dope the whisky—well, he might just as well have left a note behind to say he'd done it.

One thing was certainly exasperating. On the Tuesday morning Mrs. Gantle had washed the decanter and so removed all traces of poison and any fingerprints that might have been on it. Presumably she had also washed the glass that Ranger had used.

"Surely there wouldn't have been any prints on the decanter," Henry said. "Wouldn't Black have wiped his off?"

"If he had," I said, "that might have been a clear sign that he'd handled it. Mrs. Gantle, you remember, had dusted that room, including, presumably, the decanter. Black would have rubbed her prints off and only Ranger's would have been found."

"Yes," he said. "But aren't these local people taking a very long time? Nothing happens except in driblets."

I told him that was both the beauty and the exasperation of murder cases. You just never knew. And for all we did know, Black might turn up at any moment and let out something that would clear the whole thing up.

"You don't really believe that?" he said.

"Why not?"

He shook his head.

"I don't know, but I've a different idea. I wouldn't tell it to anyone but yourself. What it is, is this: something keeps telling me that Black is dead."

5
LAST DISCLOSURES

YOU'RE getting better acquainted with Marstead? You think you could find your way about? You could recognise people if you met them? That's fine. So let's get on with the story. . . .

It was not till breakfast next morning that I really argued with Henry about that matter of Black's death. Maybe he had awakened with new ideas, for he assured me that all he had was a hunch. Black, he thought, had committed suicide after putting the atropine in the decanter. It was the only way to explain what had looked like sheer stupidity in letting himself be left alone, to Mrs. Gantle's knowledge, in the bungalow.

"He might be in one of the local ponds," he said. "Or somewhere in the wood by the bungalow."

"You really think he was the suicidal type?" I said.

"I do know he'd gone badly to pieces. The last time I saw him he was all on the shake. He must have been sodden with drink."

"Well, you never know," I said. "What about going along the pathway this morning and having a private look in the wood?"

It was all very conspiratorial and I think I'd have felt a bit of a fool if a local inhabitant had caught me there. But no one did. We walked round by the road to Sterne's house and hoped we'd not be spotted while we made our way from the stile to the almost immediate shelter of the trees. Once in the wood there was no danger, for a thick hedge ran along it on the village side and no one could have seen us from the back windows of the main street shops and houses, even if the whole lie of the land was upwards towards the west. When we came to where the wood thickened and the path ran through it instead of alongside, I took the village side and Henry the other. The wood was largely oak and there wasn't all that undergrowth. Paths or tracks, made probably by birds-nesting boys, were everywhere, and when at last we came in sight of Ranger's bungalow, we could say for certain that if Black had decided to shuffle or stagger off this mortal coil, it hadn't been there.

We had halted, naturally, for a look at the bungalow from the path, and, as we stood there, Tagg came out of the back door. I hailed him. We found ourselves making for the back gate.

"Anything new?" I said.

"Only an idea," he told us. "We didn't realise what minute quantities of anything can be detected, so I thought I'd make sure once and for all about that poison being in the whisky—his own whisky."

"How're you doing it?"

"If you come in, I'll show you," he said. "We'll go to the kitchen."

It was a small kitchen with a window overlooking the back. The very small pantry had its window and a wired grating for ventilation. There was a dresser with crockery and a couple of small cupboards. The porcelain sink was under the window and drying racks were fixed to the wall on each side. On the draining-board was a set of spanners.

"What're those for?" Henry asked.

"I'll tell you, sir," Tagg told him. "I've just had another talk with Alice Gantle and about what washing up she did when she came in on Monday evening. All she did was wash the plate and things he used for his meal when he came in. Next morning she washed the decanter and that's all, so she couldn't have used a lot of water. What I thought was that if I took off the U-bend, here, I could send the contents for analysis."

"An excellent idea," Henry said. His nose was almost over the sink and he began to sniff. "I'm probably wrong but do I detect a smell of whisky?"

"You're probably right, sir. I could smell it too. Alice Gantle told me just now there was quite a smell of it when she was doing that washing up on Monday night. Still, we shall see what we shall see."

He found the right spanner and got to work. The nut didn't budge but he had a short length of pipe for better leverage and slowly the nut began to turn. I kept the down-pipe firm. Tagg held a clean jar to catch the drippings and, when the nut was off, he brought down the debris with a bent wire. It was a greasy looking mess of almost everything, from fibre to small pieces of potato peel. It all went into the jar. Among its varied odours, that jar had definitely the smell of whisky.

Tagg put on a paper top and tied it. He wrote on a label what the contents were and said I might as well sign it.

"And what now?" I said.

"I'm taking this in straight away to the county analyst," he told us. "By this afternoon I ought to know the verdict. If I get a chance I'll let you gentlemen in on the confidential report."

The holiday was melting away: far too quickly for my liking. There was only one other engagement: tea that Friday afternoon at the rectory. Henry said wryly that it was something to which one couldn't exactly look forward: just something that had to be done. I asked what the snag was.

"Well," he said, "the Andovers, like so many clergy, are not too well off. Mrs. Andover does her own cooking and you can't avoid her scones. And, take my advice: don't touch her damson jam."

"She's nice in herself?"

"Oh, yes," he said. "A cheerful, massive, homely sort of woman. Just the wife for him."

"Any family?"

"At home, no. A daughter was married last summer and she's living, I think, in Somerset. The son, Peter, is doing his military service. He's now in Germany."

We arrived at the rectory at half-past three, since Andover wanted to show me personally over the church. It was another of those things one couldn't avoid, for in matters of church architecture I'm probably the most ignorant person alive. However, I did try to show an intelligent interest and I did like the carved pew-ends and the fragments of mediaeval painting that had recently been discovered on the south wall. It was about half-past four when we walked back through the churchyard to the house. Marstead had been connected with the woollen industry and there were some fine tombs.

Mrs. Andover met us at the door to say that tea was ready. Henry had described her well. She was mastodonic in build, lively, thoroughly self-possessed and undeniably good-humoured. She had to be. No other wife, I thought, would have allowed a husband to appear abroad, even at golf, in that eye-dazzling collection of garments that the rector strategically wore. A worthy woman, I'd call her: the kind who writes letters about programmes to the *Radio Times*.

Both the Andovers were chatty and it was quite a lively meal. The scones looked nice enough to me and I tried one to my cost. It had a rubbery consistency. The famous damson jam with which I tried to get it down, was solid and a mass of stones, and it had a kind of alcoholic smell, as if it had been kept far too long. The home-made cake wasn't bad. On the whole I got off easily, and Henry more easily still. He had taken the coward's way and spoken of a slight stomachic disturbance that was keeping him for the moment to a kind of diet.

But they were nice people. I told them so in a roundabout way.

"I think the lines have fallen to Sir Henry in very pleasant places, here in Marstead," I said. "He seems to have everything he can wish for, including some excellent friends."

"It *is* nice," she said. "I oughtn't to say it, but it should be even more so after—well, now that man Ranger has gone."

The rector expostulated mildly.

"Now, Harry," she said. "We're among friends and you know I'm not one to gossip."

"It's that business of Major Black that's so peculiar," Henry said, and probably as a diversion.

"Yes," Andover said, and somewhat heavily. "Isn't he supposed to have left his wife?"

"That's the general opinion," Henry said. "Shall I say 'the gospel according to the Slacks'. I hadn't seen her for quite a time till I caught sight of her the other day. If rumours were true and she really was having an affair with Ranger, then she didn't appear to me to be suffering unduly from grief."

"There was something funny about that," Helen Andover said. "After what Peter told us, I thought it was Colonel Sterne she was after."

"Really, Helen. . . . Really!"

"What was that?" Henry asked unblushingly.

"It was like this," she said. "When Peter was commissioned he had to have a Sam Browne belt and they cost a lot of money, as you know, so we thought perhaps Colonel Sterne still had his and if so Peter might borrow it. So Peter called—one afternoon, it was—and he saw the Colonel and Mrs. Black in a most compromising position."

Andover protested more sharply. His wife merely waved a hand.

"Well, she had her head on his shoulder and Peter thought they'd been kissing."

"Incredible!" snorted Andover. "I told Peter he'd been mistaken. And I strictly forbade him to repeat it. It's ridiculous to imagine such a thing about Sterne."

"He's a very charming and attractive man," she said. "And still waters always run deep."

"Ah, well," Henry said. "The proof of the pudding's always in the eating." It'd have been a tragedy if he'd made a slip and mentioned scones instead. "If Black's left her and they're divorced, then we should know. Not that I'm ever likely to mention the matter."

"I sincerely hope not," Andover said with unaccustomed tartness. "It never should have been mentioned. I'm really ashamed of you, Helen."

"He'll get over it," she told us amusedly. "But I'm really not one to gossip. This was something quite personal in a way."

I couldn't help chuckling as Henry and I walked back by the path across the sports meadow.

"What an old humbug you are!" I told him. "Are there no depths to which you won't descend now this Ranger affair's got into your bones?"

"All in a good cause," he told me imperturbably. Then as usual he was catching me by the sleeve. "You think there was anything in that tale about Sterne?"

"There must have been something," I said. "Either that or the boy suffers from a too active imagination."

"You can't imagine a son of the Andovers suffering from that," he said. "I know the boy. He seemed normal enough to me."

"Well, suppose Sterne did kiss her," I told him. "She's said to be a man-hunter. I'm not without the old Adam. If she made up to me at the right time and place, I might even kiss her myself. I don't know that you wouldn't too."

He looked prim and shocked for a moment. Then he gave that enigmatic smile and I wondered again if he knew far more about Mrs. Black than he'd ever divulged to me.

We were in the dining-room, just sitting down, when Mrs. Slack said I was wanted on the telephone. It was that police inspector again. I went out to the hall at once and Henry padded along behind me.

"That you, sir?" Tagg said. "I've got that analysis. And very queer it is."

"In what way?"

"It's completely different from the stomach content. That had a fairly strong solution in whisky. This one has only a very minute trace but there's a strong impregnation of whisky."

I said I followed him, and I didn't—if he knew what I meant.

"Well, put it this way, sir," he said. "What's been found now is"—I caught a rustle of paper as if he were consulting his notes—"is consistent with a microscopic trace of the poison from when Alice Gantle washed the decanter out. But there was a strong whisky content in those fibres and stuff we got out of the U-bend."

"Isn't that what you'd expect?" I said. "Atropine's soluble. The sink water washed all except a minute trace away."

"Then why didn't it wash away the whisky?"

"The whisky *was* the solvent," I said. "That and the water."

"I know that," he said patiently. "But where'd the whisky come from? She wouldn't have washed out that decanter if there had been anything but the smallest quantity left in it."

"Don't know," I said. "I'll think it over. If I get any ideas I'll let you know."

Henry and I worried our wits over that problem during the meal and without getting much further. The annoying thing was that what should have been satisfaction was now cluttered up with bewilderment. It was proved that there had been atropine in the decanter that Alice Gantle had washed, and the smaller the amount the clearer the proof. But what about that surplus of whisky? Where could it have come from? Not from the decanter, that was a certainty. Both sherry and port may leave lees that will stain a decanter, but there's no stain or sediment with good whisky. If there had been anything more than a few drops in the bottom of that decanter, Mrs. Gantle would have left it there. Sometimes from a decanter of sherry or port you can throw away as much as half an egg-cup of waste but never from a decanter of whisky.

I forgot about it temporarily after dinner and because Henry wanted to play chess. It wasn't a game: it was butchery. That was why he had ample time to think of other things while watching me floundering to avoid a quick and ignominious mate.

"Curious?" he said. "Why should anyone want to pour good whisky down a sink."

I looked up. He repeated the question and suddenly something clicked into place.

"Henry, you've got it!"

"Got what?"

"The answer to Tagg's puzzle. Whisky was poured down the sink!"

"Who poured it? That silly woman?"

"No," I said. "Listen to this as a theory and tell me if it doesn't explain the whole thing. Black came provided with his own Irish whisky, *already drugged*. That's the clue. As soon as

Mrs. Gantle had gone, he emptied Ranger's whisky down the sink and replaced it with the same amount of poisoned whisky. When Mrs. Gantle did her washing-up, what pure whisky was in the U-bend was considerably diluted. Probably Black ran some water off too, but there was still too much whisky to be consistent with the salt-spoonful or so that Mrs. Gantle washed down when she cleaned the decanter."

"It's right," he said. "It must be right. It's sheer hard sense. But what're you going to do? Ring Tagg and tell him?"

I said frankly that I didn't think that fair to Tagg himself. Why not wait a bit and see if he stumbled on the answer himself? For me to tell him the answer was like putting myself far too forward.

Then I had a brain-wave.

"Look, Henry. It was you who really hit on the answer. You ring Tagg and put it up to him. That should put you in well with the police after I've gone."

He tried to look shocked.

"You think that's strictly honest?"

I laughed.

"What an old humbug you are! You do as I say. Ring Tagg and claim the credit."

He went off with a deprecatory shake of the head, just for appearance's sake. I cleared the board and put the chessmen into their box and was seated by the fire when he came back.

"He was delighted," he told me. "And most grateful. The trouble is, he thinks it a bit too late. Bestable, his Chief Constable, is thinking of calling in the Yard, as he put it."

"Maybe it's the sensible thing," I said.

"You'd be likely to be sent here yourself?"

I had to explain. No one did any sending as far as I was concerned. George Wharton had come to rely on me as a kind of personal aide, but this was far too unimportant for Wharton to handle. A Chief Detective-Inspector and a Detective-Sergeant would probably be sent down. Which would be all to the good. Hardened professional minds would be at work: people who didn't give a damn about local taboos or hierarchies: who'd ask awkward questions and insist on answers: who'd have an enormous machine behind them and could throw a very wide net. Henry wasn't in the least degree enthusiastic. He'd have liked the Ranger affair to remain what one might call domestic, and, above all, he'd have liked to go on having a personal finger in the pie. It was tantalising, as he said. A wholly new experience and a very crafty insinuation of himself, and now he'd know no more than what he read in the papers.

I don't say it affected his golf the next morning. We played by ourselves and I actually beat him. Then that afternoon he pretended to have forgotten that I was going back on the Sunday evening.

"It's foolish of you," he said. "Stay another week. Stay a fortnight. . . ."

It was good of him, but there's nothing so bad as outstaying a welcome, and, as I said, there could always be another time. He shook a very gloomy head, but neither of us could have guessed what the morning had in store for us. We'd arranged to go to church and I'd thought about leaving in time to break the back of my journey before dark.

It was about nine-thirty and Henry was impatiently awaiting the arrival of the Sunday papers when the telephone rang. The call turned out to be for me. Henry said, hopefully and just a bit awe-struck, that it was from Scotland Yard.

"That you, Travers?"

So it was George Wharton. He and I had had a meal together the day before I left town and he knew all about my holiday.

"Glad I caught you," he said. "I didn't know if you were on the way back. Thought I might save you a journey."

"How d'you mean?"

"Well," he said, "it's this business that's cropped up at where you're staying. We've been asked to lend a hand. Jewle's coming down, and a Sergeant Allman, but you were specially mentioned. I gather you're mixed up in things in an unofficial way."

"Purely by chance," I said. "I just happen to have learned quite a bit about some of the people who might be involved. Am I to gather you'd like me to stay on and work with Jewle?"

"That'd be fine," he said. Since he wasn't likely to be involved himself he was being uncommonly charming. "You and Jewle ought to dovetail pretty well. You've known each other long enough. He'll be at this Edenthorpe place some time this evening. I expect he'll give you a ring. Anything you want to ask?"

I said there wasn't—unless it was the little matter of a raise. He took that as great joke. And I was glad he rang off because he mightn't have agreed to what I had in mind. Chief-Inspector Jewle would have been more amenable.

"So there we are," I told Henry. "Saved by the bell."

He said he was delighted; he certainly looked it, and he's not a demonstrative man. I was glad, too. At Bendacre life was gracious and urbane, with Henry himself someone with whom one could not possibly dream of ever having anything even remotely resembling an angry word.

"You'll really go on putting me up?" I asked. "My movements may have to be pretty irregular. But don't you think it advisable for me to stay in the village, clean in the middle of everything? And under cover, as it were?"

He said it was the only thing to do. If I were merely his guest and my connection with the Yard unsuspected, I'd be all the more free to probe into practically anything. He was so enthusiastic about it all that I hadn't the heart, even in jest, to accuse him of using me as a stalking-horse for his own inquisitorial ends.

PART II
THE PROFESSIONALS

6
SENSATION

OFF and on I'd worked with Jewle for some twenty years, dating from the time when he was a young detective-sergeant. He had thickened out since then, and was something of the build of Andover, though more lithe in his movements. The clipped black moustache, more prominent than my own, and the in-curve of his rigid back gave him the look of a sergeant-major. But there was nothing martial or hectoring about him. Like so many big men, he was quiet in manner and little ever ruffled him. Where George Wharton would have raised hands of despair and upbraiding to high heaven, Jewle would shrug his shoulders and carry on. I wouldn't call him brilliant. Intuition wasn't a word to be found in his vocabulary, but he knew his job. There was little that he missed and less that he forgot.

His sergeant—Allman—was still under thirty: of medium height, dark like Jewle himself, and rather thin in the face. He would be to Jewle what Jewle had once been to Wharton—occupying a footstool, as it were, at the feet of Gamaliel: in other words, learning his job. His would be the routine work with such men as Bestable was able to spare him. Bestable was at that Edenthorpe meeting. He and Tagg had been outlining the case: Jewle had been taking notes and consulting that rough map of Marstead which I'd drawn for him.

"Well, I think I've got a clear outline," he said at last. "This man Ranger was lured to Norwich in order that his bungalow might be empty for two periods: one from, say, half-past eight in the morning till ten o'clock, the arrival time of Mrs. Gantle, and the other from midday when she left, till the earliest time of Ranger's return: say half-past twelve. Your opinion is that it was the second period that mattered. Would you tell me why you've concentrated on that second period and cut out the first altogether?"

That was something I'd never thought of. I doubt if it had occurred to either Bestable or Tagg. Both of them looked at me, as if it were I who'd committed some sin of omission.

"The second period seemed to have fact in it," I said. "It was the period when Black was actually there."

"But couldn't he have come earlier and done the poisoning business then? Mightn't the second visit have been to see if everything still looked right?"

"No," I said, "and for this reason: if Black had poured the original whisky down the sink in the first period, then Mrs. Gantle would have noticed the smell. She didn't actually notice it till that evening when she washed-up the few things from Ranger's late meal."

"Exactly."

I said he rarely missed anything, and he nodded as if he'd tidied up a loose end.

"Ranger's belongings that were found on him?"

They were on a side table—keys, a few notes, loose change: just the usual, but no letters.

"What about the house?" Jewle said. "Nothing there?"

"Not a thing of the slightest importance," Tagg said. "His desk was open but there was nothing in it but his cheque-book. A few locally receipted bills and that kind of thing, but nothing personal. You'll be able to see for yourself. Everything's as he left it."

"I wonder," Jewle said. "What about the man Mrs. Gantle surprised in the house? Mightn't he have taken something?"

Quite an argument began. I kept neutral. Tagg and Bestable came down heavily on the side of a purely chance burglary, independent of the virtual killing of Ranger.

"In any case," Bestable said, "we'll never know if anything was taken from the desk. Nothing—silver or so on—was taken from the house."

"This Major Black. You've a photograph of him?"

Tagg produced one obtained from Mrs. Black. He said it was a good likeness, though about three years old. Copies had been circulated to neighbouring authorities. I had a look at that photograph—head and shoulders only. Henry's word "dapper" seemed reasonably correct. Every sleek hair on the head was in place. But it was a weak kind of face, in spite of the upswept military moustache.

"Know anything more about him?" Jewle asked.

Quite a lot of work had been done behind the scenes. Mrs. Black, Tagg said, had been very co-operative. She'd given details, as far as she knew them, of her husband's military career. He had been shell-shocked early in Korea and, according to her, the drinking had begun as a steadying of nerves. Confidential medical opinion was that he was drinking himself to death. There's no other end for a man whose breakfast is a large brandy and soda.

"He'd ceased to take part in the life of the village?"

"He had," Tagg said. "He even dropped going to Marstead Lion. His outside drinking was done at the Crown here in Edenthorpe. They knew him. Several times they arranged to have him driven home when he wasn't fit to drive himself. It appears he could hold his liquor just so far and then he'd suddenly keel over. You never knew when."

"I don't know," Jewle said, and gave a dubious shake of the head. "Maybe I'm being a bit obtuse, but something's surely wrong somewhere. Perhaps you'll put me right, but here's an alcoholic wreck who nevertheless is able to plan a nasty kind of murder and carry it out. And to disappear himself and keep under cover. How? Wherever he is, he's surely still drinking heavily? What about money? Did he have plenty with him? Had his bank verified a drawing-out of cash? You say he didn't have even his cheque-book with him."

The eye and the hard logic of the trained professional: Bestable couldn't have many doubts about the man the Yard had sent along. He shuffled uneasily on the hard seat of his chair. I thought I'd better try to do some face-saving.

"For what it's worth, my idea's this," I said. "Doping that drink wasn't all that difficult. But after it, Black just hadn't what it takes to carry on. I think he just crept off somewhere and did himself in."

"It's a solution," Jewle said. "Have likely spots been searched?"

Bestable cut in. There weren't sufficient facts, he said, to warrant it. That was one of the reasons why help had been asked.

It was a patent shuffle and Jewle slid past it.

"There were no footprints whatever in the neighbourhood of the bungalow?"

"None," Tagg said.

"And the wreck of Ranger's car?"

"In a local garage," Tagg said. "Only a few yards away from here. The case has had a lot of local publicity and some national, but no one's come forward to claim relationship. As Mr. Travers put it, the man was a mystery inside a mystery. We knew nothing about him except that he hadn't a criminal record, and was Irish and cantankerous and about as unpopular as they make 'em."

"What did his bank say about him?" Jewle asked, and gave a dry smile. "Money's supposed to talk."

"We've done nothing about that," Bestable said. "Our inquiry was into his death."

He left it at that. Tagg added that it was a matter of first things first. Jewle nodded amiably. He agreed that it mightn't be necessary.

It was getting late and he got to his feet.

"I think that's about all, gentlemen, thank you. I've got a tongue in my head and anything I may happen to want I know you'll tell me. In the morning I'll go to Marstead first thing and have a general look round. Mr. Travers is going on staying there with a friend. He thinks it better to stay under cover and I agree. No one need know of his association with us on this particular matter."

Tagg cleared his throat.

"I'm afraid it's a bit late in the day, sir."

"How do you mean?" I said.

"Well, sir, you don't know village life as we do. It's all over the village already that you're something to do with Scotland Yard."

"Good lord!" I said. "How on earth did they get hold of that?"

"Well, sir, Warner knew, and he wouldn't see any particular reason to hold his tongue. No one warned him."

I had to smile. The native drums and smoke signals had been in action. Jewle said it might be all to the good. He and Allman were putting up at Edenthorpe Crown, but he walked with me to the police car park.

"Anything you're keeping up your sleeve, sir?" he asked me.

"I don't know that there is," I said. "All I've amassed is a lot of village gossip concerned principally with those who might wish Ranger dead. That's pretty useless if Black is really our man."

"We may be in for a surprise," he said. "My idea is that the people here started off with certain things that looked a bit too obvious and disregarded everything else."

He didn't enlarge on it. He held out his hand and asked if nine o'clock at the bungalow would be convenient. He'd have that woman of Ranger's there and get her story at first hand.

It was after eleven o'clock when I got back to Bendacre. Henry was up, tackling a chess problem by the fire. He hastened to get me a drink. I told him to consider it a nightcap. I had to tell him, of course, just what had happened. As for Tagg's disclosure that my somewhat artless plan of remaining incognito in Marstead was already out of the question, it didn't perturb him in the least. He even told me, and whether or not he was serious I couldn't tell, that he'd now be able to bask openly in reflected glory. He merely gave that enigmatic smile when I told him that, if he considered himself a shareholder in Scotland Yard Investigations Limited, he might find himself not only with no dividends, but with a danger of bankruptcy.

I didn't get up the following morning at eight-fifteen as arranged overnight, and make a leisurely way to Ranger's bungalow at nine. Something startling was to happen to upset every plan.

I woke at my usual town time of just after six o'clock and thought I might try to get to sleep again. In fact, I was sound asleep when a knock at my door disturbed me. I hooked on my glasses, looked at my watch, and it was just short of half-past seven. Mrs. Slack came in, and it wasn't with early tea.

"Sorry, sir, but you're wanted urgently on the 'phone."

"Who is it, Edith?"

"He wouldn't say, sir. He only said it was urgent."

I pushed my feet into the slippers, put on a dressing-gown and went downstairs. It was Jewle who was calling.

"Something's just happened," he said. "Black's body's been found."

My fingers went to my horn-rims: an old nervous trick when I'm suddenly taken aback.

"Where was it found?"

"At a farm just short of Ranger's bungalow. I'm just coming out there."

"It's called Culver's Farm," I said. "I'll be with you as soon as I can make it."

Edith Slack hadn't yet taken up Henry's tea. I told her not to tell him I'd suddenly been called away till I was out of the house. That, unwashed and unshaved, was five minutes later. If Henry didn't know where I was, then he couldn't contrive to follow. I didn't even disturb him by taking the car. There wasn't a soul in the main street as I strode out up the slight hill. Long before I got to the farm I could see a car by the verge. I caught sight of Warner, just beyond the car, and that was all till I was quite near. Then, through a gap in the straggly overgrown hedge, I saw Jewle and Allman. Old Culver was there, and two of his men.

"No one's to go through there, sir," Warner told me, pointing to the gap. "You can go in the main way."

Perhaps you remember the lie of the land. There was the open shed that stood longways to the road. It, the farmhouse, the track and the main road made a big rectangle. In the half of that rectangle nearer the road was the untidy mass of trussed and untrussed straw and, nearer the house, the shelter which the men had begun to build. Black's body had been found by a man who was clearing up the corner nearest Edenthorpe and right by the gap.

As I came up, Jewle was thanking Culver and saying he'd call him and his man if he wanted them. Old Culver gave me a quick, questioning look as if he didn't quite recognise me and then moved off with his men towards the house. I had a look at Black's body.

"Better get along to that builder's Warner told us of," Jewle told Allman. "Get some iron stakes and some rope and we'll cordon the area off. Take the car."

I was looking down at Black. He occupied a mighty small space, for his legs were drawn-up, kneecaps almost at his chin. The grey overcoat, covered with straw debris, trailed behind him. There was straw in his hair and on the grey felt hat that lay flattened down just beyond. The arms were across his chest.

"He wasn't moved at all?" I said.

"Not an inch, so they say. The two men came to work at seven and one of them—the short one—started to get this straw away from the hedge. His fork struck something and he cleared just enough to see what it was. He told the farmer and he rang Warner and Warner rang me. I told Warner to get here and see nothing was further disturbed."

I straddled across the body and had a good look at the dead face. I was wincing as I stepped back.

"You think what I think?" Jewle said.

"Don't know," I said. "He's a pretty horrible sight. And those eyes!"

Then I knew what he meant. Those horribly protruding eyes were almost the eyes of Ranger. Once more my fingers were at my glasses.

"You think he died of poisoning, too?"

"More than likely," Jewle said, and turned to look along the road. "This looks like Tagg's men. The sooner we get the body away from here, the better."

Ten minutes, and the photographs had been taken and the position of the body marked. Allman came back with stakes and ropes and they began enclosing the site, even through the gap and clean up to the road. There was no ditch and quite a large section of the grass verge was shut off. Then the ambulance men came. There was more than a whiff of decay as they carefully moved the body. Tagg said he'd get the post-mortem in hand at once. The cars moved off. Jewle, Allman and I still stood there.

I broke the brief silence.

"No possibility of suicide? He couldn't have crawled in here to die?"

Jewle looked almost startled.

"You're not really serious?"

I had to tell him that I didn't know whether I were serious or not. It had merely seemed logical for him to have committed suicide after virtually killing Ranger.

"He didn't crawl under that straw, sir," he said. "No one in his right senses would have done that. It was all wet and half rotten for one thing. You can see it now. Besides, we think it was atropine that killed him. A pretty horrible death to choose? And for a military man who's probably got a gun at home."

"You're probably right," I said. "But if he was put here, he'd have had to be carried from the bungalow."

Then I changed my mind.

"That way his legs were drawn up: you think that was all due to the agony of the poison?"

"Some almost certainly was," he said. "My notion is that the rest of it was from being rammed into the boot of a car."

"Ranger's car?"

"Don't know," he said. "But we've been lucky—or so I think. Have a look at this."

He led the way round by the farm track and back along the road to that fenced-off part of the grass verge. But he called Warner over first. He was to go to the house and warn Culver and his men that nothing was to be said about that morning's discovery.

"If anything does get out, say I'll hold them responsible."

Warner went off. Jewle gave a wry smile.

"Pretty optimistic, hoping to keep this quiet. And now look here, sir. You see that long depression? That's where a car drew in. It's only last week they had fine weather here. Up to then it was very wet. All this verge was soft as putty. You can see it was."

He was right. You could see where the car drew in, and the deeper tyre depressions where it had stopped just beyond the hedge gap. But it wasn't the body of the car that was level with the gap; it was the boot.

"There's something else," he said. "I don't expect you can see them from here, but there're a few feet marks through that gap. Probably someone taking a short cut to the farm. But there're two other sets that match: one going in and the other coming out. The ones going in show that whoever made them was carrying something pretty heavy. Mind you, I don't put Black at more than nine stone, but that's heavy enough when it's dead weight."

"What're you going to try to do?" I said. "Check the tyre and feet marks?"

"Yes. Tagg's bringing some plaster. The tyre marks are going to be harder. You might know more about them than I do."

He ducked. Allman held up the rope and we went under it. That verge wasn't wide enough, or the car hadn't drawn over far enough, for more than one set to be seen. The rest had just stayed on the hard road.

"The treads look to me to be practically new," I said. "Ranger had an almost new car."

"I don't suppose you recognise the pattern?"

I had a close look. I had to admit that I couldn't identify the make. What I was sure was that the pattern was out of the ordinary run. And that the car had been a biggish one—say a six-cylinder saloon.

"Well, we'll have a whole lot of answers before tonight," he said as we ducked back under the rope. "What about you, sir? You had your breakfast?"

I said I'd arrived virtually warm from my bed.

"You get back then," he said. "There's no hurry about all this. I'm going back to Edenthorpe to get my own breakfast and I'll check up on Ranger's car before I come back. I'd also like to hear the doctor's opinion about Black's death."

"Anything for me to do?"

"I was coming to that," he said. "What I'd like you to do is break the news to Black's widow. Just see how she reacts."

"And then?"

"I'll be back here," he said. "Allman here will have taken the casts. We might have a look at the bungalow and see that Mrs. Gantle. But there's no hurry. Nothing's going to run away. Have a good breakfast, sir, and spruce yourself up and see what you make of the widow."

It was that last word I was thinking of as I made my way back to Bendacre. Mrs. Black was now a widow. Would it be the

Merry Widow? If Black had made no will and she was due for the money with which report had credited him, then I doubted if Marstead would see her much longer.

I put some of that to Henry while I was having that belated breakfast. I'd had to confide in him and, though he hadn't actually descended so low as an I-told-you-so when he learned of Black's death, he had given himself a very self-satisfied nod. I suppose I was being a bit smug when I told myself how curious it was that he, a really important person who'd been accustomed most of his life to deal with the hush-hush and important, should now display the almost shameless curiosity of a newspaper reporter who scents a coup. And, though he might not be a transmitter of scandal, there was no doubt that he was taking an enormous pleasure in having it in his possession.

"She might get married again," he said. "She's not more than forty, if that. She looks younger. A lot of men would find her very attractive."

"But not you?"

"Heavens, no," he said. "At my time of life one thinks of one's latter end, not of marrying and giving in marriage."

Then his teeth suddenly came down on his lower lip as if he'd thought of something.

"Was there anything in what we happened to learn about her and Sterne?"

"Don't ask me," I said. "And wasn't it you who said that time would show?"

At Henry's insistence I'd had breakfast first and then I went up to bath and shave. I put on an almost new brown suit. My wife had chosen the material. Brown, she claims, goes splendidly with dark hair and brown eyes. I put on the Old School tie—not that Lucia Black would recognise it, but because it, too, happened to go well with the brown. When I looked in the glass at the general effect, I was looking—if not like a lounge lizard—as little like a representative of the law as could possibly be imagined. It was a good thing that Jewle had brought down with him my warrant card. Even then I doubted if the lady would accept it as genuine.

Henry went with me to the garage and it was regretfully that he watched me drive off alone. I took the car because I wanted to get back quickly up the hill and miss nothing of what Jewle and Allman might be doing. Jewle might say there was no hurry and I might know that he was right, but he hadn't my restless sort of brain. Interviewing Lucia Black should have been ample for most people, but there was I, looking ahead. That was why I drew the car just in at the narrow entrance to Black's garage, reversed it and left it heading back towards the main road.

I pressed the bell-push and heard the ringing inside the house. The door opened almost at once. I'd wondered if she'd be up, and, before the door had actually opened, I'd wondered if she'd be wearing a dressing gown. But she was dressed and the make-up looked immaculate. In her left hand was a lighted cigarette in a long, amber-coloured holder.

She gave me a frowning sort of look. I wasn't quite so much at ease as I'd thought I'd be. I said I'd come about her husband, and I showed her the warrant card. She gave it the merest glance.

"Oh yes," she said—it was a precious kind of voice—"you're the Scotland Yard official who's staying with Sir Henry Morle."

"Not an official," I said. "Just an ordinary sort of person."

It was awkward in a way. There was I on the doorstep and she making no move to let me in.

"If you've come about my husband, I ought to tell you, I know he's dead. I heard it nearly an hour ago."

My eyes nearly bolted from my head. It was incredible, as I told her. News travelled fast in Marstead, but this was sheer black magic.

"Perfectly simple, really," she said amusedly. Then she drew back and was asking me to come in.

7
Some of the Truth

ATTRACTIVE in a hard, modern way, Henry had called her. There was a callousness about her at that moment that had in it something almost frightening, but who was I to judge? To state categorically that in order to understand people you must aim not only at comprehension, but also at compassion may sound priggish but I believe it to be true. One may have even to divorce one's self from one's own moral standards in order to understand fully those of others, and by others, I mean those who so often come under scrutiny in the course of an investigation.

We sat in the small drawing-room which she called the lounge. A dull fire showed hardly a glimmer in the grate: the furnishings of the room were unusually sparse and had no distinction, and to me the whole atmosphere was depressing, with the bright yellow of her jumper and the light brown of the skirt things that were somehow out of place. I didn't feel a lightening of spirits when she explained about her husband's death. Robert Laving, who would conduct the autopsy, had rung his brother Frank to arrange about general work, and Frank had taken it upon himself to ring Lucia Black. She thought it kind of him, and considerate, and her face softened somehow as she said it.

"You'll have a cigarette?"

She passed me the packet from her bag. I said I'd prefer my pipe if she didn't mind. The visit was all highly informal, though later she'd be asked to make an official statement.

"But I've already made one to that Inspector from Edenthorpe."

I explained, and after that she made no bones about going over the whole thing. There was nothing new—till the recital was over. Then things began to arise out of her question.

"I suppose he died of exposure. Isn't that what they call it?"

"How do you mean?"

Her lip curled slightly.

"My dear Mr. Travers, you needn't think you have to be polite. Before you'd been here a day you must have known all about him. He was drunk—that's what I mean. He slept out all night, and the exposure killed him."

The lip curled again.

"You think I've no heart, perhaps. You probably expected to find me in tears. Well, let me tell you something: my tears were shed long ago, as soon as I discovered what I'd really married. I wasn't married to a man. My husband was a fish—if fish drink what he drank."

"I'm sorry," I said. "But I didn't come here to cause you distress."

She didn't let me go on. She didn't even seem to have heard what I'd said.

"Do you know there were actually people who thought I was lucky? Lucky? My God!"

"But you're free now. You can live your own life."

"On what?"

"Well, on what he's left you."

"You're joking?" She gave a little snort of contempt as she stubbed out the cigarette. "He had his pension. The rest went long ago."

She leaned towards me from her low chair.

"You ought to be an understanding man. Let me tell you something, just between ourselves. All I've been doing here is keeping up a front. Do you know what it costs to live as he did? Ask Butt and Hewland: they were his wine merchants. Look at this room, and ask Smedland, the antique dealer at Edenthorpe. Ask him what I sold him from time to time, just to keep things going." The lip curled once more. "My husband never even noticed. The only thing he noticed was if a bottle was full or empty. Now his pension will be gone, and all I've got is this house and what's in it. And a car that's done fifty thousand miles."

"You don't want any pity of mine," I said lamely. "All I can say is that you've had a pretty bad time."

"That's nice of you. You're probably the only person who's had a good word for me."

"That's because you did too well what you thought was your duty," I said. "You put up too good a front. But what do you think of doing now? Selling up and going away?"

"Don't know," she said. And then abruptly: "What d'you think of Marstead?"

"Well, frankly, I like it."

She smiled.

"You would. But it's my idea of hell. You don't stay in hell when the gate's open."

I rose to go. There was something I felt it my duty to tell her, even if it could only be a hint.

"Mrs. Black, I must tell you something in strict confidence. You promise you won't mention it unless it should happen to become common property?"

She gave me a long, level look.

"Depends what it is."

"It's this," I said. "There's the possibility that your husband didn't die of exposure. The possibility is—I won't call it a likelihood—that he was murdered."

She didn't turn a hair. The dark eyes narrowed a bit and seemed to be boring into my own. It was I who looked away.

"Murdered," she said, and as if to herself. I looked at her again and now she was frowning. Then suddenly she smiled. All sorts of things were in that smile—irony, satisfaction, even a kind of gloating—but there wasn't one of which I could be sure. And then she seemed to straighten herself. There was a livelier difference in her voice.

"Is that all you can tell me?"

"I shouldn't even have told you that."

She smiled to herself again, looking beyond me across the room. She bit her lip. She shrugged her shoulders and then the smile—a different one—was turned on me.

"It was good of you to tell me, and I do appreciate it. It was horrible to hear it. But there—"

I moved towards the door.

"Do come again," she said. "I won't say a word about what you told me, but I'd like to know the truth. The whole truth."

I said that if what I'd said had had truth, then she'd be the first to be told.

"Come in any case," she said as she reached beyond me to open the front door. "You're the first person for years who's had the least bit of sympathy."

She touched my arm as if to hold me back. I thought for a startled moment she was going to tip-toe up and kiss me, but the smile must have been for something else. She merely held out her hand. It was a firm hand and the grip more strong just then than my own.

She waved cheerfully to me as I moved the car on. I didn't move it far. Just out of sight, round the bend into the main street, I drew it to a halt and I was there for a minute or two thinking of that half-hour I'd just spent with Lucia Black. Before I moved the car on again I knew that only one thing really mattered. That mention of murder had had in it, for her, nothing of the horrible. That, for her, had been a moment of sheer pretence, for that one word had changed the whole tenor of her thoughts. It had changed the woman herself. It was almost as if I had told her something pleasing: something that gave an ironic satisfaction. And yet that couldn't be right. Or was it? Might it just be possible, for instance, that, in the moment of that, sudden revelation that her husband had not died of exposure after all, Lucia Black had known beyond all doubt who it was that had murdered him? I didn't know. I had no means of knowing, and yet the thought stayed with me. As I drove up the incline towards Culver's Farm, distance weakened it. All I knew was that for the moment it would be better to keep it to myself and make no mention of it to Jewle.

Warner's job was a sinecure—if Jewle had intended him to keep back the curious. Marstead's men were at work, the women busy indoors and the children at school, and, except for that leakage of information by Doctor Laving, no one had been told that Black was dead.

I couldn't see Allman, but the car was by the bungalow and I drew mine in just beyond it. The front door was open and Jewle came out.

"Everything very peaceful?" I said.

"Yes," he said. "Allman's fetching Mrs. Gantle. How did you get on down the road?"

I told him the kind of life Mrs. Black had led with her husband and that his death was going to do her little financial good.

"She may have all the feminine trappings, but she's tough," I said, "and embittered. I think she'll leave Marstead as soon as she possibly can."

"That's the queer thing about Major Black," he told me. "She described him to you as a more or less hopeless alcoholic and yet he was supposed to have Irish whisky already doped and to come here on a faked errand. I never did like it, even when I first heard Tagg expound it last night."

"What've you got in its place?"

"Don't know yet," he said, "but I'm hoping to prove something very different."

He cocked an ear. Allman and Alice Gantle were at the door. We had been in the kitchen, but now we went through to the lounge. Alice Gantle was already expostulating about not having had time to tidy herself.

"We shan't keep you five minutes," Jewle told her. "Just answer one or two questions. Very simple ones. For instance, just where did the decanter stand?"

She showed him.

"And the glasses and a carafe of water were in the cupboard underneath?"

She said they always were. And any bottles.

Jewle opened the cupboard door, and there were glasses and tumblers and a carafe of water. There were three empty whisky bottles. He slipped on his gloves and began looking at the glassware, moving things aside with a finger. All at once he picked up a glass and brought it out. He held it to the light.

"Have a look at it, Mrs. Gantle, while I hold it. Would you call it clean or dirty?"

"Why, it's dirty!" she said, and stared. "How'd that git there?"

"I'll tell you," he said. "Mr. Ranger always left his used glass out for you to wash. Somebody else used this glass and put it back in the cupboard. You washed a glass of Mr. Ranger's on that Monday night?"

"Why, yes. He allust had a drink with his meal."

Jewle laid the glass carefully down on the top of the desk. "One other thing. Just what washing up did you do when you came in on that Monday morning?"

"There weren't practically nothing." She looked at the three of us as if wondering what it was all about. "He didn't have any breakfast—only a cup o' tea."

"I know," Jewle said. "He was called on the telephone and hadn't time for breakfast. You washed the cup?"

"No—o," she said. "Far as I remember, he'd swished it round hisself and put it in the rack. He often did that. I rinsed out the pot."

"And no other washing-up that morning?"

"No—o," she said again. "All I did was wash my hands after I'd peeled that onion."

"Onion?"

"Yes. Just one small onion. I was going to lay him out some cold meat and tomatoes and a bit o' lettuce, and he allust liked an onion with it."

"I see. And when you came in the evening, you washed up the glass he'd used at that meal?"

"That's right," she said. "I washed up all that he'd left. And that weren't much."

"Fine," he said. "That's all we want to know. We're much obliged to you, Mrs. Gantle."

Allman saw her out. Jewle's smile was slightly ironic as he turned to me.

"Don't think I pulled any rabbits out of the hat when I found that glass. I actually spotted it an hour ago. Allman's taking it in now to check prints. Another ten minutes and we'll know things. Or do you think you know them already?"

He offered me his cigarette case. I preferred the pipe. We took the two easy chairs. As he said, we might as well be comfortable while waiting for Allman's telephone call.

"I've been very obtuse," I told him. "I ought to have spotted something in what you mentioned last night—the significance of that first period when the house was empty. And I ought to have remembered that Black was a lush."

"The vital point," he said. "Ranger was rung at about eight o'clock that morning. He rarely got up before nine, so he just had time to shave, dress and make himself a cup of tea before going to Norwich. He had to allow himself a good two hours. That left the place empty till Mrs. Gantle's arrival at round about ten, and that was what the poisoner counted on. That was when he nipped in here, poured the contents of the decanter down the sink and substituted the poisoned whisky ready for Ranger to drink when he ultimately came back here. So much for the first period. The second period begins when Mrs. Gantle left at midday. Black came just before midday and he'd got himself into the state where he was going to have a show-down with Ranger. He sat here alone and waited. He kept on waiting. Maybe he took a look or two out of that window to see if Ranger was coming. Then he kept seeing that decanter. Finally he kept an eye out of the window and poured himself a tot. Maybe he had two tots. He slipped the glass back behind the clean ones and went on waiting. But in his general state of health he didn't wait long. He had that stifling sensation in the throat, he collapsed on the floor: he tried to drag himself towards that door. I've had my glass on that linoleum and you can actually see what I think are the marks of his shoes. All right so far?"

"Dead right," I said. "That's the only way it could have happened."

"That's what I think myself. And now to Ranger: when he came back here he must have gone into the kitchen first and begun his meal. He may even have eaten what he did before he came in here. He saw Black lying dead and he was scared out of his wits. I'm told that he and Black had already had one stand-up row, and so he knew he must get rid of Black's body. He took a drink to steady himself: he emptied, in fact, what was in the decanter. Then he got to work. It must have been dusk by then."

"Yes," I said. "It must have been. Also he was lucky in the siting of this bungalow. It isn't overlooked. The front hedge even keeps it from being overlooked by Culver's Farm. It'd have been easy to slip the body into the boot of that big car of his."

The telephone shrilled. Jewle moved quickly across to the desk and lifted the receiver.

"Yes," he said, and, with a nod, "I see. Better stay there and get a vacuum on that car boot and send the contents and his clothes straight off to the Yard. Warn them that they're coming. . . . Yes, I'll be along."

He hung up.

"Black's prints on that glass," he said. "That means everything's as we worked it out."

His lips clamped together and he frowned.

"What's worrying you?" I asked. "You ought to be pretty pleased about things. You also know now, without having to waste time on enquiries, how Black's body got under that straw."

"That's just what we don't know," he said. "All we've done is solve one problem only to find ourselves up against another that's a damn sight harder."

"How d'you mean?"

"Who put the body under that straw," he said. "I had a good look at those tyre tracks and I also had a good look at Ranger's wrecked car. You know what we're up against? *The car that brought Black's body there wasn't Ranger's.*"

It was incredible! But to Jewle's mind there wasn't a doubt about it. The tyre pattern on the grass verge and the pattern of Ranger's tyres were utterly different. It was in order to make assurance doubly sure that he was sending the contents of the car boot and all Black's clothing to the Yard laboratories. It was billions to one that the results would be negative.

"Still, we oughtn't to grumble," he said. "We do know one important thing. No one murdered Black. He virtually killed himself. The whole thing centres round Ranger. Black is only a side-line. The man we're after is the one who tried to murder Ranger. A local job. You agree on that, sir?"

"Must have been. He certainly knew Mrs. Gantle's hours and when the house'd be free. And that the back door would either be open or have its key under the mat."

"It's a pity about that onion," he said. "It was the smell of it that kept Mrs. Gantle from smelling the whisky during the morning and not spotting it till she came in in the evening. But for that you people might have tumbled to it that the first period was the really important one. Not that it matters now. But about it being a local job: did I gather that you had one or two people in mind?"

I told him about Old Culver and Frank Laving.

"Culver wouldn't need a car to get the body across to that straw," he said. "Laving's more interesting,"

"You mean, for instance, he rather took it upon himself to ring Mrs. Black about her husband's death?"

"That's one thing. But that Gantle business and Ranger getting her to pour the medicine down the sink. Let's suppose that Ranger really knew what he was talking about. Suppose he'd threatened to report Laving to the G.M.C. for a dangerously wrong diagnosis. Or to get the woman herself to bring an action."

"Not too far-fetched," I said. "Ranger might have been holding it over Laving's head. That taunt Ranger made after the row they had at the Bridge Club rather confirms it."

"Laving," he said. "Any relation to the one who did the post-mortem on Ranger?"

"His brother. They're identical twins."

I told him of that rather amusing meeting of mine with Frank Laving. I recalled Robert Laving's attitude at that conference I'd been invited to attend at Edenthorpe after the post-mortem, and how he'd been unduly persistent in the matter of Ranger's death being possibly an accident: that the atropine, for instance, had been taken by mistake.

"Could have been an attempt to shield his brother," he said. "Maybe he had a few private ideas. Not that we want to get ourselves in as deep as that—not yet."

To me it had begun to look attractive, and I didn't want to drop it. The fact that those brothers were so alike would make an alibi easy. Robert Laving might have been manoeuvred by his brother into some position or other which involved such an alibi, and he had become aware of it.

"Plenty of time," Jewle said cheerfully. "The one we want isn't going to be so mad as to bolt. What he'll do when he reads his paper tomorrow morning is quite a different matter."

"You're spilling the beans?"

That was the idea. The whole truth was going to be given to the Press as soon as the post-mortem proved that Black had definitely died from drinking the atropine. He was going to do more.

"I'm like you," he said. "I think there was something highly mysterious about Ranger himself. This afternoon I'm going to see his bank manager. If I find anything the least fishy I shall have Ranger's picture in the *Police Gazette* to see if anyone can identify him. It's a long shot but it may work out."

He looked at his watch.

"What time do you have your meal?"

"One o'clock."

"It's not far off that now," he said. "What I'd like you to do is to be at Edenthorpe at about two. The photographs of the tyre casts ought to be ready by then. If we can't get the information at Edenthorpe, you might get it from one of the big stockists. Soon as we identify the tyres, we'll get the man who bought 'em. It may be a long business but we can get more men on the job." He smiled a bit grimly. "And when we do get him we ought to be listening to quite an interesting tale."

Lunch was on when I came down from the bathroom. Henry was thrilled when I told him what the morning had brought forth. Mind you, I didn't tell him everything. He heard nothing from me, for instance, about that extraordinary look on the face of Lucia Black when I'd hinted that her husband might have been murdered. He heard nothing about the brothers Laving. And when I mentioned my afternoon, he did suggest that Ipswich might be the best place to find a stockist. And if I were going to Ipswich, there were things he wanted to do there himself. I might pick him up on my way back from Edenthorpe. He was so Machiavellian about it all that it was hard to keep a perfectly straight face.

8

PROGRESS

I MET Jewle at his hotel and we walked to the garage—the largest in the little town—to which the wreck of Ranger's car had been brought. We had half a dozen photographs of those tyre impressions—the selected, clearest portions from the total length—and all considerably enlarged. The garage proprietor was in. He rubbed his chin a bit dubiously when he had his first look.

"It's funny, but this isn't the sort of thing you carry in your mind. I don't know that I've realised it till now."

Jewle named a few well-known makes.

"You mean you wouldn't be able to identify them by their treads?"

"One or two—yes. But not these ones. They all run somewhat to a pattern, you know. There's what we know as the Big Five. I could spot any one of them at a glance, but not the rest. Tell you what, though. We'll have a look at what we have in stock. There might be some of the smaller firms' makes. Sometimes we order a set or an odd lot for a customer and some get left on our hands."

We went out to a brick building at the back. Along one side tyres of all sizes were stacked, from the huge balloons of tractors to slim bicycle tyres. Where he was in doubt he ripped off the wrappings and exposed the treads. It was wasted time.

"Sorry, sir, but I can't do anything for you. If it had been one of the Big Five or one or two more, I might have helped you."

His stock was small, as he said. The real place to go was Mattersons of Ipswich. He told me the easiest way to find their depot.

"By the way," Jewle said, "there was something I meant to ask you when I was in this morning. Do you happen to know where Ranger bought his car?"

"Know?" he said. "I ought to. He bought it from me. He traded in an old Standard he had when he came here first."

"Then tell us something, in confidence. Did he pay for it on delivery? Or was it, say, on the instalment plan."

"Oh, he paid for it."

There'd seemed a slight hesitation.

"By cheque, or how?" Jewle asked. "And, just in case, let me assure you I'm not an income-tax snooper. That isn't the kind of information I'm after. My interest is where the money came from."

"That's all right," he said. "He paid cash. Mostly pound notes. And a few fivers."

That was that. Jewle went straight on to the bank and I left for Ipswich, calling for Henry on the way. I was to have another view, as far as Bedham, of the road I'd taken in reverse on the night of Ranger's death. Beyond Bedham I'd travelled the road only once—that day when Henry and I had gone on our sightseeing tour of Suffolk—so that stretch of the journey was comparatively new to me. Not that I would see much of it. The sharp bends and unexpected turns would keep my eyes very much to the road.

But there was something that I remembered from that other daylight trip and which I wanted to see again. It was a really superb day of late autumn—that sad apotheosis of the year—and the light was mellow and curiously serene. Just after we left Bedham I spotted well ahead the blob of orange that marked an old gravel-pit that lay just off the road at the crest of the hill which I was then beginning to climb. I stopped the car there and looked out towards the east.

Then we both got out. It was a grand view, as Henry said. We didn't exactly see the coloured counties—no Suffolk hill is big enough for that—but we did see the coloured countryside. Oaks were still green but elms and the tall poplars had their yellowing. There were patterned fields, some still in stubble, some ploughed and some with the green of young winter wheat or the darker green of sugar-beet. A few yards away to our right the old gravel-pit was part orange, part brown, according to the sun's direction, and scattered everywhere were the reds or slate blues from farms and cottages: apart, almost on the horizon, rose a couple of church towers. In all that patchwork of colour there was easily discernible that meandering lane which had ultimately brought me out that Monday night at Bedham. I pointed it out to Henry.

"That's one reason I stopped here," I said. "I wanted to lick some sort of sense into Ranger's movements on the night he was killed. Think it out: he got home from Norwich in the late afternoon and he had his meal. Black's body doesn't enter into things. It had already gone. Someone—not Ranger—had taken it away: the someone whose car tyres we're hoping to trace.

"But about Ranger. He'd had a trying and a puzzling day. He'd had the best part of four hours' driving in all, and yet, as soon as he'd had his meal, he went off in his car again. And he went somewhere that brought him back through Bedham. Why?"

"Can't for the life of me think," Henry said. "You'd have expected him to light the fire and get into an armchair."

He remembered something.

"He *ought* to have stayed at home. It was a Bridge night at Edenthorpe. I'm practically sure he never missed his Bridge."

"And yet he went out," I said. "But something else. You see that road I took myself: you can see it almost as far as Bedham. Was he on that road behind me that night? Or did he come by this road we're on now?"

Naturally he couldn't tell me, for we'd never a clue. As I said, it was a loose end I'd have liked to clear up. And clues themselves were queer things. You had them under your nose and didn't spot them, or you might spot them and not be able to evaluate them. And something, I said, had been telling me that if we knew why Ranger left his bungalow again so quickly that night, then we'd know a whole lot more about who killed him.

We went along that small plateau for a bit, and then dropped down into Little Warbridge. Henry was still puzzling his wits about Ranger's Monday night.

"One thing he would have done," he said, "or so it seems when I try to put myself in his place. I'd have been furious about that false call that took me to Norwich, and I'd have wanted to know a whole lot about it."

We were through the tiny village and ahead was a large direction board about a hundred yards from a fork. To the right was Colchester; our way was to the left. Just as we took it, Henry thought of something.

"Colchester! That's where he was going. Colchester!"

"Why?"

"Well, because for telephone purposes, Marstead is in the Colchester area. He'd be going there, hot-foot, so to speak, to get the head office to trace that telephone call that took him to Norwich."

It was as good a solution as any. Henry had more than earned his ride.

"If it becomes necessary we could find out from Colchester whether or not he did go there. I don't know what their closing hours are. But there's something else about that telephone call. I wonder why the person who made it was pretty sure Ranger would fall for it. Would you have fallen for it?"

"Yes," he said. "I'm practically sure I would. No one could disregard a request by the law. And I wouldn't have thought it all that peculiar that the caller wouldn't tell me exactly why I was wanted. I'd take his word that it was both urgent and confidential."

I said he was right. What we did know about that call was that it had been made by a man, and a voice so disguised that Ranger hadn't come anywhere near recognising it.

Mattersons, Ltd., was a huge place: wholesale and retail business in tyres merely an adjunct to three or four acres of repair shops, display rooms and a service station. The chief reception engineer sent a boy with us to the tyre depot, and we were to see an elderly employee by the name of Tom. It turned out that he'd been concerned with nothing but tyres ever since he'd been with the firm, and that was nearly forty years.

"Yes, sir," he said, when he'd inspected my warrant card, "I reckon if there's anyone knows more about tyres than me, then he'd take some finding."

He put on his glasses and had a look at the photographs. He frowned.

"No, sir. We've never had a tyre with a pattern like that. You can see for yourself."

He showed us brochures, all illustrated, of what must have been every known tyre, and some of which I'd never heard.

"Might be a foreigner. A firm that hasn't an agency here as yet. Wait a minute, though. I may have thought of something— something that came in only a few days back. We haven't done anything about it yet."

In another drawer was some more advertisement matter. And among it was what we wanted. It was one of the new tube-less, unpuncturable varieties of tyres that had only recently come on the market. The parent firm was Italian: the name, Colonna. Henry said he'd seen it advertised a few days ago in the Press.

"No use asking you, Tom, if you've sold any," I said. "I take it you haven't applied for the agency yet."

He said they probably wouldn't apply. They already had two agencies for the same type of tyre. I told him of my predicament. We were on a crime job near Edenthorpe, and we'd found those tyre tracks of the car concerned. What did he advise?

"Ring up their head office," he said. "We've got the number here. Get them to give you a list of the stockists in the Eastern Counties that they've supplied."

He did the preliminaries himself, then handed me the receiver. I must have spent half an hour getting the right depart-ment and then the right man. All I was promised was that the information might be in the post the next morning. Henry took it on himself to give Tom a tip. I didn't see what it was, but Tom's finger went to his forehead. Then we went to the main office and paid for the call. By then it was dusk. The labourers were worthy of their hire so we had tea in the town at the ratepayers' expense. It was six o'clock when we got back to Bendacre.

I tried to get Jewle but couldn't locate him. A few minutes later, he rang me. Henry, at my elbow, whispered that I might ask him to dinner. I thought that a bit too grandiloquent and might scare Jewle off.

"Run out here for a change," I said. "And Sir Henry would like you to have a bite with us. It'll be ready by the time you get here, or soon after. No need to wash behind your ears."

"That's capital," Henry said. "We must get a fourth. What about Andover?"

Andover had a meeting that evening. Henry managed to secure Colonel Sterne instead.

I kept an ear cocked for Jewle's car. As soon as I heard it I was out of the front door and showing him where to park. What I wanted, of course, was to make a few things clear. Before Jewle had taken over, I'd been consulted unofficially by Bestable and Tagg, and, as I pointed out, I couldn't be a guest in a man's house without advising him to some extent of what I was doing. But Sir Henry, as I said, had been a distinguished public servant. One could rely absolutely on his discretion. Moreover, his intimate knowledge of the village might be of considerable value.

By that time we were entering the house and Henry was coming forward with outstretched hand. I think the two took to each other from the first, but before much was said, along came Colonel Sterne. Henry had asked him not to dress specially but he was looking very smart in brown velvety corduroys, brown jacket and regimental tie. I'd been wrong, I told myself, and Mrs. Andover right. Even that scarred flesh on Sterne's cheeks couldn't detract from his look of distinction. Women—Lucia Black for instance—would find him a remarkably attractive man.

Over sherry Henry apologised for what he called a scratch meal. I'd have called it an uncommonly good one. We'd been having a steak pie in any case, and there was ample for the four of us. The soup was good and a cheese souffle came last. The two bottles from Henry's cellar that we killed were good for the palate and loosening for the tongue. Henry, I should say, was tactfulness throughout. He introduced Jewle by his official title and left it at that. Sterne had seemed rather taken aback for a moment.

"You're enquiring into that accident of Ranger's," he said, "I should say, according to the village. You've no idea how things get about."

Jewle modestly admitted that that was why he was now at Edenthorpe.

"I don't want to sound inquisitive," went on Sterne, "but I should have thought it all cut and dried. The locals have it he was drunk and his car got out of control. Still, it's no business of mine." He gave his dry smile. "I expect you fellows will tell us all about it in your own good time."

I learned a whole lot about Sterne that night. There was, for instance, what arose out of the death of Black.

"They tell me poor Black's dead and his body was found at old Culver's place. You heard that, Sir Henry?"

"It's all over the village," Henry said. "Would it be tactless, Inspector, to ask if it's true?"

"It's true enough," Jewle said. "Afraid I can't say more. You might, however, see something in the papers in the morning."

"What about Mrs. Black?" I cut in. "I suppose you've no idea of what she's going to do, Colonel?"

"No," he said. "I thought I'd drop in on her in the morning when I knew he was really dead."

"A very attractive woman," Henry said. "What d'you think of her, Colonel? You're her neighbour."

Sterne pursed his lips.

"Well, strictly between ourselves, she was just a bit too attractive, and I was rather foolish." He laughed. "Not what you may think. She had a devilish bad time with Black and I'm afraid I was a bit too sympathetic. She'd got recently to coming and weeping on my shoulder. Still, I expect she'll be leaving. I don't see what there is to keep her here."

So that explained what young Andover had seen on a certain afternoon. But about Sterne in another light. It was a mellow evening, as I've indicated: a brisk night outside and a good fire indoors: excellent company and excellent whisky and some of Henry's treasured cigars at which even Churchill might appreciatively have sniffed. And Jewle happening to ask Sterne what his regiment had been.

A long story, Sterne had said. He'd been fruit farming with his father in British Columbia and had joined up at the outbreak of war, leaving his father in charge. He'd got a commission and had come to England with the very first Canadian troops. He'd been in that Commando raid on St. Nazaire. He'd been one of the lucky ones who'd got away. It was there, incidentally, that he'd got his D.S.O.

"My young brother was a Commando," Jewle said. "He was at Narvik. Later he was killed in Normandy. What happened to you, Colonel?"

There'd been considerable reorganisation and he'd been transferred to a Canadian regiment. In France he'd been attached to an English regiment and, after the war, he decided to take advantage of the chance to stay on in the army. He got leave of absence and induced his father to sell the business and had then come back. Owing, he modestly admitted, to casualties, he'd been in command of his regiment when he was wounded and captured in Korea. On release he'd been invalided out. He'd wanted to stay in England and his only regret was that his father wouldn't leave Canada. However, in the spring he would be visiting England and Sterne hoped he could persuade him to change his mind.

"And what made you come this way, Colonel?"

"As a matter of fact, my regiment happened to be at Colchester for a time. I liked the country round here and—well, there you are."

"And what made you come here, Sir Henry?"

That made the conversation more general. But the time went fast. Jewle heard the tall walnut grandfather strike and got to his feet.

It was ten o'clock and I'd no idea it was so late. For the country, that is, and, as Jewle said, for a working man like himself. Henry talked about a final drink but had no takers. It was Sterne who actually left first. In the morning he was meeting some boyhood friends from British Columbia who were spending a day at Cambridge.

Jewle was staying on for a few minutes to hear my report. He was quite pleased about the identification of the tyres. As for himself, he'd had some very interesting hours. Take, for instance, the bank.

"This is the real point," he said, looking at his notes. "Ranger opened an account virtually on a shoe-string when he first came here. He left it untouched till about three months later, and from then on he replenished it with cash. Every month regularly, the deposits varying from twenty pounds to thirty. He rarely signed a cheque against it and his balance at death was about three hundred pounds. There're some other peculiar things, but I'd like you to notice that there wasn't any transfer of a banking account when he came here. Everything was strictly a fresh start, so to speak."

"What about his bungalow?"

"He paid cash for that, too. He got it cheaply as things go nowadays—for nicely under fifteen hundred pounds. I understand it wasn't in too good order. I'm told he did some exterior decorating on it himself. And spent a little money. Some of the cheques went to an Edenthorpe builder. Allman enquired into that while I was looking into that car of his that he traded in when he got a new Ford."

He'd had some luck over that, since the Standard had been bought by a local man. Through the registration book it had been established that Ranger had bought the car—second-hand, of course—from a Cambridge dealer about a week before he arrived in Marstead. It had cost him a flat hundred pounds. Once more, he had paid spot cash.

"Allman's at Cambridge now," Jewle said, "trying to find out where Ranger stayed while he was there, but the overall picture, as I see it, is this: Ranger turned up there—possibly by train—

and he had just so much money in hard cash. He proceeded to invest his money frugally because there wasn't much of it. First he bought the car which our Edenthorpe friend describes as a poor bargain even at a hundred pounds. He also bought about as cheap a bungalow as he could, and he had only enough left over to open a banking account at Edenthorpe. *But here's the important point.* Within three months of his arrival here, he was getting money again, and not by dividend vouchers or by cheques. He was getting it in cash. And very soon after that he bought a new car, again paying cash. Where'd that cash come from?"

"The answer's obvious," I said. "The trouble is, it's too obvious. I'd call it a clear case of blackmail. No person paying blackmail would pay by cheque, nor would the blackmailer take it. Transactions would always be cash."

"Yes," Jewle said. "That was my first idea, but I've had others. He might have been some kind of remittance man, collecting an allowance from relatives in, say, Ireland. The money may have been sent to Cambridge or anywhere by money orders and he collected it at an accommodation address. But what's your idea about this blackmail business, Sir Henry?"

Henry had been unobtrusively listening. He smiled as he shook his head.

"I can't speak for anywhere else but I think I can vouch for Marstead. There's nobody here, I imagine, who hasn't got a perfectly clean record."

"One thing I might add," I said. "It was a queer remark that the rector, Andover, made to me. It seems to have a bearing on that matter of Ranger's being here for three months before he apparently received any money from anywhere. According to Andover, Ranger was quite a different man after his first three months here from what he was at the beginning. He almost went out of his way to be pleasant to everybody. That was at the start. After that, he began throwing his weight about. He almost went out of his way in another direction—putting people's backs up."

"Do you know, I think Andover was right?" Henry said. "Now I look back to the little I had to do with Ranger, I'm sure he became a different man."

Jewle said he'd sleep on it all and maybe he'd be able to see things in the right perspective in the morning. He'd give me a ring after the post had arrived and he'd heard from Allman.

Henry and I sat talking for a few minutes after he'd gone. I thought blackmail was at the heart of the whole business. As Henry had to agree, nobody kills a remittance man.

"And it was a local job," I said. "Only someone who knew Ranger's habits could have slipped into that bungalow and done the poisoning. And, wait a minute. There's something else that fits in with blackmail. You blackmail a person because you've acquired some very dangerous hold. What we've been forgetting is that burglary. In the light of what we know now, it wasn't a sneak thief whom Alice Gantle disturbed: it was the one who was being blackmailed. The one who hoped to have already killed Ranger."

"Then what was he looking for?"

"Don't know. Probably letters that Ranger had somehow got hold of. Incriminating letters. Or photographs. If that's so, then I was all wrong about Doctor Laving. It was a pretty fantastic theory in any case."

I had to explain it: the badly false diagnosis of Alice Gantle's illness or whatever it'd been, and the possibility of Ranger's threatening him with exposure.

"Frank Laving would never have stood for blackmail," Henry said dryly. "He'd have been at Ranger's throat as soon as he had the nerve to suggest it, and he'd have told him to go to hell. I know Frank Laving."

We left it at that. Upstairs in my room I had one gratifying thought, that everything that was happening was pointing to the mystery of Ranger as the solution to the murder of Ranger. Jewle had made admirable progress and, with Allman ferreting at Cambridge, there seemed every reason for at least some mild optimisms. That, maybe, is why I slept what they call the sleep of the just. I admit that when I woke, the cool clear light of morning made the night's views less roseate. Like Henry, I couldn't think of anyone in Marstead whose life shouldn't have been an open book. Not that there weren't skeletons in the very best of cupboards.

9

THE LATEST IN THUNDERBOLTS

WITHIN a few minutes of Marstead's receiving its newspapers the next morning, it was an ant-hill disturbed. Jewle hadn't divulged the whole truth, but, if his object had been local publicity, then he'd divulged more than enough. The vital facts were there: the accidental killing of Black and the main object—the killing of Ranger. Henry's two papers were of the staider kind and their reporting decorous, but one could imagine the headlines in the popular Press. Unless I was very far wrong, within a very few hours Marstead would have an influx of reporters and photographers. Marstead, in other words, would soon be an excellent place for Jewle to avoid. My name, of course, hadn't been mentioned.

What interested me most was the request for information about Ranger himself, and the photograph that was printed by the less staid of Henry's two papers. Jewle must have telephoned his day's discoveries before coming to dine with us, for everything he had mentioned to me was there on the printed page. I was pointing that out to Henry when Mrs. Slack suddenly announced the rector.

I could never have dreamed of Andover's showing so much perturbation. His plump cheeks were red, too, and he was blowing slightly, as if he'd fairly scurried across the sports field path as soon as he'd gobbled down the murder details.

"Ah, you've seen it!" he said. "It can't be true, Sir Henry. No one in Marstead could have done such a dreadful thing."

He switched his look, almost an accusatory one, to me. I shrugged my shoulders and said mildly that I didn't think one would dare to have such things printed if they weren't largely true.

"Sit down, Andover, and let me get you some coffee," Henry said.

"Good of you, but I'm afraid I can't stay," he said. "I feel I ought to call on Mrs. Black. This must have been an overwhelming shock to her."

He was already backing out. Henry went with him. Then the telephone went and I heard Henry taking the call. A couple of minutes and he was back.

"That was Sterne," he said.

"Is he also going to console the widow?"

Henry chuckled.

"Quite the reverse, my dear fellow. I gather he doesn't want any more weeping on his neck, so he's very glad he'd arranged to be away for the day."

His face straightened.

"He didn't seem inclined to believe it, either. He called it something out of a horror comic. Curious, isn't it, how one reads about such things and never expects to be involved in them oneself."

We exchanged newspapers and relighted our pipes.

"Wonder what Mrs. Black's reactions to Andover were," I said. "If she spoke to him as frankly as she did to me, then he must have had a shock. I'd have liked to listen in."

"I think you might do worse than ring her yourself," he told me. "If this village is going to be invaded by London crime reporters, she might do worse than get away for the day herself. It's something she probably won't have thought of."

I waited a few minutes and then I did ring Lucia Black. She said that Andover's call had been very short and she had thought it rather sweet of him. So sweet, in fact, as she added with a certain cynicism, that she hadn't had the heart to disillusion him about Marstead's idea of the relationship between her husband and herself.

"It was funny in a way," she said. "He tried so hard not to keep looking at me as if I were Mary Magdalene. You could see his brain ticking over."

"Thinking of what?"

"All that gaff about me and Norman Ranger. Don't tell me you believed it?"

"I'm not the Great Inscrutable," I said. "I have to hear all, but that doesn't mean I necessarily believe it."

"Well, don't believe that one," she said. "Perhaps I had my own reasons for letting Ranger give himself ideas. And they weren't what you think."

"My dear lady!"

"Drop it," she said. "But thanks for ringing up."

I told her hastily that she hadn't heard all the reasons why I *had* rung her. But that advice about reporters seemed rather to amuse her.

"I'm not budging an inch. I shall bolt all the doors, and short of breaking the windows they won't get a word out of me. But thanks all the same. By the way, don't forget you promised to drop in some time when all this blows over."

I reported back to Henry. A minute or two and I was wondering when I'd hear from Jewle. It was after ten o'clock and I was more or less tied to the telephone. Then I heard a sound like a car drawing in at the short drive. I looked through the side window and, sure enough, there was Jewle. I met him at the front door.

"You're not looking too good," I said. "Not a hangover, I hope?"

"To tell the truth," he said, "I've had a bit of a shock this morning. May I come in?"

We went in. Henry appeared. He congratulated Jewle on what had been in the morning's papers. But Jewle did a curious thing. He had a look into the hall and closed the door. He looked through the door to the kitchen and closed that.

"Something extraordinary has cropped up," he told us. "As my old Chief, George Wharton, would have said—it beats cock-fighting. I still can't believe it. It just couldn't have happened."

I suppose our ears were stretched and our eyes bulging a bit. My fingers had gone instinctively to my hornrims. It was to me that he turned.

"You remember I had Allman vacuum the boot of Ranger's car and send the contents, and Black's clothes, to the Yard for a laboratory check? Well, I was rung up this morning bright and early. And what do you think? *Black's body had definitely been carried in Ranger's car.*"

The three of us looked at each other. Stout Cortez and his men had nothing on us in the matter of wild surmise. As Jewle had said, it just wasn't credible.

"Don't your laboratories sometimes make mistakes?" Henry asked mildly.

"Oh, no," Jewle said. "Maybe occasional doubts, perhaps, in some highly involved analyses or so which I couldn't begin to understand, but not in anything so dead easy as this. Everything fitted. What was on the clothes was in the car. There were even microscopic fibres. Black's body was put in Ranger's car and no one could have put it in but Ranger. He shifted it to just as far as that straw."

"Then why did he go off in his car again? What was he doing out beyond where he was killed? Trying to establish some kind of alibi, or what?"

Jewle shook his head.

"You want it both ways, sir. Once he'd got rid of the body by hiding it under that straw, he didn't need an alibi. No one was to know where Black actually died."

"But what about the other car? The one with the Colonna tyres?"

"That's what I've come over for," he said. "I thought we might go along there and have another look. And a word with Culver."

He gave a wry smile.

"But that's not the half of it. Let's put it this way. Black's body was in Ranger's car and therefore Ranger moved it to where it was found. He must have stopped his car on the actual road so that none of the wheels ran on the grass verge. That's why there aren't any tracks."

"Might I say something?" Henry cut in. "Did Ranger put the body under that straw so as to cast suspicion on Culver? After all, Ranger and Culver were on pretty bad terms."

"A good point, Sir Henry. The trouble is that we're assuming it *was* Ranger who put the body there."

"But wasn't it?" I said.

"Listen," he said patiently. "I told you that you hadn't heard the half of it. Now take those casts of the boots. Feet went through the gap and feet came back. Those that went through were more deeply embedded than those that came back and therefore something—and something heavy enough to be Black's body—was taken in. *But the feet-marks weren't Ranger's.* His shoes were nines. The marks were made by elevens at the very least."

What could we say? Jewle knew what he was talking about. If it had been incredible before, it was fantastic now.

"But that's still not all," he said. "The most puzzling thing has yet to come. I wouldn't be surprised if this business doesn't become known as the case of the flowery corpse. Listen to this, for example: on Black's clothing was chlorophyl. His body had been in very close contact with green Vegetable matter—in fact, chrysanthemums. One or two petals adhered to the clothing—his overcoat principally."

"That's pretty macabre," I said. "Where the devil could the chrysanthemums have come from? Almost as if someone'd anticipated the funeral."

"And even that's not all," Jewle said. "In the boot of Ranger's car there wasn't a trace of chlorophyl or petals."

There wasn't an adjective for it. Fantastic had ceased to be the word.

Henry gave a little clearing of the throat.

"It's probably a foolish suggestion, Inspector, but—well, are there any chrysanthemums in Ranger's garden?"

"Yes, sir, there are. But Black's body was never laid on top of them for any reason. They're scrubby, neglected sort of plants that ought to have been divided years ago. Tiny flowers and too many of them. And they're bolt upright. Now the flowers that Black's body came into very close contact with were florists' specimens. You can tell that by the size of the petals."

It was the most amazing thing I'd ever been up against. It had neither rhyme nor reason. It was, when one thought of those queer happenings in the dead dark of that Monday night, a something nightmarish, surrealistic.

"The only solution I can think of is even more incredible than what's been discovered," Jewle said. "It's that there must have been two cars. But how two people in two different cars could have had a hand in shifting Black's body is something that's got me beat."

He got to his feet.

"Do stay and have coffee," Henry said.

"Good of you, Sir Henry, but I'd like to clear some of this business up. The way I feel now, I shan't eat nor drink till I can lick some sense into things. So if you're ready, Mr. Travers, what about having a word with Culver?"

Marstead was astir. A few elderly men and some women with prams were standing about near Ranger's bungalow or looking over the hedge and gate into the garden. Three cars were drawn up at the verge. The posts and rope that had fenced off the verge, gap and the resting place of Black's body had gone. Warner stood in front of the gap as if ready for anyone who might want to go through. Jewle turned the car into the farm track and drew it to a halt at the farmhouse door.

Culver was somewhere about the farm. His housekeeper found a man to go in search of him. Jewle and I walked back and across to the gap. Those footprints from which the casts had been removed still stood clear. The shoes must have been large. Both soles and heels looked smooth with no signs of heavy nails or cleating.

"Ranger's feet could have swum in boots that size," Jewle said. "You see these coming in and the difference in depth and spacing from those going out? That's about the only thing no one's been able to disprove—as yet. Someone definitely carried something heavy through that gap."

The housekeeper was calling to us and we went round to the back of the house. Old Culver was just coming through a field-gate and we went to meet him.

"Bin some rum goin's-on accordin' to the papers, hain't there?" he said, finger flicking to forelock and eyes moving questioningly from one of us to the other. "You reckon it's all true?"

"It's true enough," Jewle assured him. "But we'd like your help in clearing something up. Tell me: didn't you catch Mr. Ranger helping himself to some straw of yours a few months ago?"

The old man's eyes narrowed. He took a step forward and was peering at Jewle from under his heavy eyebrows. His look was queerly menacing.

"What're you bringin' all that up for? Tryin' to make out as though I had somethin' to do with what happened to him?"

"Not at all—"

"You speak your mind. Don't you try them roundabout tricks wi' me, sir. I won't stand for it. If you've got anything to say, do you say it straight out."

"Now, now, now," Jewle smiled. "You mustn't fly off the handle like that. I'm not insinuating anything. Why should I? You had nothing to do with Ranger's death, nor Major Black's. All we want from you is some help. Where, for instance, did Ranger get that straw from? That lot there in the yard?"

There was still a suspicion in Culver's look.

"Not from there it weren't. From some what I had up the Edenthorpe Road."

"A pity," Jewle said. "I was hoping it had been from here. What I was trying to get at was this. Ranger took something out, but could anybody have brought anything in—and I don't mean Major Black's body. Let me show you something."

He led the way to the hedge gap. Culver was still faintly muttering to himself—the last reverberation of his outburst—and he took his time.

"See these foot-marks?" Jewle said. "They're coming in, as you see. They're pretty deep and they're closely spaced—the sort of marks anyone'd make who was carrying in something heavy, like a body. Now look at these others: they're going out. The heels hardly touch the ground, which shows he was in a hurry. You follow all that?"

Culver had been interested. He'd bent right down over the feet-marks.

"Yes, sir, I can follow that all right," he said as he straightened himself.

"Right," Jewle said. "Now look out here. See those tyre marks? We thought they were made by the car that brought Major Black's body here and that someone took it out of the boot and carried it to where it was found. You've got that?"

Culver nodded importantly.

"Yes, sir. Reckon I have."

"Right," Jewle said. "And now let's suppose we were wrong. The car didn't come here to bring a body and those prints weren't made by the feet of anyone carrying a body in. Let's suppose a car pulled up here for a perfectly legitimate reason—say a tradesman's car or van. And say something was carried through this gap as a kind of short cut to the house: a crate of beer, for instance, or a box of groceries. What would you say about that?"

Culver shook his head.

"'Tain't a short cut in the first place. Anyone comin' through here'd have to walk all round that straw, wouldn't he? Why should he go sploddin' through all that muck and stuff when he could drive right up to the house?"

"That's a sound answer," Jewle told him. "There's no reason in your opinion for anyone wanting to carry anything through that gap?"

"It don't make sense," Culver said. "Don't make no sense at all."

"Well, that's cleared up that point." Jewle let out a breath. "We're much obliged to you, Mr. Culver. Keep it to yourself, by the way. We don't want everyone to know what we've been talking about."

Culver nodded knowingly as he shook Jewle by the hand.

"You can rely on me, sir. I know when to talk and when not."

I had a grip, too, from that rough bony hand, and then we went out to the road through the gap. More cars were parked by the roadside. We stood there while Warner was sent to move the sightseers on.

"Well, it was a good try," Jewle told me philosophically. "I'd hoped we might have washed out that car business."

It'd been ingenious and I told him so. But there was just one thing: a tradesman's delivery van would hardly have been fitted with new Colonna tyres which cost more than the very best of the ordinary types.

"I know," he said, and grinned. "Don't rub it in. It was just one of the things you do when you're at your wit's end. You hope for miracles, and there just aren't such things. Besides, even if we had eliminated that car, we'd still have been left with two other cars on our hands. Black's body was in Ranger's car, and in the chrysanthemum car."

He looked back over his shoulder.

"Culver seems to have gone. A bit touchy, wasn't he?"

"Maybe he's heard something already," I said. "The village may have him in mind for Ranger's murder."

The bungalow was clear of sightseers when we moved across. Jewle unlocked the front door. We went through the tiny hall into the lounge. It struck cold and damp.

"Anything you've come for particularly?"

"No," he said slowly. "Hoping for the same old miracle. I've often gone back to the scenes of crimes when I've been stuck and picked up something that I'd missed. Know what I'd like to do? Come in here at about four or half-past when Ranger came in that afternoon. The same light: the same everything. Try to put myself in his shoes."

"One thing we know happened," I said. "He found Black's body here. And he must have put it in the boot of his car. But what happened then? All I can think of is that he had a confederate who transferred it to *his* car. And that's absurd."

Jewle had gone over to the window that overlooked the back. His hand went to the curtain as if to draw it and begin darkening the room. The hand fell.

"Hallo, what's this?"

"Look," he said. "The catch is back. I'd bet my life it wasn't when I was in here last."

He got his glass from his breast pocket.

"Have a look yourself."

On the brass of the catch were friction marks where a knife had been forced up from outside and pushed it back. Jewle slipped the catch into place and went out by the back door. He forced his own knife up between the sashes and pushed hard. The metal couldn't have done the cutting edge of the knife much good, but the catch went back. With my gloved hands I pushed the bottom window up. Jewle put a leg across and got back into the room. He put his glass once more on catch and woodwork. Mrs. Gantle hadn't cleaned that room for days and here was a film of dust. You could see where it had been disturbed, and by a gloved hand.

"Hopeless to look for prints," Jewle said. "Even babies in arms know all about prints nowadays. Who made the entry, do you think? The one who was here before? The one Mrs. Gantle disturbed that Monday night?"

I thought there wasn't a doubt about it. And, if that was so, it scotched Tagg's fluent theory of a sneak thief.

"That blackmail idea looks good," Jewle said. "I'm beginning to like it. Wonder what our friend was looking for? Letters or photographs, like you said?"

"The thing is, did he get what he was looking for?"

"No harm in having another look ourselves."

We kept together, and we looked. We went through each room with a small-tooth comb. We felt and we prodded: we even looked on top of the closet cistern and took off the lid to look inside. When we'd finished we were pretty sure there was nothing on which one could rely for blackmail hidden anywhere in that house. We went into the outside shed and explored that too, even shifting aside a couple of hundred-weight of coal. We went through the garage just as carefully; finally we looked under the eaves along the gutter-pipes.

"Whatever was there must have gone," Jewle said. "The devil of it is, he must have had all the time in the world in which to explore." He clicked his tongue in annoyance. "It's my own fault; I ought to have taken that first entry far more seriously and had the place under observation."

I didn't think it as serious as all that. And there were still plenty of avenues, as the politicians say, we had yet to explore.

"It was bad handling," he said. "If we'd caught whoever it was red-handed, this case might have been over."

He looked at his watch.

"Let's get out of here. Trying to lick sense into things is driving me crazy. We'd better go to Cambridge. I promised to pick Allman up. We might see things a bit differently if we get far enough away."

An excellent idea, but it didn't stop us from beginning all over again when we were on the road.

"When you look at it, the whole thing's simple," Jewle said. "Just the matter of Black's body being in two different cars. Ranger took it away in his own car and then, for some reason or other, it had to be put into another."

He drew his car to a halt.

"Wait a minute. He might have had a puncture or something, and helped himself to that second car. And taken it back when he'd finished the job."

Then he smiled wryly. That idea was as full of holes as a tennis net. All Ranger had had to do was get Black's body across the road to Culver's straw yard. If his car had been punctured, he could have carried it there. The whole idea of a second car was sheer lunacy. And yet Black's body *had* been in two cars— Ranger's, and what we called the chrysanthemum one. And to complicate things still more, there was the fact that Ranger had been well away from Marstead when he'd been killed. Where had he been, and why?

"Leave it," Jewle said, and moved the car on again. "All the same, something tells me the whole thing's as simple as ABC. It's like when I was a boy and couldn't get a key to open a lock. I knew it was the right key, and yet it wouldn't turn. I would oil the lock and do everything and then my father would produce a pin and poke a bit of fluff out of the key, and everything was as right as ninepence."

Something made me smile. I explained.

"Maybe my mind isn't as pure as it ought to be, but when you mentioned a little bit of fluff, I couldn't help thinking of the other meaning—the slang one. There *is* a little bit of fluff somewhere in this case: *Mrs. Black.*"

We talked about her and I told him at last about that peculiar expression that had come over her face when she learned that her husband had not died of exposure. I think he was coming round to the idea that she might be far more deeply concerned than we'd thought.

"Chrysanthemums," I said. "Ranger might have been bringing her a dozen of the best."

"Damn the chrysanthemums!" he told me exasperatedly. Then he grinned. "I thought we were running away from this case and here we are back at it. How much farther to Cambridge?"

10

THE RANGER TRAIL

TEN minutes later we picked up Allman in Cambridge and the three of us had lunch at the hotel where he'd put up—the one where Ranger had stayed when he had first come to the town. There were one or two ends still to tie up but by the time we were ready to return to Edenthorpe, we knew quite a lot about Ranger. The trouble was that we still hadn't the faintest inkling as to who might have killed him, or anything beyond guesswork as to why.

Ranger had come to Cambridge by motor-coach and his luggage had been two suitcases. All he had let fall about himself at the hotel was that he had been in business in London and had now retired and was looking for a little place in the country. The morning after his arrival he had called on two different estate agents and had asked about small properties near Edenthorpe. He left the office of the second of those agents with descriptive lists of about twenty properties within some ten miles radius of

Edenthorpe, and it was not till the late afternoon of the following day that he came back.

It seemed almost a certainty, although he said nothing about it to the agent, that he had meanwhile gone to Edenthorpe by bus and then on to Marstead and had made his own inspection of the bungalow which he subsequently bought. At any rate, when he came to the agent's office that afternoon, he said that he'd looked the lists over and thought the bungalow known as The Briary, at Marstead, might be the kind of place he was looking for. He was a bachelor, he said, and had no liking for gardening.

The Briary belonged to a widow, who'd continued to live on there after her husband's death some two years prior to Ranger's arrival. She had become something of a recluse and the place began to suffer. There was also some mental trouble and finally her daughter took her away to her home in Nottingham and the bungalow was put in the hands of the agent—first to be let furnished and then, since there'd been no applications, to be sold together with the furniture.

The price had been gradually lowered. Eighteen hundred was being asked when Ranger visited it officially with the agent. His final offer was fifteen hundred and another hundred for the contents. The vendor, tired of the delay, accepted. The agent, by the way, was given the same story—that Ranger was a retired businessman from London. He was asked something else that struck us as interesting.

"I shall get the place in better order," Ranger had said, "but it's possible, of course, that I shan't find it suitable after all. If I decide to sell, could you get me my money back?"

The agent said he certainly could. The only thing that had militated against an earlier sale had been the admittedly poor condition of the place and the unwillingness of the owner and her daughter to spend money on it. If Ranger put it in really sound order, he could count on getting his money back, and more.

"That's something else that fits in," Jewle said. "Ranger did do some repairs and decorations. But principally in the first three months. Doesn't it look as if he really came to Marstead to look for something and, if he didn't find it, he was going to look elsewhere?"

I agreed. Ranger was looking not so much for something as for somebody, and that somebody might be the one about whom he'd somehow acquired incriminating evidence.

"And there's that other business," I said. "That during his first three months in Marstead, he laid himself out to get friendly with everybody. After that he suddenly changed. It was as if he were in a position to be himself. His was a kind of *folie de grandeur*: you know, a sort of swollen-headedness you might get when you know you're all at once sitting on top of the world."

"Yes," Jewle said. "There's also the fact that here in Cambridge, and everywhere else, for that matter, he let out virtually nothing about himself. I can't see him as a retired businessman; I'm pretty sure he had a past, and a none too clean one either and that he must have been worried about it. Marstead's a remote kind of place and what he might have been cocksure about was that after having lived there three months, nobody had the faintest idea that he might have that kind of past. All he had to do was keep his hair dyed and he could end his days there. And with an assured income, of course, if he'd found the person he'd hoped to blackmail."

"What was the general opinion of him here?" I asked Allman.

"Everyone got on well with him," Allman said. "They thought he was very nice indeed. All of them—the staff here, the bar, the proprietor, the people in the agent's office—nearly shed tears when they read about his death."

"He never came back here?"

"Never. The agent was that way some four months after Ranger'd bought the bungalow and he found him at home. He told him he liked Marstead and was staying on. The agent mentioned certain things that might still be done to improve the place—clearing up the garden was one of them—if Ranger should decide to sell at any time, and that was about all."

"Except," Jewle said, "that Ranger never did clear up the garden, except perfunctorily, and he didn't make any more improvements—at least to the extent suggested. He did buy some furniture at auctions and got rid of some of the old. That bureau in his lounge, for instance, and the easy chairs. And he'd had loose covers made for the chairs, by an Edenthorpe firm, and new curtains."

As I said, we knew quite a lot about Ranger and we could guess still more, but how to use it as even a basis for finding out who'd poisoned him was a vastly different matter. Ranger was still a mystery as far as concerned essentials, and how to proceed further was beyond us. All we could hope for was some response to the photographs in the *Police Gazette* and the Press. And in the meantime, all we could do was to follow up that clue of the Colonna tyres.

It was about five o'clock when we got back to Edenthorpe. Jewle suggested tea, and then he'd run me back to Marstead. There was nothing from the Colonna people, but we hardly expected anything till the morning.

"You carry on with tea," Jewle told me. "I'll just slip along to the police station in case anything's turned up."

I had a couple of cups of tea and a cake. I got my pipe going and still Jewle hadn't come back. I had a second pipe and altogether it must have been best part of an hour after he'd left that he appeared again. He was looking on remarkably good terms with himself.

"We've got something," he said. "We know who Ranger was and where he was—at a certain time. I'll lay you a hundred to one you'll never guess."

I didn't even try.

"He was at Parkways Jail!"

I must have gaped.

"But how could he be? He hadn't a record."

"I know," Jewle told me, and grinned. "He was probably a Medical Officer there from 1945 to 1948."

"I see," I said slowly. "But why *probably*? Aren't you sure?"

"They're not," he said. "We're seeing the Governor tomorrow morning. That was deliberate on my part. We might pick up a whole lot we'd never discover over the phone. But I'm pretty sure and I'll tell you why. This is how it was passed to me by the Yard. Parkways saw that *Police Gazette* enquiry and someone thought he could spot Ranger as their M.O. at the time I said. Only, he didn't call himself Ranger. His real name was Nicholas Riley. Nicholas Riley: Norman Ranger. The same initials. They all do it."

"Yes," I said. "And that Alice Gantle business. Something tells me I ought to have spotted the fact that Ranger'd been a doctor."

"It wouldn't have got us anywhere," he said. "We could only have got at him through medical enquiries if we'd known his right name."

It was great news. We didn't disagree about that as he drove me back to Marstead. As for the morning, we'd have to make an early start. Parkways was a hundred and fifty miles away and he wanted to get there at about eleven o'clock.

As a matter of fact, it was short of seven o'clock the next morning when I drew in at the police station. Inside a couple of minutes I'd switched to Jewle's car and we were off.

We had an hour and a half of fast travelling with little traffic on the roads. We were crossing the main arteries in any case and there wasn't all that much traffic later on, but it takes a fast car and a lot of luck to average forty on English roads. We were only a quarter of an hour late when we reached the jail. The morning had been dull with a threat of rain, and that old-fashioned prison and its grey Victorian Gothic looked a depressing place. If they'd put out the window boxes and hung out flags it would still have been depressing. Even from the long window of the room we entered, our view was across the exercise yard with its tall, grimy-looking walls and frieze of spikes.

It was better inside that room when you turned your back on that window. Colonel Otway was a burly, genial man and there was a roaring fire in the grate, and in less than no time you knew yourself in a little comfortable oasis that had nothing to do with crime. We shook hands and he waved at a table on which were a good many documents.

"I think we've got everything ready for you. I'm really interested in this business. If your man Ranger is our man Riley, it looks as if there might be developments."

"You think he is, Colonel?"

"Both were Irish. Height and colour of hair seem to agree. Not bad for a start. Still, have a look at this photograph."

"You knew Riley personally?" I asked.

"Unfortunately, no," he said. "He was before my time. But I got into touch with my predecessor and he told me some very interesting things. Still, they'll keep for a bit. What do you think of the photograph? I took it out of the frame, as you see. There's another in the infirmary, so it's at your disposal if it's any use to you."

It was a photograph of the infirmary staff: a group of some twenty men arranged in three rows. In the middle of the front row were what I took to be a couple of doctors. One certainly wasn't Ranger: he was far too big and had a beefy kind of face. The man on his right was the problem.

"The one with the moustache might be our man Ranger."

"That's what we think," Otway said. "But I've got one of our senior warders outside. An excellent fellow called Hobbis. You'd like to discuss it with him?"

Hobbis came in. He was a tall, loose-limbed man of about forty-five. We shook hands. Little courtesies like that make the wheels go round.

"It's this moustache that bothers me," Jewle said. "Amazing what a difference it makes to the look of a man. And, of course, if Doctor Riley was the man we know as Ranger, then a few years have rolled by. You knew him well?"

Hobbis smiled.

"I don't think many knew him better, sir."

"And what'd you think of him?"

"Well, sir, personally, I liked him. I think everyone did. He was easy to get on with. Mind you, sir, he had a tongue on him when anything went wrong, but it didn't last. Free-and-easy, sir: that's what I'd call him."

"Did you form any opinion of his actual doctoring?"

"He was good, sir. At least, everyone said he was."

That photograph had been taken in 1946 when Riley was assistant medical officer. Two years later he was in charge. No photograph was available for that particular time.

"Let's try and get at things in another way," Jewle said, and produced one of those retouched photographs of Ranger from his case. "I'll just pencil in lightly a moustache on this—so. Now have a look."

Hobbis had a look. He frowned just for a moment. Then he smiled.

"That's him, sir. I'd bet a month's pay on it."

"It shouldn't get to that," Jewle told him. "Let's put it officially. You'd swear to it in a court of law?"

"Every time, sir."

"That's fine," Jewle said. "Now we've really got something to start on."

Another shaking of hands and Hobbis went out.

"What next?" Jewle said.

Otway thought we might look at Riley's records. They were remarkably complete, and even included copies of various testimonials. I've grumbled enough at red tape in my time, but I did feel a little glow of gratitude to the officialdom that had had those records filed.

Nicholas Riley was born near Belfast in 1900. He had taken his medical degree at Queen's University in 1927. That looked a bit late and we thought it might be enquired into. In 1929 he had bought a partnership—he was one of a triumvirate—at Harrenden, in Worcestershire. Jewle, methodical and logical as ever, looked the place up. It was a small market town of some four thousand souls. The senior partner was a Doctor Wormgay, whose practice was in the town itself. Riley had a country area adjacent, with his headquarters at the village of Tedfold.

Riley was there till 1939, when he either joined up or was called up. At the end of the war he didn't go back to Harrenden but applied for a post under the Prison Medical Service.

"Isn't there something wrong about that?" Jewle asked. "Riley was forty-five and I had the idea that the P.M.S. liked their people to be thirty-two or under."

"Those were difficult times," Otway said. "They'd want some experienced newcomers as well as the younger men. Also I rather gathered from my predecessor that Riley had some influence. There's a testimonial from his R.A.M.C. Colonel, who'd once been in the Service himself."

It was an excellent testimonial, even if it was also from a brother Irishman. The one from Doctor Wormgay of Harrenden was quite good, too.

"Well, all that seems clear enough," Jewle said. "He came here as assistant and learnt his new job and then he moved up. Later, in 1948, he resigned from the service. Isn't that rather peculiar? He'd a first-class job here, so why'd he throw it up?"

"Ah!" said Otway. "That occurred to me, too. This is what my predecessor told me. You remember what Hobbis said about Riley: that he was quick-tempered and it soon wore off? Well, my information is that that was true and what little squabbles did arise were when Riley regarded himself as being interfered with. It was something of the sort that made him resign. According to Gasport—my predecessor—the whole thing was ridiculous. Not only was it unnecessary but Riley went out of his way to be objectionable. I know Gasport: he's a most reasonable man. Anyone can get on with him. But not Riley. Gasport asked him to think things over but Riley was positively insolent. I can't credit this, mind you, but Gasport had the idea the whole thing was staged and that Riley had his own reasons for leaving. I think Riley just worked himself into a rage and got himself to a state where he just couldn't draw back."

"Well, it's hard for an outsider like me to judge," Jewle said. "It certainly seemed damn silly of Riley: giving up a good job and forfeiting pension rights and so on. But what did Gasport think of him as a doctor?"

Otway chuckled.

"Between ourselves, he thought he was competent but not exactly brilliant. What he did have was a wonderful bedside manner: a sort of Irish blarney or gift of the gab. Maybe that's most of the battle in the medical profession. I wouldn't know."

We laughed. I said I thought he was right. I had a doctor of that kind myself. The last time I'd had influenza and was feeling a longing for the pearly gates to open, he'd come into the bedroom like a tornado and practically accused me of malingering. When he'd gone I'd decided that there might be something in going on living after all.

"Well, that's the end of the records," Jewle said. "But where'd he go from here? You don't happen to know that?"

"But I do," Otway said. "That's one of the things I happened to get from Gasport and I've been trying to work things out. I haven't got all the answers but I think there's enough for a basis for you to work on if you think it necessary. What you may find is that Riley did nothing for a year and then he applied for a National Health job—if that's what you call it—through the Leicestershire Executive Council. At any rate, he was back in practice again towards the end of 1948." He looked at his notes. "A country practice at a place called Helmsby. I looked it up and it's near Market Harborough. He was there till the autumn of 1951."

"And then?"

Otway gave a queer sort of smile.

"I won't ask you to guess, but he was struck off the register."

Our eyes popped a bit.

"Thought that'd surprise you," Otway said. "Gasport wouldn't probably have known about it if he hadn't been a Leicester-shire man himself. He has a married sister living not far from Helmsby."

"What were the grounds for striking him off?"

"One of the usual: grossly unprofessional conduct with a patient. In this case it happened to be what I'd call a bit of a fool of a widow with money. It was the brother who made all the stink and managed to turn her against Riley. There'd been other women, too, it appears. But I don't know all the ins and outs of it. Gasport and I were talking on the telephone and I got only the highlights, so to speak."

"That bedside manner must have been pretty good," Jewle said dryly. "He was a man of fifty-one."

"I'm told he never looked his age," Otway said. "He was as active and alert as men many years younger. And he was very good-looking. You can even see something of it in that photograph. And don't forget he had a marvellous way with him. When that red hair of his began to grey a bit he must have been pretty attractive—to middle-aged widows."

"And after he was struck off," I said. "You don't know what happened to him?"

"No one has the faintest idea," he said. "He just disappeared."

The room had a heavy silence. From somewhere beyond the yard was the faintest sound of a machine in the prison workshops. Jewle's fingers slowly began caressing his chin.

"A most interesting morning, sir. It strikes me you might like to hear our side of things."

Otway glanced up at the clock.

"Lunch should be ready. In fact we're late. Why not talk things over while we're having a meal?"

Mrs. Otway had tactfully absented herself and we three lunched alone. By the time the meal was over, Otway had heard all about the man who had called himself Ranger and the problem that still faced us. We agreed that our journey had been more than worth while, if only because we now had a much clearer picture. Ranger, as we still preferred to call him, was a flesh and blood person, not a mere name or something on the tray of a morgue.

"About these blackmail ideas of ours," I said. "I'm beginning to have an idea. While he was here, Ranger must have become acquainted professionally with quite a few inmates. Let's suppose that after he was struck off he happened to get wind of one who was going straight—shall we call it?—and perhaps under an assumed name, and he traced him to Marstead."

"That'd be too easy," Jewle said. "You know everyone in Marstead. It'd be child's-play to find out where everyone was during the time Ranger was here, from 1946 to 1948."

"Why confine things to Marstead?" I said. "There's the whole immediate area, including Edenthorpe. We know that whoever slipped that atropine into Ranger's whisky must have been familiar with his habits, but that needn't mean he had to be an actual inhabitant of Marstead."

"I suppose not," Jewle said it reluctantly. "It's a good idea, but what I'd like to do is learn a whole lot more about Ranger. You've got a reference book here, Colonel? I'd like to get into touch with the Belfast police."

Otway took him into another room. It was a quarter of an hour before they came back.

"Well, that's that," Jewle told me. "I've asked them to dig up all they can on Nicholas Riley and to let me have it at Edenthorpe. Got any maps here, Colonel? I left my own in the car. Just a large scale map of England will do."

Otway produced a map and Jewle bent over it. It didn't take him long to make up his mind.

"No use being in a hurry about all this," he said. "When we get back to Edenthorpe we want to say we know everything there is to be known about Ranger. What we'll do is make for Harrenden straight away. We'll pick up all we can about him there and then tomorrow we can circle through Leicestershire. It'll only mean an extra day."

That made him think of something else. He ought to get into touch with Allman and hear any news, and let him know about our movements. An adjourned inquest on Major Black might be got out of the way, and there was no reason then why both Black and Ranger shouldn't be buried. I asked him to get Allman to ring Henry.

It was almost three o'clock before we could finally get away. We had a journey of a hundred miles in front of us and some of it would be done in the dark, but we'd be striking a main road before then and it ought to be easy to find our way. We shouldn't have to worry about a hotel. Harrenden had been in the A.A. guide-book and Otway would be ringing the White Lion to book rooms for the night, and, old hands as we both were, we'd taken the precaution of bringing with us what we might need for such a night. And it was good in some ways to leave that jail behind, profitable though the day so far had been.

"Never a word this morning from those Colonna people," Jewle said as we emerged from the speed-limit area of the little town. "They're certainly taking their time."

I think that was all the harking back that we did. It was new country for both of us and Jewle had to keep his eyes on the road. Towards dusk there was a certain amount of mist and it was after six o'clock when we got to Harrenden. The hotel was in the little market square. The rooms were waiting for us but when we came down we found that dinner was not till half-past seven. Jewle thought it a pity to waste time. With any luck we might get started at once on our way back along the Ranger trial.

11

TRAIL'S END

THE hotel manager knew nothing about a Doctor Riley. Nor did his odd man, for he too had only been in Harrenden for about ten years. Tedfold, where Riley had actually practised, was in any case four miles away which, for that part of the world, was pretty remote.

"There was a Doctor Wormgay actually here in Harrenden," Jewle said. "Ever heard of him?"

The manager smiled.

"Why, yes. He's still hale and hearty. Retired about three years ago, just after I came here. He's living in Pershore Road—a detached, red-brick house covered with creeper. You must have passed it as you came in: about a couple of hundred yards away. You can't miss it. Left-hand side."

He was right. We found it without the least trouble—a small-ish Georgian house with a particularly fine fanlight. A plump, middle-aged woman—the housekeeper—admitted us and took Jewle's warrant card. A couple of minutes and we were being shown into the doctor's den. It had a look of the most comfortable untidiness: books everywhere, *The Times* on the floor, a score of pipes in a long rack and more on the table, and, believe it or not, a cat asleep on the rug in front of the friendly fire. The only thing missing was a kettle singing on a hob.

Doctor Wormgay laid his pipe alongside the ash-tray and got to his feet as we came in. For just a second he had a grave courtesy. Jewle identified himself, and me.

"Sit down. Sit down." He gave us both a quick, shrewd look and handed the warrant card back to Jewle. "Scotland Yard," he said and chuckled. "Don't say my sins have caught up with me at last. But take a seat, gentlemen. Just put those things on the floor."

He was exactly eighty and he didn't look it, except for the slight stoop to his broad shoulders. His mop of grey hair still had the yellow flecks of its younger colour as did the untidy moustache that straggled below and round the full lips. The eyes twinkled beneath the heavy eyebrows and it wasn't hard to tell that for Doctor Wormgay life still had its zest. He picked up his pipe, puffed hard at it to get it going again, and waved a hand at an exceedingly handsome cigarette box—a present, one could guess, on his retirement.

"A cigarette? . . . Help yourselves. There're matches inside, or should be. . . . And now," he said, surveying us from under those heavy eyebrows. "Just what is it you want from me, gentlemen?"

Jewle told him.

"Riley?" the doctor said. "What's he been up to now? The last thing I saw about him was his getting himself into serious trouble. You know about that?"

Jewle said that if he meant that business of being struck off the register, then he did. But this was a bit different. Riley had been murdered and we were in charge of the Yard enquiry.

"Murdered, eh?" The doctor gave a slow shake of the head. "I oughtn't to be, but I'm sorry to hear it. There were times, mind you, when I'd have liked to do something like that to him myself. Not that I'm being serious, of course." He shook his head again. "Nick Riley murdered. A bad ending, however you look at it."

Jewle told him the whole story. He listened with only an occasional nod of the head. But the pipe was cold when Jewle had finished and he didn't trouble to light it again.

"And now you want to hear anything else I can tell you about him," he said. "Naturally I'm prepared to do it, though I must say I never thought of revealing it to a soul. My other partner, by the way, died some four years ago."

Riley, he said, had been one of the most likeable and, at the same time, the most exasperating of men. He had, he said, all the blarney and blandishments and inconsequence and irresponsibility and illogic of all the stage Irishmen that ever were.

"It wasn't his fault entirely," he said. "It was his upbringing. But you don't want to hear about that."

"It's one of the things I *would* like to hear about," Jewle told him. "I've asked the Belfast police to make enquiries but I'd certainly like to hear what you know yourself."

Riley, Wormgay told us, was the son of a doctor. The mother died when the boy was at school and thereafter he was brought up by a spinster aunt. She spoilt him and, when he went to Queen's, he was very much of a playboy. Then the worst possible thing happened. The father died and his son was the sole heir. He sold the practice and, altogether, he came in for about fifteen thousand pounds. At Queen's he did most things but work. In fact, it was only when most of the money had gone that he at last succeeded in qualifying. But for the aunt's death and another, smaller, legacy, he'd never have been able to buy the practice.

"But you couldn't help liking him," the doctor went on. "The trouble was—well, that there began to be trouble. Riley's idea of a country doctor's life was Riley first and the patient second. That might do for Ireland but it didn't do for Tedfold. The upshot was that I had to do some pretty straight talking after one case of really bad neglect that might have landed him in very serious trouble. That sobered him and he began to settle down. He never was brilliant but he was competent." He smiled to himself. "Inside a couple of years he was the most popular man in the place. I never contemplated for a moment that he'd be leaving us, but he did. That's the queerest story of all. By the by, it's dry work talking and you people would like a drink? You'll have some sherry?"

He produced a decanter and glasses from a hanging corner-cupboard. We took the first sip to each other's health. He wiped that moustache of his with his handkerchief.

"Where was I?"

"At where Riley left you," I said. "I take it that was when war broke out."

"Yes," he said, and chuckled. "I was blinding mad at the time but now I can see the other side of it. We assumed he'd been called up. Don't think us utter fools, by the way, but he was a man you could never pin down. When he really got busy in that delightful brogue of his, he could talk you into anything. At any rate he said he didn't know what was going to happen and he got us to buy back the practice." He chuckled again. "We thought we were doing pretty well. Two thousand five hundred was what he took, which wasn't bad considering the circumstances. And then later, when we had to have everything enquired into on behalf of his successor, we began to unearth things."

"He'd cooked the books?"

The doctor smiled dryly.

"Well, that's what it amounted to. Monies that should have gone to the common fund had never found their way there. We made the deficiency over eight hundred pounds."

"And he got away with it?"

"Oh dear, no. We didn't let him get away with that. I tracked him down through the War Office and threatened all hell and over. And you know what happened? We got his cheque and it was good. And the letter that came with it! I kept it for years and then that fool of a woman of mine burnt it by mistake. It was really a gem. Honestly, when I'd read it I felt ashamed about having worried him for a trifle of eight hundred pounds. Full of thanks for all we were supposed to have done for him here, and what he thought of us and how he'd never forget us—you know the sort of thing."

Jewle smiled.

"And never a word about the deficiency?"

"Not a word. Just the cheque."

"Yes," Jewle said. "He certainly seems to have had the gift of the gab. But didn't you send him a testimonial when he wanted to enter the Prison Medical Service after the war?"

"I did." He didn't chuckle this time and the smile was just a bit wry. "He wrote me one of his famous letters and it mesmerised me. Believe it or not, I honestly didn't see why I should hold that eight hundred pounds against him and the way he'd contrived to break up the partnership, so I said all the good about him and kept quiet about the rest. And I thought the P.M.S. ought to be the very best thing for him." Then he did give another chuckle. "Any monkey tricks there and he'd be nice and handy for a cell."

"What was he like with women?" I said. "Any trouble?"

The doctor pursed his lips.

"Yes," he said slowly. "Soon after he came here. A young nurse at our local hospital. I won't say it went beyond getting himself talked about but I had to have a word with him. After that he was more discreet. I think he had a lady friend or two but that was no business of mine."

"So long as he kept his nose clean."

"Exactly. Help yourselves to the sherry, by the way."

Jewle said we'd already taken up too much of his time and we ought to be going. There was, however, just one question—a confidential and ticklish one. It was that matter of blackmail.

"Yes," the doctor said. "I definitely wouldn't put it beyond him. What you've got to remember is that apparently when he left Helmsby he was a ruined man. He was debarred from doing the only thing he could do. Would you mind telling me those dates again?"

"Struck off in 1952. Arrived in Marstead in 1954. The actual gap is about eighteen months."

"I see. Looks to me—I don't know if it does to you—as if he spent those eighteen months looking for some kind of work. Why he should go to a village in Suffolk is altogether beyond me."

"What about the money? We calculate he arrived in, Marstead with getting on towards a couple of thousand pounds. Where'd that come from?"

"Don't know," the doctor said. "It sounds curious to me. He was always a spender. And he never seemed to get anything for it."

"All I can think of," Jewle said, "is that he must have brought off some swindle or other."

"Maybe. A desperate man is capable of most things. He'd dyed his hair, you said, and shaved off his moustache, so he probably wanted to keep out of somebody's way. All the same, I'm like you. I think he must have had some good reason for going where he did."

"Yes," Jewle said. "And there you can't help us. No use asking you if you knew of anyone he'd be likely to blackmail. But just one other thing: any point in us going to Tedfold and trying to pick up anything about Riley there?"

"I think it would be a waste of time," the doctor told him frankly. "I've told you more than anyone in Tedfold's likely to know. No one knew Nick Riley as well as I did. And sixteen years is a long time."

Jewle agreed. One thing he said he'd be most grateful for. If anything else came back to the doctor's memory which had a bearing, however remote, on Riley's death, then he'd be glad to be told of it. And that was about all. A minute or two later we were walking back to the hotel.

It had been, as we both agreed, an interesting hour, and an enjoyable one. Our picture of Ranger was more and more clear—up to a point. And it was that vital point at which our knowledge and understanding stopped short that was the thing that worried us. Eighteen months of Ranger's life were unaccounted for. At the end of them he had emerged from nowhere and had made a bee-line for Marstead, or Edenthorpe. Where had his money come from? Those were some of the questions and with them was the tantalising feeling that in learning the much that we had, we ought somehow to have learned just that little essential more.

And the queer thing is that we were right. We weren't to know it for quite a time, but the solution to most of our problems had been there in old Doctor Wormgay's study. Everything had been balanced, as it were, upon a razor edge. If, instead of making a categorical statement, Jewle had put the same words in the form of a question, then Wormgay would almost certainly have given us the answer. But that's just how it goes. And, after all, unless you've at least some idea of what an answer might be, how can you ask the right question?

After dinner that night when we were going over what we had learned from the old doctor, a something did occur to us.

"Give him a ring," Jewle told me. "He's almost certainly not in bed and he might clear it up."

The doctor wasn't in bed.

"No," he told me. "I think he made very few enemies. He had what I'd call a witty tongue but I can't say it was ever a bitter one. He was outspoken, mind you, but I can't think of him making enemies. He was the sort of chap whose throat you'd like to cut one minute, and you'd be standing him a drink the next."

So that was that. Perhaps there wasn't any illogic about it after all. Even at Marstead Ranger had been said to be very much of a wit, even if the wit itself was barbed and he had allowed it to get so far out of control as to let it make him enemies. And, as Jewle and I agreed, Ranger at Marstead was a far different man from the Riley of earlier years. Things had caught up with him at Helmsby and when he had left it, little had been left but an illogical sense of grievance. The old smooth tongue had taken on a rasp. The Norman Ranger who had tried to ingratiate himself in his first three months at Marstead had been far from the ready-witted and natural hail-fellow-well-met of the earlier years. Everything had been nicely calculated. Ranger had been playing a part.

But to find a logic out of illogic was not much good to us. It still didn't explain why he had played that part. But maybe, as Jewle said, we should find some sort of answer to that at Helmsby.

At half-past eight the next morning we were on the penultimate stage of our trip. The morning was misty and Jewle had to switch on the wipers to keep the windscreen clear. But the sun broke through just short of midday and the church clock at Helmsby was striking twelve as we came into yet another little country town. We parked the car in front of the Greyhound and went into the bar for a drink. Lunch, we learned, would be on from twelve-thirty.

I did the talking as arranged. There were three people, local businessmen by the look of them, in that saloon bar. A man in riding breeches, younger than the others, came in later. I spoke to the middle-aged woman behind the bar. She had poured us a couple of tankards and I was picking up my change.

"Where's Doctor Riley hang out here?" I said.

"Doctor Riley?" She stared. "He's gone. Been gone quite a time now."

"Gone!" I said. I turned to Jewle with a look of exasperation. "You hear that? He's gone!"

Jewle shrugged his shoulders.

"I told you he was a slippery one."

Ears were pricked. A man with what looked like a double whisky spoke up from the corner by the fire.

"He got himself into trouble here. You wanted him badly, did you?"

"Just a little matter of a couple of hundred pounds," I said ironically. "I've been abroad and I only just got wind of his being here. I thought I'd look him up. Where's he gone to? You don't happen to know?"

"No one knows," the woman said.

"He was struck off the register," another man said, "but he cleared out long before that."

"Struck off the register!" I said. "Then what's going to happen to my two hundred pounds?"

He didn't know. But they all knew about the widow, and her brother. The big, hearty man with the whisky—I was soon buying him another—told us all about it. What he didn't know, the others did. But no one seemed to be blaming Riley. There was even an undercurrent of admiration at which only the woman behind the bar protested.

"I know," she said. "Butter wouldn't melt in his mouth. But a doctor oughtn't to do such things. There ought to be only lady doctors to attend to women. You can say what you like, Mr. Gotch."

Gotch was my friend with the whisky. The woman behind the bar turned out to be a Mrs. Newby.

"He used to come in here a lot?"

"Quite a lot," she said. "And I will say this for him, he was a regular gentleman. A rare one for a joke." She sniffed. "A pity he had to go and carry the joke too far."

Gotch laughed.

"That's one way of looking at it. But about your two hundred, sir. I reckon you can say goodbye to it—unless you find out where he's gone."

"Not much good that if he hasn't got the money," I said gloomily. "What debts did he leave behind here?"

He laughed again.

"He didn't. That's the point. They reckon he had quite a packet from her before the brother found out."

Her referred to the widow, a Mrs. Yandall. She'd lived at the Old Hall in a village about two miles away.

"But didn't they make him disgorge the money?"

"The doc was too smart for 'em," another man said. "He reckoned it was a gift and they couldn't get her to say otherwise." He appealed to the room. "How much do they say he had out of her from first to last? No end o' money. Hundreds and hundreds."

"She could afford it," Gotch said. "And she got something for it, didn't she?" He grinned as he nodded to himself. "I'll bet the doc used to make the old bedsprings creak!"

"That'll do, Mr. Gotch," he was told severely. "We don't want that kind of talk here."

Gotch gave me a wink. Maybe the bar-lady was putting on an air of propriety for my benefit. The younger man in the breeches and leggings must have thought so.

"I always reckoned there was something in that Irish whisky he always had. Don't know as I won't start on it myself. I could do with a bit of gingering up."

There was a general guffaw.

"So he was still drinking nothing but Irish whisky," I said to the bar-lady.

"That's right," she said. "Never anything else. And always with water."

"And the lady? This Mrs. Yandall: where's she living now?"

"Sold up and gone," she said. "She couldn't show her face round here after what came out."

"It was that brother of hers that spoilt all the sport," Gotch said. "But for him we'd have had the doc here now. I'll bet he'd have married her. That's what his game was all along."

Riding-breeches snorted.

"Don't you believe it. The doc wasn't the marrying kind. You've heard him say so, and in this very bar."

The lunch gong went. I finished what was left of my second half pint and announced gloomily that we might as well eat, and that one way and another it would be the most expensive meal I'd ever had. The bar gave us a friendly farewell as we went through to the dining-room. Once we were out of earshot I'd no doubt they'd be running me down as a first-class fool who'd let himself be tricked by a far cleverer man.

"What's the local paper here?" Jewle asked the waiter when he brought our soup.

It was a weekly—the *Helmsby Weekly Advertiser*, with its offices in Tanner Lane, the entrance to which one could see from that dining-room window. Jewle thought it might be profitable to look up their files for the time of the Riley-Yandall affair. There was no point in two of us going, so I had coffee alone. He was gone for only half an hour.

We'd thought that gossip we'd heard in the bar would have to be heavily discounted, and now Jewle was saying that in the main it was true. The widow had been induced to bring an action for recovery of the money, in the course of which she had had to confess to intimacy with Riley. The action hadn't succeeded, and Riley had got away with between two and three thousand pounds.

That was virtually all we'd learned from Helmsby—the source of the money with which Ranger *alias* Riley had arrived eighteen months later at Cambridge, and we doubted if a study of the proceedings of the General Medical Council would tell us more. Riley couldn't have been judged on that matter of money since the court had cleared him: the striking off had been on account of the intimacy.

It was half-past two when we set off on that last and homeward stage of the journey, with a hundred and twenty miles ahead of us, and I know now that when we tried to sum up the results of two days' work we were trying to be more optimistic than we actually were. We could follow the career of Nicholas Riley almost from the day he was born to the time he had left Helmsby, and from what we had learned we could follow almost the very twists—gay, inconsequential and yet always calculated—of his fertile mind. But after Helmsby—what? That was what pulled us up short. We'd have given most things till Helmsby in exchange for what happened after it, and especially those lost eighteen months.

For it was in those eighteen months, or so it seemed to us, that Riley, looking about him for a job, had come across a certain blackmail prospect who had finally brought him to Marstead. When Jewle said that if a good few men were put on the job by the Yard, Riley's tracks might be picked up from Helmsby, I knew and he knew the words had little conviction. It was just one of those things one might do as a very last resort.

My own optimistic contribution was the claim that two things—the brief absence from Marstead and the Riley background we'd learned—ought to act like a kind of vacuum cleaner on our minds. With a whole lot of uncertainties cleared away, we'd see the Marstead end of things far more clearly.

"Take what worried us for a time," I said, "about the difference between Riley and Ranger. Riley got through life on the strength of a specious and calculated charm. He could get away with anything short of murder, and he used that charm deliberately the first three months he was in Marstead. It was a bit faded and tarnished by then but it served the purpose of getting him accepted by Marstead and Edenthorpe. Then he became Ranger, the man who'd been kicked out of his profession and had only escaped jail through possibly some legal quibble, and who now had a last final chance of financial security for what might have been some pretty grim last years. He'd had lucky breaks before—those that Doctor Wormgay told us about, for instance—but never one like that. That's why after those three months at Marstead, when he'd found the one who was to be his source of income, he had those delusions of grandeur. All the time, as Ranger, he'd be chuckling to himself and wondering what people would say if they only knew he was Riley. He even went so far as to take a chance when he told Alice Gantle to pour Laving's medicine down the sink. What I'm getting at is that we not only know the main events of Ranger's life; we can see clean into his mind. That ought to give us something for a fresh start. Or don't you think so?"

Jewle had been driving. The road was good and the car had been gliding comfortably along. I had been lying back in my seat, eyes closed, prattling away complacently: deluding myself, maybe, into thinking that word; and theorising were major contributions. Jewle brought me down to earth.

"You know, sir, you ought to write a book," he said, and when I glanced at him he was grinning. "Not that you mayn't be right, mind you. But I'm not too strong on that psychological stuff. What I was wondering was how Allman is getting on about those Colonna tyres."

It was a quarter-past six when we reached Edenthorpe, but this seems as convenient a place as any to add a postscript—what was in that confidential report that arrived from Belfast the following morning. What it did was confirm implicitly what we had learned from Doctor Wormgay—that Riley had been a playboy and had passed his finals with difficulty and virtually at the eleventh hour. He had no real police record except a fine for assaulting the police in the course of a hospital rag, as a result of which he had been sent down for a term. All of which, as Jewle said, merely clinched some comparatively unimportant nails that had already been driven home.

12

Colonna Tyres

RANGER had been buried the previous afternoon at Edenthorpe, Allman told us. Now his real name was known, relatives could be advertised for in the Northern Ireland papers, with a possible settlement of his small estate. Black was being cremated at Ipswich the next afternoon.

Allman's afternoon and early evening had been spent at the telephone, for he'd received the information asked for from Colonna Tyres Ltd., and had got to work at once. Several tyre distributing firms had received tyres on sale or return conditions, but, thanks to what he knew of the treads of the tyres at Culver's Farm, Allman had been able to whittle the likely prospects considerably down. We wanted, for instance, a complete set of tyres: four at least, though it was claimed that with unpuncturable tyres a spare was unnecessary. We also had a rough idea of the size. Allman, who'd had time to go into things more fully during our absence, thought the tyres we wanted would be 700 X16, or thereabouts. He'd already eliminated a set of 550 X15 supplied for a Wolseley and one of 450 X17 for a pre-war Ford.

I gave Henry a ring, picked up my car at the police park and made my way to Marstead, and there was something agreeably strange about driving down the main street again and turning into Henry's drive. By the time I'd had a bath and a change, dinner was on the table. There was quite a lot to be told that night. I was pretty tired and went up to bed at about ten. Henry's last comment—Ranger's epitaph, if you prefer it—was apt.

"What a life spoilt!" he said. "Somehow I can't help being sorry for him. It's a kind of Greek tragedy. It was that aunt of his who spoilt him—she and his father—who really put the atropine into that decanter."

I slept that night like a log. Just as I was drinking my early tea next morning Mrs. Slack came up again to say I was wanted on the telephone. It was Jewle.

"Thought I'd get you before you made any sort of a move," he said. "There's two likely prospects for those Colonna tyres. One's near Cambridge, and I'll see into that myself; the other, at Ipswich, will be handier for you. A garage run by a man called Fitchling, just short of the town as you come in from Stowmarket. A biggish place. I'm told you can't miss it. I tried it on the telephone this morning, but it isn't open yet."

I said I'd get there straight away after breakfast.

"But suppose I unearth something: what am I to do? Follow it up or wait for you?"

"Better follow it up," he said. "I'll do the same at my end."

I set off alone. Henry, to his great regret, had a dental appointment that couldn't be postponed. Short of Ipswich I took a by-pass that was said to bring me out on the Stowmarket Road. It did, but it took me miles farther than I'd have had to go if I'd gone through the town. It was half-past ten when I got to that garage.

It was one of those medium-sized repair and service stations, all very trim and smart. The proprietor was a man of about fifty who was doing sufficiently well not to be wearing dungarees himself. My warrant card took him considerably aback. We talked in his cubby-hole of an office.

"Yes," he said. "I did sell a set of four: 700 X17s. I got them from my tyre distributor."

"Why that particular make? I mean, there're others that've been on the market much longer."

"It's a bit of a story," he said. "The customer—he was an American staff-sergeant—drew in here with a puncture, and his tyres were pretty bad. It was a second-hand Buick and the tyres were practically down to canvas, and I told him so. Then I did a bit of sales talk. 'Another year or two,' I said, 'and people won't know what punctures or bursts are.' You know: just getting him interested. In fact, I talked him into it, not that he wasn't going to do himself a bit of good too, mind you. I showed him the literature on three different sorts and it was he who chose the Colonna."

"Why?"

"Well, sort of sentimental reasons. He had an Italian name and he told me he'd been in Italy during the war, and he reckoned the Italians made damn fine cars, so they ought to make damn fine tyres. I didn't argue the toss. It made no difference to me: my profit's the same. All I wanted was to clinch the deal."

"Which you did."

"That's right. He was game to pay cash down but all I took was a deposit."

"Got all the details in your books?"

He had. There was the date of the order, and the date of delivery. It was that last that made me a bit excited. Those tyres had been fitted and the Buick driven away on the afternoon of the Monday on which Ranger had met his death.

The purchaser was a Staff-sergeant L. Porelli, stationed at Brackenham Aerodrome.

"Where's that exactly?"

He showed me on the large-scale map that was hanging on the wall. It was about the biggest in the country, he said, and entirely American. All I saw about it was a snag. The direct route back to that aerodrome from Ipswich would have been via Stowmarket and Bury St. Edmunds. How, then, could that car have been a good fifteen miles out of its way at Culver's Farm, Marstead?

"He wasn't going that way," Flitchling told me. "He'd come in that way the afternoon when he had his puncture, but he wasn't going home that way. He had a pal with him, another staff-sergeant, and this pal was spending the night with some friends of his at—wait a minute now. Where was it?"

He had another look at the map.

"Here we are. A place called Felworth. I remember he had a look at this very map, just for a check-up. How we worked it out was he'd take the main Colchester road, and then turn off."

That was clear enough. And after he left his friend at Felworth, he'd naturally take the reasonably direct road to Bury and the aerodrome rather than try the winding minor roads across country.

"What time did he leave here?"

"What time?" He frowned. "Be about three or so. That's right. He brought the Buick in soon after two. We fitted the new tyres and did a bit of a check-up. About three o'clock it'd be."

I thanked him, told him to regard our little chat as confidential, and asked if I'd have any difficulty in finding the aerodrome myself. Another look at the map showed me I couldn't very well miss it, so I had four gallons put in the tank for the good of the house, and moved the car off in the direction of Stowmarket. I couldn't help smiling at his last words as I was getting into the car.

"Those tyres of yours don't look too good, sir. What about a set of Colonnas for yourself?"

If I'd thought I should be on a fast-travelling road I was mightily mistaken. After the first five miles I was back at the same old twists and turns, and it was like that till I got to Bury. They leave out the St. Edmunds in this part of the world. After Bury it wasn't so bad, except through four or five villages. Then I came to the open Brecklands: lovely and lonely country with stretches of heath and clumps or rows of ancient pines. The air was good there and the roads more open and almost straight. When it seemed that I must be getting close to that aerodrome I pulled up at a lonely cottage and asked my way. All I had to do was take the next right-hand turn and a couple of miles would bring me there. I glanced at the dashboard clock as I had my first sight of the aerodrome buildings. It was just after midday.

That aerodrome was a colossal place. In the distance the grey blue of hangars looked miles away, though already I was at the tall, wire enclosures that marked the boundaries and kept intruders out. There were rows of houses—married quarters, I guessed—and groups of administrative buildings everywhere along the network of concrete roads. There were huge car-parks, a sports' stadium and shops. There was never a sight of a grounded plane, for I wasn't even on the fringes. Transport was moving along the roads and the drivers seemed mostly to be coloured men. More of them, off-duty, stood about by the various entrances and I beckoned one over. He didn't seem to know what I meant by headquarters but he suggested I take the first turn on my left. He had a fine, natural courtesy.

I took that turn and nobody halted me. I'd had visions of sentries guarding entrances but there were none. What I'd planned was a call at what I'd call headquarters for an interview with some high-ranking officer or other, and so proceed downwards from him to Staff-sergeant Porelli. That would have been the procedure at an English aerodrome or army camp, but it didn't work out like that. I didn't know it, but I hadn't even penetrated into that aerodrome. A quarter of a mile along the concrete road I saw a big notice and what looked like gates and sentries. The notice told me to have my pass ready. I drew the car up. The men on duty were white.

"Your pass, sir, please?"

"Sorry, but I haven't got one," I said. "I'm looking for headquarters."

"Provost Marshal's headquarters," he told me, and waved a hand. "You'll have to report there if you haven't a pass. That way, sir. Better get your car off the road first."

I backed the car into the handy park and went where I was told. Signs and arrows pointed the way. There was only the one entrance door. A passage gave the choice of two ways and I took the right and stepped into a fairly large office. A sergeant was typing at a side table in front of a row of filing cabinets. Another sergeant was reading a newspaper at a table in the far corner. At the desk by the main window a young officer was writing. Nobody paid any attention to me. Then the officer looked up. He had a slow, friendly smile. On his feet he looked as tall as myself.

"Good morning," I said. "I'm looking for your headquarters."

I gave him my warrant card. He looked at it, and at me. He handed it back.

"What's the trouble, sir? Perhaps we can help you."

"What's your rank?" I said.

"Lieutenant."

He had a nice voice, soft as Irish rain. He waved a hand at the chair by the desk and I sat down. I told him I would like to interview, in his presence, a Staff-Sergeant Porelli. We thought he would be an important witness in a case we had in hand. He leaned back in his chair and gave a beckoning nod to the sergeant who'd been reading the paper.

"Will you write the name down, sir?"

I wrote it. The sergeant took the sheet of paper and went out.

"You know this man, Porelli, Lieutenant?"

"No," he said. "But we'll get him here. I hope he hasn't been in any trouble."

I told him the little that I thought advisable. He seemed to take it all as a matter of routine. I don't think he'd have turned a hair if I'd said I'd come to arrest his O.C. Aerodrome. Then we had some general talk, such as how he liked England and about his wife and two children. I liked him—his smile and the young friendly voice—but I doubted if he was just the rank I wanted to see. Maybe he'd pass me higher up when he'd heard the preliminaries.

A man from the entrance gates came in with a report. A civilian pass was checked. Ten minutes had gone by and then I heard feet in the outside corridor.

The sergeant who'd gone out was reporting back that Porelli was outside.

"Don't mention Scotland Yard," I said to the lieutenant. "I'd be glad if you just told him my name. And if we could talk at ease."

Porelli came in. He stepped smartly to the desk and saluted. He was a stocky man of about thirty-five, thick-set and with dark hair and a sallow complexion.

"This is Mr. Travers," the lieutenant told him. "He thinks you can help him."

The sergeant who'd been typing brought a chair. Porelli sat down. He was looking uneasy. His feet were large. I put them at about elevens. We two and the lieutenant made a perfect triangle, each facing inwards as it were. The lieutenant sat back at ease.

"You're Staff-sergeant L. Porelli?" I said, and I made it as friendly as I could.

"Yes, sir."

"The L. stands for what?"

"Louis, sir."

"You've been here long?"

Just over a month, he said. He'd been posted to Brackenham from Pinecastle, Florida. He was married and his wife was with him. They had no children.

"There's a little matter in which we think you can help us," I said. "I'm from Scotland Yard, by the way."

You may read of people's faces going white, but it's something you rarely see. Porelli's face did whiten. Then it flushed.

"We'd like you to tell us all about it," I said. "Just what happened on the night of last Monday week."

He couldn't speak. Something seemed to be contracting his throat.

"You remember?" I said. "You had a set of new Colonna tyres fitted to your old Buick and you and a friend left the garage on the Stowmarket Road at about three o'clock. You carry on from there."

"Okay," he said. He shook his head determinedly, and once the words came, they came fast. "I've been wanting to get this thing off my mind. I knew you'd catch up with me."

I can't reproduce the words exactly as he spoke them. And I'm no authority on what we'd call American colloquialisms, so if what I set down seems too English and a trifle phony, blame it on me.

"Who was this friend of yours?" I asked.

"Technical-Sergeant Grunbaum," he said, and gave a quick look at the lieutenant as if for confirmation. "He had a forty-eight hour pass and I was dropping him at a place called Felworth, but we stopped in the town first. I'd bought my wife a new coat for her birthday and she'd seen it but it had to have some alterations and I was collecting it, and then Joe—that's Grunbaum—chipped in with a couple of dozen chrysanthemums. Big ones, like this. We put them in the boot with the coat and then I stayed on a bit at this Felworth place with Joe and his friends, and it'd be about six when I left. I went through another place: little something—"

"Little Warbridge?"

"That's the place. You go up a hill when you get out of it and I was coming round the bend at the top when I had to jam my brakes on hard. There was another car there well out in the road and it hadn't any lights on. I just managed to squeeze past and I saw a fellow standing by the back of the car so I stopped the Buick and came back. I said, 'What's wrong, mister? Your light fused or something?' Then, as soon as he opened his mouth I knew he was drunk. He couldn't get his words out properly. I just made him out when he wanted to know if I was a Yank, and I said I was and then I thought I'd better take a look, so I tried to get a look at his dashboard to see where the light switches were and when I backed out again to ask him if he had a torch, he hit me. Must have been a heavy spanner or something. Look. You can see."

He took off his cap and there was the scar. It was more of a scab, still there in the thick black hair at the back of his skull.

"And then?"

"Well, sir, I didn't even know I was hit—not till I came round. I was on the grass, just off the road, and his car wasn't there any longer. I guessed I'd been out for a good ten minutes. I didn't feel so good and I sat there for a bit and then I made it to my car. Everything seemed okay so I drove on and I took it slow. Then, just as I was almost through the next village but one, I thought of something and if it was robbery he'd been after. He could have got my keys and unlocked the boot, so I got out and had a look. Soon as I looked in the boot I saw a body. I didn't know what it was at first, not till I looked. I was so scared I don't know how I moved the car on and then I stopped and started thinking. I knew I had to ditch that corpse some place, and then I caught sight of all that straw. I'd seen it before when I was driving my wife round the country, so I shut off my lights and moved the Buick across and there happened to be a gap in the hedge. . . . I guess that's about all."

I looked at the lieutenant. He was as imperturbable as a Buddha. The sergeant who'd been typing when I first came in, was sitting with pencil poised. The other sergeant was sitting, arms on the table, chin in hand.

"You believe it, sir? What I've been telling you?"

Porelli's eyes were boring into mine. I could see the white on his knuckles as the fists clenched.

"I do," I told him. "I believe every word of it. And for the very good reason that I happen to know it's true."

He let out a breath. The whole of him went limp. We sat there like that for a good minute and then he roused himself.

"And what happens now, sir? I guess I'm under arrest."

I smiled.

"Listen to me, sergeant. I read a lot of American books. What I've read about your cops in America scares me stiff. So suppose this had happened to me in America. What would I have done? Reported it to the nearest police? I don't know. I don't think so. I wouldn't have wanted to get tangled up with the law. I hadn't done anything. I'd have had a clear conscience as I ditched that body and then I'd have got to hell out of it fast. So how could I blame you? You probably feel the same way about English cops as I do about American ones, so you ditched the body and got back here to America. It is America in a way, or that's how I felt about it when I drove in."

I got to my feet.

"I'll have to have a formal statement," I told the lieutenant. "Win that be in order?"

He gave the same slow smile.

"It's in hand, sir. It'll be typed right now."

That sergeant had taken everything down in shorthand and in five minutes he was producing in duplicate what had been said. Porelli and I read the typescripts and we each signed, I—L. Travers, as of New Scotland Yard. The original was mine. The lieutenant took the carbon, then he waved a hand at Porelli, who saluted and went out, the other sergeant at his heels. My guess was that he wouldn't be going far.

"You're satisfied with everything, sir?" the lieutenant said.

I don't think I made too good a hand of what I told him. Had that business been handled at a comparable English aerodrome I'd probably have just been getting over the first hurdle and, after that, I'd have been passed upwards for at least the rest of the afternoon. But there it was. Not an unnecessary word and in a matter of half an hour the whole thing had been cleared up. I said I'd remember it as an example of unobtrusive efficiency and I must say that he looked pleased.

"About Porelli," I said. "I'm pretty sure we shan't want him again. I hope he doesn't get into any trouble with you people."

"Maybe not," he said. "I'll have to pass it up to Special Investigations. What you said about yourself might be a help."

I wondered how my own powers-that-be would take it if they read that verbatim script I had in my hand. Not that I was worrying.

"Just one other thing," I said. "Might I use your telephone?"

He got the Edenthorpe number for me, and it took quite a time. Jewle was at the other end.

"Travers here," I said. "That matter's been cleared up and I've got a signed statement. I gather you've had a wasted morning. . . . But just one little thing wants clearing up. Can you get out straight away to the top of that hill between Bedham and Little Warbridge? I'll come on from here. . . . Yes, I'll explain when I see you."

I shook hands with the lieutenant and thanked him. I thanked the sergeant who'd typed the statement and I guessed that when I left that room it would settle again within a couple of seconds to whatever routine it was that I'd briefly broken. In the passageway Porelli was standing and the sergeant with him. Porelli drew himself up. I thought it his way of showing gratitude.

"Good luck to you, Sergeant," I said. "And, by the way, what happened to those chrysanthemums?"

"No good at all, sir." He managed a smile. "But my wife didn't know anything about them, sir, so I slipped into Bury next day and bought some more. Just so she could thank Grunbaum."

"Well, good luck again," I said. I shook hands with the sergeant and went out to my car. I reversed it out of the park and set off back the way I had come. In the stadium the football teams were limbering up and the tiers of seats were filling. There were white men and coloured, and wives and children. I'd have liked to stay and watch, but I had a pretty long way to go compared with Jewle. Once out of the gates through which I had come I pushed the car on. Five minutes later the last tall wire fencing was behind me. I was out of America and in England again.

13

WELL OF TRUTH

JEWLE had guessed that it would take me best part of three-quarters of an hour to reach that hill top, so he hadn't hurried to meet me. His car was parked just short on the Bedham side and I drew mine past it on the verge. I took that typed and signed statement out of the envelope and he read it where he stood. When he'd finished he nodded to himself. I gave him the envelope.

"How'd you actually get on to him?"

I filled in the gaps. He said it was good work, and quick. Then he looked about him.

"This'd be about the very spot. What was Ranger's idea? Where was he off to with that body?"

I said I thought I could show him. We walked on about fifty yards round the slight bend to the very top of the hill—the spot where Henry and I had halted one day and admired the view. On our left the remnant of hedge was gapped and I went through. In front of us was a strip of hard, dry ground, about thirty yards across, and then came an old post and rail fence. It was in bad order, with some of the rails missing. We stepped across a bottom rail and only a couple of yards on was that derelict gravel-pit. It fell sheer. Its sides were overgrown with weeds and trailing brambles. About forty feet down was water, a pool that looked about twenty or so yards in diameter. Some large flint stones were lying about near the fence and I threw one into the pool. You couldn't tell how deep the water was but the plop of that heavy stone made one think somehow that there were a good few feet. And there was no rise of mud or the red of gravel—only the ripples that slowly spread. Beyond that pool, the lane rose green from the cup that held the water, and you could still see the ancient ruts from the tumbrils that had once drawn the gravel out.

"Yes," Jewle said. "I begin to see. Ranger must have seen this pit scores of times. He was going to drop Black's body into that pool."

That was it. It just had to be it. He'd put Black's body into the boot of his car and left the bungalow at dark. Probably while he was actually driving towards Bedham he had felt the first constriction of the throat. A doctor he might have been, but we doubted if any doctor would diagnose what he was feeling as poisoning from atropine. And, as the effects of the poison took hold, his mental processes would be weakened. There would be the beginnings of that ultimate lack of control.

He arrived at the nearest point to the pit and, naturally, extinguished his lights. He was actually about to take the body from his car boot when he saw the lights of an approaching car, so he stood behind his own car till it had gone by. But the car halted, went slowly by and then pulled up again.

His own speech was now becoming indistinct and his mental processes less sure. He knew from the stranger's speech that he was an American. He knew that he himself had been seen, if only in the comparative dark. What brief logic or illogic made him then act as he did was hard to work out, but he seemed to us to have acted in a confusion of thoughts—that an American could never have known him, that the American would be going somewhere away and that he might take that body with him. Speed must have seemed the essential thing at that moment. But what he struck the American down with might have been not a wrench, but one of those big flints that were scattered about in the neighbourhood of the pit.

The effort of shifting even a body as light as Black's to the other car must have made the throat constriction worse. When he'd reversed his car at the side road just short of Little Warbridge—and that must have been a tremendous feat—his fuddled mind must have had only two ideas: to get away as quickly as possible from the neighbourhood and, no doubt, to get to a doctor. But the toxic progress of atropine is geometrical, not arithmetical, and he wouldn't have gone far before control had almost gone and the only thing left would have been the urgency for speed.

But all that didn't really matter. What stood clear were the things themselves that must have happened, and as we walked back to the cars we ought to have been feeling mildly elated. But we weren't. It was like that return the previous day from our tour, with practically enough material to write a life of Nicholas Riley. We ought to have felt elated then, but we hadn't.

"Well, what now?" I asked Jewle.

"I don't know," he said. "We've cleared a lot of rubbish out of the way but we still want a lead. It's a queer case. You can't go to everyone in the district who might have been an enemy of Ranger and enquire into alibis. Too much time's gone by in any case. I think that the first thing in the morning I ought to report back at the Yard and hear what the really big brains have got to say. Anything you can think of yourself?"

"Only spilling the whole of the Nicholas Riley story. Publishing the photograph brought in dividends, so why shouldn't the story?"

"As a matter of fact, I got that off this morning," he said. "It took me most of last night, after you'd gone, to get it all down."

I ought to have known he'd have thought of that. The best thing to do, it seemed, was to wait till he'd had his conference at the Yard. I asked him if he'd stop at Bendacre for a cup of tea, but he said he ought to be getting into touch with the Yard and he might even be going back to town that night. I think it was the word night that made me think of something.

"You never got a chance to go to the bungalow after dark to try to reconstruct things? You remember—putting yourself in Ranger's place and hoping it would give you ideas."

He must have read the rest of my thoughts, for he was already feeling in his pocket for the keys.

"This is the spare for the front door," he said. "Try it yourself. If anything happens at the Yard I'll give you a ring. In any case I'll ring you as soon as I'm back. Allman'll be at your disposal if you should happen to need him."

As we slowed into Marstead I saw two people standing talking at the junction of the Pinfold Road—Andover and Sterne. Andover spotted me as we neared and he waved. Jewle slowed the car still more, then drew in.

"Did he want to see you about something?"

I said I didn't know, but in any case we both got out. Jewle shook hands with Sterne, who introduced him to Andover.

"Did you want me for something, rector?" I said.

Andover looked at Sterne.

"Well, in a way—yes," he said. "Or rather Sterne here did. I suppose, Inspector, you don't know any relatives of Ranger's?" He turned to Sterne. "You tell the Inspector what it's all about."

Sterne smiled a bit sheepishly.

"Well, it was just being talked about, that's all. The question of Ranger's bungalow. You remember I was meeting some old friends from British Columbia? They gave me some unexpected news about my father. It seems he's got a hankering for ending his days in England after all, so Andover and I were wondering if there might be a chance of buying the bungalow."

"He wouldn't live with you?"

He smiled.

"Not he. He's a cantankerous old cuss in some ways and he's got pretty settled habits. Besides, I'm not so sure he *would* like to live here. What I was hoping to do was buy that bungalow and smarten it up and have the garden spick and span and everything, and then sort of suggest it to him when he comes over in the spring. I think he'd fall for it."

"How old is he now?"

"Seventy-six," he told me. "But he doesn't look a day over sixty. His back's straighter than my own."

"Seems a good idea to me," Jewle said. "We haven't found any relatives yet, but as soon as we do I'll put you in touch, Colonel. That be all right?"

Sterne's thanks were almost embarrassing. Jewle merely waved them away and we got back into the car.

Who should be at Bendacre but Frank Laving. Henry had needed gas at the dentist's that afternoon and Laving—it was his free afternoon—had officiated, and Henry had brought him back to tea. They were in the middle of it when I arrived. After those two extractions Henry wasn't eating much. But I'd had no lunch.

"Well, any more news of that fellow, Ranger?" Laving asked me. It was more of a demand. "Sir Henry professes to be ignorant of what's going on."

"Come, come, my dear fellow," protested Henry. "Professes is hardly a good word."

Laving shrugged his shoulders.

"You don't tell me you've got a Scotland Yard expert in the house and don't pick his brains?"

"There's something about which I'd like to pick yours," I told him. "I wouldn't mention it if it weren't common village property, but about that little tiff between you and the late Ranger which arose out of a certain illness of his daily woman, Mrs. Gantle: what actually was she suffering from?"

His look was first a reproof and then almost a glare.

"You ought to know I can't tell you that."

"You see?" I said, and helped myself to the last piece of toast. "A doctor doesn't discuss his patients. And yet you expect me to discuss things with Sir Henry."

Henry laughed.

"He had you there, doctor. You fell right into the trap."

Laving smiled glumly. And he changed the conversation. Or maybe it was a trap of his own to find out how much longer I should be in Marstead. Was there a chance for a game of golf with me before I left? I said I very much hoped so and switched the talk to Sterne and his hopes of buying Ranger's bungalow. That seemed quite exciting news to both of them. Henry hoped that Sterne's father would be a bridge player. Marstead needed a local four. That lasted us till Mrs. Slack came in to take the tray. Laving and I lighted our pipes. Henry didn't light his usual cigarette. He said the smoke might cause some infection. Laving gave his thin laugh.

"Rubbish, my dear fellow. What old wives' tales you people do perpetuate!"

"Well, if that's the case," Henry said, and his hand went out to the cigarette box.

"I don't think I *would*, Henry," I said. "If you do, the doctor might think himself justified in sending a bill for advice."

"He can afford it," Laving said with that dry smile of his. He let his eyes wander round that delightful room. "You've got some valuable stuff here, you know."

You'll see in a moment the queer way in which ideas can suddenly and unexpectedly present themselves. It's possible— it's even probable—that if I hadn't made that far from brilliant quip about a bill for professional advice, the Case of the Flowery Corpse might never have been solved.

"You've got some good stuff yourself," Henry told him. "But tell me: I suppose those tales one heard in one's youth about doctors taking valuable antiques from villagers in lieu of bills is a thing of the past?"

"Everyone knows too much nowadays," Laving said regret-fully. "Mind you, some of my things were acquired by my father in possibly that way. He had a very shrewd eye for what was good. That Chippendale writing desk of his, for instance. I believe he got that for a song."

Henry had had to start from scratch on his retirement but, shrewd man that he is, he put himself in the hands of an antique dealer who'd been recommended by an old Cambridge friend, and that friend's knowledgeable wife, and between them they'd made a fine job of furnishing Bendacre.

"I'm not all that good a judge," Laving said, "but wouldn't that knee-hole writing desk be about your best piece?"

It was an early walnut piece which he was indicating. I'd admired it myself.

"I couldn't say offhand," Henry told him. "I admit I like it as well as anything I may happen to have acquired."

"Has it got any secret drawers?"

"It actually has six," Henry said. "I'm told that's very rare in a knee-hole desk as early as that. I expect that big secretaire of yours has got more."

"To tell the truth I've been meaning for years to get an expert to have a look at it. I only know of five but I wouldn't be surprised if there're more."

"You should get it done at once," Henry said. "Who knows what might be in one of those drawers. Wasn't it in something like that that someone unearthed a whole lot of envelopes with extraordinarily valuable stamps on them?"

Laving gave a little grunt.

"That sort of thing only happens to other people. Besides, I know nothing about stamps."

"I wonder where that collection of mine is?" Henry said reminiscently. "I was getting on quite well as a young man till I had to give it up. Maybe my daughter has it in Kenya. I must remember to ask her when I write."

About five minutes later Laving got up to go. I'd had only the most casual of washes in the downstairs cloakroom as I'd come in, and now I thought I'd rather like a bath and a change. So I went up to my room and began emptying my pockets, and when I took out my loose change, I saw a Yale key. For a moment I wondered what it was. Then I remembered: the front door key to the bungalow. I looked at my watch. It was just about the time when Ranger had set off that Monday night with Black's body in the boot of his car.

I shook my head. Somehow I didn't think that if I went up there and into Ranger's kitchen and lounge I'd have a blinding flash of revelation. Maybe Jewle's brain worked differently from mine and, in any case, I could stand there in that bedroom, close my eyes and see both kitchen and lounge as clearly as if I were actually in them. Especially the lounge. The sideboard on the right as you come in, and the decanter standing clean in the middle on top of it. Then a chair by the corner and then the bureau . . . the bureau! A kind of cold shiver ran over me. I pushed that loose change back into my pocket, switched off the light and nipped down the stairs. Henry was just coming out of the lounge and he must have wondered what was possessing me.

"Suddenly remembered something I've got to do," I told him, and hurried on to the cloakroom. I put on hat and coat and went out. Henry said afterwards that he thought I was hurrying to the post-office, and maybe to send a telegram.

That bungalow struck icily cold as I entered it. I switched on the lounge light and went through from the tiny hall. I drew the curtains and then set to work on that bureau. I knew I should have thought of it from the very first. I had a family bureau myself that had a couple of secret drawers, and there had been a case which George Wharton and I had solved because of something that was unearthed in the secret drawer of a bureau, and yet there had been myself, that bureau under my eye—Jewle and I had even searched it together—and I hadn't thought of secret drawers. I could tell myself that it was inexcusable neglect, a failure to concentrate, a slapdash approach and all the rest of it.

I pulled out the runners and let down the front flap. The usual place to look would be behind the small drawers that were each side of the central, tiny cupboard. In every case I've known, such secret drawers are behind the bottom drawers on each side of the bureau. You pull the drawer out and feel at the side. If you feel a slot, that's because a kind of long handle to a small secret drawer is nestling in that slot, and all you have to do is edge out the handle with your thumbnail, pull it out and there is the tiny oblong drawer at the end. My heart gave a quick leap as I felt a slot. I edged out the long strip of wood, and sure enough, there was the tiny drawer. It was empty.

There was a similar secret drawer behind the corresponding drawer at the other side. That, too, was empty, and I stood there, utterly deflated. Then I tackled the other drawers, but they all went right into the bureau back. I'd seen that the bureau had a well that took the place of a long top drawer, so I pushed the cover back along its slot and felt round it. Jewle and I had looked in that well before, but now I felt everywhere inside it, even beneath the cover as far as my wrist could wriggle round. There was nothing there.

I consoled myself, as Jewle would have done, with the thought that there'd been nothing wrong with the idea. But that brought another thought, and another cold shiver. Maybe there *had* been something in one of those secret drawers. Maybe that intruder—the one whom Ranger was blackmailing—had found what he wanted at his second attempt. Secret drawers weren't specialised knowledge, and probably the idea had occurred to him later, just as it had to me. And if that were so, then just an unpardonable forgetfulness on my part had lost us what simply had to be a vital clue. As I walked far more slowly back to Bendacre, I told myself that it was something I'd do well not to mention to Jewle.

I heard Henry in the bathroom so I contented myself with a clean-up at the bedroom basin. When I came down, Henry was stirring the fire in the lounge. While he was pouring me a sherry I decided to tell him where I'd been.

"I don't think there's anything to upbraid yourself with," he told me consolingly. "It's pure surmise on your part. There might never have been anything in those drawers at all."

It didn't console me. After all, there had been two unlawful entries. Someone had been looking, and most urgently, for something. Jewle and I had searched the rest of the premises and found nothing. The only possible inference was that the intruder had been more lucky.

"Don't let it worry you," Henry said. "Sleep on it. Maybe you'll think of something else."

I did sleep on it and I did think of something else, even if the hope was exceedingly forlorn. The idea came to me after breakfast when I'd rung Allman who'd told me Jewle had gone to town by a late train the previous night. It was the day for Henry's local paper and I was glancing at it when I came to the page of advertisements of auctions.

"You don't happen to know, Henry, where Ranger bought that bureau of his?"

"Why, yes," he said. "He bought it at an auction at Bedham. I was there myself. I never could resist an auction. It wasn't all that long after he came here. Probably four or five months. I remember having a word with him there. He told me he'd had some stuff of his own there that he wanted to get rid of and how well it had sold. It practically paid for the bureau."

"You don't know who the auctioneers were?"

"I believe they were Bellings of Edenthorpe," he said. "I think I can verify it. I bought that little Rockingham cottage there that's in the cabinet. I ought to have a receipt."

A few minutes later I said I thought I ought to run into Edenthorpe and see Allman. I'd most certainly be back for lunch. But I didn't see Allman. I went to the office of the auctioneers and I saw one of the principals. When I told him the date and place of that auction, he remembered it well. He remembered the bureau. He even remembered something about secret drawers: something he might be able to check.

"It went cheap, that bureau," he told me when he came back. "Eighteen guineas. A dealer'd give more than that today. Three secret drawers."

"Three!" Then I thought I'd better go warily. "I suppose the buyer knew about them?"

"Oh, yes," he said. "I conducted that sale myself and he came to me afterwards and asked about them. The catalogue description had merely mentioned the three secret drawers and he wanted to know just where they were."

"The usual thing? Behind the inner drawers?"

"Two of them—yes," he said. "The other, as far as I remember, was in the well-cover. One of the usual places in fine old mahogany bureaus and secretaires but you don't often find them in a bureau like that." He gave me a roguish sort of look. "Are you hoping to buy it from the man we sold it to?"

My smile was as arch as his own. I hadn't produced my warrant card and I didn't want him looking up that sale again and finding Ranger's name, so I thanked him and made my way out. Just as I turned into the market square, I literally ran into Lucia Black. I was wool-gathering and knew only that I'd bumped into somebody, and when I turned to apologise, there the lady was.

"In for some shopping?" I asked.

"In Edenthorpe?" She laughed. "No, I brought my car in to be overhauled and I'm just passing the time till I can get a bus."

"Why do that? I'm just going back to Marstead."

We were practically at my car so there wasn't any talk till I'd turned into the quieter street that led to the Ipswich road.

"What about your plans?" I asked her. "Made up your mind yet?"

"No—o," she said. "Not really."

Heaven knows I'm no authority on women, but I did think there was a kind of purring satisfaction in the way she'd said those last two words. I gave a quick look. She was smiling to herself: the same sort of smile, or so it seemed to me, that I'd seen on her face that morning when I'd hinted that her husband might have been murdered.

"Well, there're worse places to live in than Marstead," I told her. "But not, of course, if you're thinking of taking on the role of Merry Widow."

That seemed to amuse her.

"That's an idea. Do you mean in a decorative sort of way, or have you a dirty mind?"

"Don't flatter me," I said. "Besides, I'm a respectable married man."

"That could be cured," she said. "But it might be a lot of fun, don't you think, really giving the busybodies something to talk about."

I'd been driving pretty fast for I wanted to get back to that bungalow, and already we were in the village. She said I might drop her at Bendacre, but I didn't want her to see me going back, so I injected a little chivalry and insisted on driving her home. When I drew the car up, I leaned across to open her door, but she sat there for a minute.

"You're not scared of me, are you?"

"Good lord, no!" I said.

"What *do* you think of me?"

"Well," I said reflectively, "that you're a very charming and attractive woman."

"Then why haven't you been to see me?"

"If I told you, you'd probably not believe me. But honestly, I've been extraordinarily busy."

"And you will come?"

"I'd love to come."

She nodded to herself.

"I'm serious about this, but you're about the only person I feel I can trust. Everything may be wrong—I mean I may change my plans and I might want you to help me."

"If so, you've only to ask," I told her soberly.

"I knew it."

She gave me a smile. She even gave me a little pat on the knee, and then she got out. I moved the car on and backed it at Sterne's entrance. When I glanced at her house as I went by again, she'd already gone.

But I still didn't manage to drive undisturbed to the bungalow. Frank Laving and Andover were talking by Laving's car outside his house, and my car must have been spotted. Andover was hailing me and I couldn't do other than stop. But I didn't get out. The two of them came to my opened window.

"Another nice bombshell you've hurled at us," Laving said, and, for a moment, I didn't know what he meant. I thought that perhaps they'd seen me go past with Lucia Black.

"Oh, the newspapers," I said. "But it oughtn't to have surprised you that Ranger'd been a doctor."

"In name perhaps," he said. "But the man was a quack."

"Come, come," Andover said. "That's a bit libellous." He had to bend right down to get his head near the window. "But tell us: don't these revelations make it look like suicide after all? He was a ruined man, you know."

He drew back.

"But you're in a hurry, perhaps."

I said I had an appointment but I might see him later. A wave of the hand and I moved the car on again. Through the driving mirror I could see him and Laving watching the progress of my

car. Then their heads went together as they resumed their inter-
rupted talk. A car drew in between me and them and it enabled
me to draw in on the verge and out of their sight. Andover, I
knew, wouldn't have scrupled to come along to the bungalow if
he thought I was there.

I let myself in and the lock clicked behind me. I had that
unreal kind of feeling of dull anticipation: the hope of finding
a something in that secret drawer and with it a resignation for
the certainty that nothing would be there. The drawer didn't
take a lot of finding once one knew it was there. That cover to
the bureau well was thicker than it should have been by a good
quarter of an inch. I moved it right back to reveal the well and
then gently pulled at the front beading. It moved. I tried it with
two hands to make a movement parallel and out came a long,
thin drawer.

Even its first revealed inch made a quick thrill. That drawer
held some papers. As it slowly slid out, I saw they were pages of
a newspaper. When I extricated them I saw they were not whole
pages but cuttings of various sizes. Once they'd been folded—the
creases were plain—but in that drawer they'd been laid flat.

They were from at least three different newspapers. The
dates ran from October 1938 to February 1939, and they seemed
to be concerned with something which was alluded to as both
the Ritz-Plaza Affair and the Cordage Case. I guessed it would
take me over an hour to read them, and it was cold in the lounge
of that bungalow. Henry's study would be a much more comfortable place. So I replaced the drawer and the flap, and made my
way out. There was no sign of either Laving or Andover as I
drove past the doctor's house.

14

THE CORDAGE CASE

HENRY and I dug ourselves in. Edith was told that on no account
were we to be disturbed. The hour that we'd thought ample for

an assimilation of the contents of those newspaper cuttings turned out to be an under-estimation: it was almost the lunch hour by the time we'd completed a précis. And the thing that made us work so carefully was the discovery, as soon as we had our first good look at those cuttings, that some of them were from the *Harrenden Gazette*. That was the weekly that circulated, of course, in Tedfold where Nicholas Riley had practised for almost ten years.

Henry didn't recall the Cordage Case, but as soon as I began to read the *Daily Telegraph* extracts, I remembered it rather well, and that was noteworthy considering that all that most of us remember of 1938-9 is the frustrating unreality and tension of those immediately pre-war months. Why it, or most of it, came back to me was because of the characters concerned and the care and ingenuity that went to the making of what was after all a *coup manqué*. And that merely made it the more sensational.

There were three principal characters: the rest are only ancillary. Two of these characters were brothers. Arthur Cordage was thirty-four and Hugh, his brother, eighteen months younger when that *coup* was attempted. The other character, even if he took no part in the dénouement, was the eldest son of the Maharajah of Serindar—the Raj Kumar.

Philip Cordage, father of the two boys, was political officer in Serindar, which was one of those princely states that had been causing a certain amount of anxiety after the first world war. He was a man of fine character and administrative ability who became as much the friend as the mentor of the Maharajah. His two sons, Arthur and Hugh, were of the same age as Govind, the Raj Kumar. The three went to school at Dehra Dun, and, later, to the same public school in England. There, during the shorter holidays, they made their home at Tedfold, where the Rev. Thomas Cordage, brother of Philip, was rector.

In 1924, while his sons were in their first year at Cambridge, Philip died suddenly and the fifteen thousand pounds that he left them was not to be handed over till their twenty-fifth birthday. Philip, by the way, had married late in life and his wife had died at the birth of the younger son, Hugh. Then, just when the boys were about to come into their inheritance, their uncle died. He was a bachelor and the boys his only heirs. His estate realised about twenty thousand pounds.

There were photographs of the brothers: that of Hugh taken at the time of his trial and the other of Arthur, taken some years earlier at Cambridge. Newspaper reproductions are never wholly reliable but Arthur was definitely taller than his brother; more stoutly built and fuller of face. Both were good-looking in an aloof kind of way. That aloofness was significant considering the delusions of grandeur that beset the pair when they came into possession of those considerable sums of money. One gathered, by the way, that they liked Tedfold. It was a period of re-adjustment of livings, and the rectory wasn't needed on their uncle's death. Arthur bought it from the Ecclesiastical Commissioners but sold it again some six years later when he was beginning to be short of money.

If all this seems tedious, I'd nevertheless like you to read on, for what happened later would seem ever more fantastic unless one was sure of the background. The Cordage boys paid several visits to Serindar—in fact they seemed regularly to have spent the winter months there—and Govind paid at least one visit to Tedfold, just before his father died in 1937. After that there seems to have been some sort of quarrel which arose out of an attempt by the brothers to obtain a considerable sum of money from the new Maharajah for a scheme which turned out to be a non-existent one. It will be gathered that the monies received from father and uncle had gone. Considering the style in which the sons had lived, it was a wonder that they'd lasted so long. At the trial it was hinted that large sums had been lent or given them by the new Maharajah while he was still the Raj Kumar. And so to the new scheme which was to land Hugh in the dock.

It was a scheme sired by Conceit out of Impecuniosity. Money was desperately needed. If the scheme succeeded they had apparently no fear of suspicion falling upon themselves. If it failed, then Govind, they were sure, would take the whole thing as an elaborate hoax. It was based upon the practice of the late Maharajah to add to his jewel collection on his rare visits to

England. The Cordages—members, practically, of the family—knew all the details and, had the care and ingenuity that were devoted to planning that scheme been put to better ends, the brothers, as the judge remarked, might have made as honourable a success of life as had their father.

The Maharajah and his son always stayed at the Ritz-Plaza. But for the fact that the hotel was under new management in 1938 the scheme could never have worked and maybe it was that fact that put it in the brothers' minds. The manager had never seen Govind. Operating then from Paris, where the new Maharajah was supposed to be staying on his way to London, the brothers arranged for an incognito visit. They would need only a small and intimate suite, since, as the visit would be for only three days, the Maharajah would bring only his secretary. No one except a Mr. Joseph Haffer, a Hatton Garden dealer in stones, would be aware of that visit. Haffer had supplied the late Maharajah with fine quality stones and would be bringing some for inspection. The Maharajah would be arriving on the 7th October and perhaps the manager would check with Haffer the time arranged for the call—temporarily fixed for four o'clock the following day.

It was a trick almost as old as the hills themselves, and yet the manager had no suspicions. Nor did Haffer, once the manager had confirmed with him the time for the call.

Moreover, Hugh, as the secretary, paid a quick preliminary visit. The brothers, by the way, spoke Mahrati like the natives they practically were. Dress, deportment—everything was at their finger-tips. Arthur always had had a strong resemblance to Govind and little was needed by way of disguise—not that Haffer had ever seen Govind. And four o'clock, at that time of year between daylight and dusk, would mean a tricky light in the Maharajah's room. Best of all were the arrangements for the getaway. Under a false English name, and with a false moustache and dark glasses, Hugh had booked a room at the hotel, almost adjacent to the suite. After bringing off the *coup*, all that the brothers would have to do would be to go to that room, become English, and walk out.

Everything went swimmingly at the start. In his pocket Mr. Haffer had brought a few choice stones—diamonds, emeralds and one superb black opal—of a total value of sixty thousand pounds. Something seemed to be wrong with the light when they were inspected and it was suggested that the three should go into the next room where the light was better. That was the crucial point of the scheme. The Maharajah would go first, carrying the stones and then would come Haffer and the secretary. There would be a slight delay as to who should go first through the door and that would give the pseudo-Maharajah time to be inside. Then the secretary would thrust Haffer violently back, slip through the door, bolt it, and make a quick exit to that room which had been taken under another name.

But it didn't work out like that. Hugh's attack on the jeweller was apparently too clumsy or badly timed. Haffer, suddenly aware of something wrong, closed with him and began hollering for help. He was a smaller man than his assailant and much older. Hugh had to silence him and he smashed him across the skull with a heavy vase. But the jeweller's shouts for help had been heard and Hugh was seized before could make his getaway.

For some weeks Haffer lay between life and death. Then he died and that meant murder. At the trial the defence was that the whole thing had merely been an elaborate hoax.

How could it have been anything else? The real Maharajah would have guessed at once who had been the perpetrators. Later the defence shifted ground. The taking of the jewels would have been only a kind of blackmail. The Maharajah would want everything hushed up so the jewels would have been returned, subject to certain terms. As for murder, never had there been any intention of doing anything but excluding Haffer from that other room. Hugh Cordage had merely been defending himself when Haffer attacked him. But two inexorable facts remained. *Haffer was dead and the jewels had gone*, and Arthur Cordage with them.

Some thought that Hugh Cordage got off lightly. Maybe the judge had in mind the fact that a man of his parentage and upbringing was already ruined for life and that the public would be sufficiently warned against him. At any rate, Hugh Cordage got off with a total of fifteen years: the sentences on the various charges running concurrently. And at that the accounts ended. Whether Arthur Cordage had subsequently been apprehended I didn't know. As for Hugh, even if he had received no remission whatever for good conduct, he should now be out of jail.

That last, of course, was the important thing. Ranger—we still couldn't help calling him that—must have known those two brothers well. A man of his charm—specious though it might be—would have appealed to those equally showy, unscrupulous and megalomaniac brothers. A village doctor moves in its best circles.

"I think we've got it," Henry said. "Hugh Cordage came out of jail and Ranger somehow picked up his trail and traced him to this neighbourhood. It must be so. He wouldn't have kept those cuttings merely out of a temporary interest—and in the secret drawer of his bureau."

But it couldn't be decided so fluently as that. I said we had to look at Ranger himself and to try to discover if his arrival at Marstead really tallied. Apparently it did. Thanks to his position in the Prison Medical Service at Parkways, he could discover just when Hugh Cordage was being released. That, allowing for eventualities, should have been in 1951 or 1952. Ranger was then in practice under the National Health Scheme at Helmsby. By rights he ought to have left that job and fastened on to Hugh Cordage.

"If there was loyalty between the brothers," I said, "then Hugh would get into touch with Arthur and collect his share of the loot. Every reason then why Ranger should pick up Hugh when he came out of jail. But he didn't."

"I think I've got it," Henry said. "Ranger had a more lucrative proposition on at the time—getting money out of that widow. Then, after the scandal flared up and he was struck off, he had to go back to his original idea. That's what he did after he left Helmsby: tried to pick up Hugh's trail. It took him a year or so and it ultimately led him here. It sounds simple I know, but what you have to do is find Hugh Cordage."

It sounded feasible enough. We tossed it all backwards and forwards during lunch and then I knew that I'd have to see Jewle at once, and maybe those whom George Wharton always ironically calls The Powers-That-Be. So I rang the Yard and asked for Jewle. His conference appeared to be still on, or maybe it had just begun. I left an urgent message. It was about seventy miles to the Yard but I'd try to make it in a couple of hours.

I didn't quite make it, but the main thing was that Jewle was waiting for me, and in a familiar spot—Wharton's room. There was a certain reserve about George's handshake. I gathered, and I can read him like a banner headline, that I was expected to produce something really spectacular out of the hat. Not that I was worrying. Don't think I'm boasting when I say that work at the Yard is for me chiefly a matter of prestige. Thanks to having had the right parents, I'm not hard-up. George can scarify the life out of people merely by puffing out that vast moustache of his or peering at them over the tops of his bogus spectacles, but most of his tricks have become so familiar that now, when he tries them on me, they've even ceased to be amusing.

"About time you got hold of something," he said. "What is it? Anything really important?"

"It has possibilities." George often rouses the impish in me and it does him no harm to be led momentarily up the garden path. "Just some newspaper cuttings that were in a secret drawer in Ranger's bureau. But you'd better read this précis first."

I caught Jewle's startled look and gave him a reassuring wink. Wharton began reading. He put on those bogus spectacles and began again, this time reading aloud.

"I don't get it," he told me when he'd finished. "I haven't got this case at my fingertips, you know."

He was an old liar. I'd have wagered he'd assimilated every detail of that case. He'd already listened to Jewle at that conference and Jewle isn't the one to leave things out.

"I'll cross the t's and dot the i's," I said, and told him in words of one syllable just why that discovery looked to me to be important. I'd put the cuttings on his desk and he was trying to tie them up with what I was saying. When I'd finished Jewle cut in with almost the very same words I'd heard that morning from Henry.

"It certainly looks as if you're on the right tack at last," George said. He just couldn't leave out that little reprimand. "One thing we can find out and that's when this Hugh Cordage was actually released." He unhooked the spectacles and screwed up his eyes. "A funny thing, you know, but I seem to remember something. Don't know what it is, but it's there. Tell you what: you'd like some tea? Then ring for a tray. I'll be back as soon as I can."

He gathered up those cuttings and the précis and went out. We guessed he was off to a tête-à-tête with Commander Crime. Not that we worried. We took our time over tea and went on talking about the Case while we smoked our pipes. A couple of evening newspapers came in and we'd had a look through them before George came back. There was a queer look on his face. His full lips pouted and that walrus moustache of his stood out practically at right-angles.

"You and your Hugh Cordage! I knew there was something I remembered. Where do you think Hugh Cordage is? In the cemetery at Parkways Jail. He died there in 1948."

It hasn't been often that George has been able to shatter me with a bomb like that. Everything was blown sky-high.

I hope I didn't show it. And George had shifted that withering look to Jewle. Jewle didn't bat an eyelid. He was actually smiling.

"That's just what we want! What about the other brother, Arthur? Did they ever get him?"

"No," George said. "Far as I can make out, he disappeared into thin air. Those two scoundrels must have been prepared for all eventualities well beforehand."

"Then Arthur's the one that Ranger managed to get wind of. No use rushing ahead, I know, but it looks to me long odds that Arthur Cordage *alias* Something-or-Other was the one that Ranger was blackmailing."

"It's up to you people," George told us largely. "You've got some new leads. There's just one thing, though. You're both dead sure those cuttings *are* a lead? The whole business couldn't depend on something else?"

"They *are* the lead," I said. "A man doesn't keep newspaper cuttings just for any old reason. Don't forget that Ranger arrived at Marstead with about a couple of suitcases, and yet those cuttings were in one of them. And there were those two burglarious entries. They couldn't have been for anything else but trying to find the evidence which Ranger was using for the blackmail. I don't think that was necessarily the letter-press, mind you. I think it was the photograph."

George beamed.

"Well, there's the photograph. Why can't you people identify it?"

"It's not so simple," I said. "For one thing we don't know the whole range of his friends. Everyone I've made contact with fails to fit. But I'd say that Ranger bluffed about the whole thing. He knew that the passage of time had changed Arthur Cordage very considerably and that that photograph wasn't now very much like him. But Cordage wouldn't know that, *provided Ranger didn't let him actually see the photograph.*"

"It's possible," George said. "At any rate you've now got much more to work on." A wily offhandedness entered his tone. "I suppose you'll be going to Parkways again?"

"I don't think there's any point, sir," Jewle said. "We've got everything we can from Otway, and most of that was at secondhand. I'd like a talk with his predecessor, Gasport. Gasport knew both Hugh Cordage and Ranger."

"Gasport's retired," George said. "I ran across him the other day and I believe he told me he was living at Wembley. Look him up in the directory: Major B. Gasport."

Jewle looked him up and there he was. George lifted the receiver and asked for the number. The call came practically at once and it was Gasport himself on the line. He'd be pleased, we gathered, to see us that evening.

"Well, there you are," George said, and got to his feet. He held out a beefy hand. "Good luck to you both. Another day or two and you'll have everything wound up or I'll be surprised."

I asked him if that was a hope or a threat. He pretended to take that as a really good joke.

We took the Underground to Wembley. It was a Saturday and no rush hour so there was no crowding. We could talk without being overheard. Jewle said the trouble with everything was that to people like George Wharton things looked so easy. Just, for instance, an identification of a photograph.

"What I told him is right," I said. "The people I know in what might be called Ranger's circle don't fill the bill: the Lavings, Sterne, Andover, Black. Their careers are an open book. That means we've got to extend the circle. Have a look, for instance, at the members of Ranger's bridge club."

"Yes," Jewle said. "That's one thing I'll see to personally as soon as I get back. But I've thought of something. Let's assume that Ranger and the two Cordages were on friendly terms at Tedfold. In some ways they were birds of a feather, so when Arthur Cordage left the hotel that afternoon, why shouldn't he have made for Tedfold? Ranger might have let him lie up there for a bit—"

"For a consideration."

"Exactly. For a consideration. But that's not all. It may sound a bit high-flown but why couldn't Ranger, as a doctor, have done some facial alterations on him?"

"Plastic surgery?"

The idea had certain attractions and yet I didn't know. I doubted if Ranger had the skill. He wasn't a surgeon: he wasn't even a really good doctor. My idea of him was a man with a mediocre knowledge but a superb bedside manner. I thought, in fact, that our main hope was not Arthur Cordage but his brother Hugh. Hugh had died in Parkways Infirmary while Ranger was its principal medical officer. And as soon as I enlarged on that, Jewle agreed. We decided that the interview with Gasport might as well be built round it.

We didn't have any trouble in finding the house. Major Gasport was a well-preserved man of over sixty: on the short side and remarkably spry and alert. We did a lot of talking about

Parkways generally, and his telephone conversations with Colonel Otway, before we got to Hugh Cordage.

"He was a queer bird," Gasport said. "A mixture of the likeable and the plausible. Never expressed the slightest regret, mind you. That type of rascal always imagines the world owes him a living and he's entitled to get it in any way he likes. He died of double pneumonia, by the way."

"Doctor Riley attended him throughout?"

"Throughout is hardly the word," he told me. "It was all very sudden. Just thought to be a heavy cold and then a diagnosis of pneumonia and then out—just like that."

"You don't know if he recovered consciousness before he died?"

"No," he said, and frowned. "Naturally that occurred to me, but as far as I remember, Riley said he didn't. Not that you could always believe Riley. He was another of the plausible ones."

"You used the word *naturally*," Jewle said. "I wonder, Major, if that means what I hope it does."

Gasport smiled.

"The way I used it is this: when a man knows he hasn't long to live, he's inclined to open his mouth. Cordage might, for instance, have told where his brother actually was. Let me explain."

The authorities, he said, would always consider Hugh Cordage as a possible lead to his brother, and the stolen jewels. He was entitled to send the official number of letters and receive them, but he never sent any letters. The very few he received were closely examined.

"I only remember him actually receiving two," he said. "I think one was in 1941 and the other in 1945. They were supposed to be from an old Cambridge friend but they bore no address so they couldn't be traced. If they contained some kind of code, then it was never broken."

"It's possible the letters were from Arthur and that they gave information as to his whereabouts?"

"Possibly—yes," he said. "They were two clever young men, you know. In spite of his superciliousness I always regarded Hugh Cordage as having a remarkably clever brain."

And that was virtually the tantalising end of the evening. Everything was hypothetical—*if* this and *if* that. Hugh Cordage *might* have told Ranger how to get into touch with Arthur. But against that was the fact that *Ranger* hadn't got into touch with him.

"There's just one thing," I said. "The curious way in which Riley left the Prison Medical Service. I believe he practically picked a quarrel with you, Major, so as to try and put you in the wrong, and then he resigned."

"I think that about sums it up."

"And that was soon after Hugh Cordage's death. Which makes it look as if he thought Arthur Cordage a much better financial proposition than going on looking after sick convicts. But then the whole thing falls to pieces. He didn't contact Arthur. It looks as if he may have tried and then he had to give it up and find another job—which he did. He went into practice under National Health. And it wasn't till he was kicked out of that that he tried looking for him again. But why the gap? If he could find him in the last resort, so to speak, why not in the first?"

We couldn't find an answer. Hypotheses, of course, but always far from satisfying, so there was nothing more to do than thank Gasport and get back to our cars at the Yard.

"Do you feel like going to Tedfold?" Jewle asked me.

"Something might be picked up. And one thing we haven't got, and that's a really accurate description of Arthur Cordage to supplement that photograph. You ought to get one from there."

15

LUCIA BLACK

JEWLE was spending the night with his wife and family. I went to the flat and it was at about nine the next morning that I set off for Tedfold. I wondered if it might pay me to call on Doctor Wormgay at Harrenden again, but Tedfold happened to come first and I didn't see after all just what the old doctor could tell me that he hadn't divulged before. Besides, what I was enquiring about was something that certainly wouldn't be common knowledge. It was a possibly private and dubious part of Ranger's shifty career, no hint of which could ever have reached the ears of Wormgay.

I'm the sort of person who's liable to cold shivers. I got one during that three hour drive, and when I suddenly remembered a forgotten person—Lucia Black. You remember that hint of Wharton's—that we might be on the wrong tack after all and those newspaper cuttings might have nothing to do with Ranger's death? Well, just for a moment, when I suddenly began thinking about Lucia Black, I had just that feeling myself. Things came to me in that moment like a cinema flashback.

I don't claim that I thought of them in their right order but when I did come to arrange them, they seemed to make a curious pattern. First had been that cryptic remark about Ranger.

"All that gaff about Ranger. I may have had my own reasons for letting him get ideas."

Was that just lies? An attempt to ingratiate herself for some reason or other with myself and explain away village gossip? If not, what had been her reasons for starting an affair with Ranger? Could the answer be—and there came another cold shiver—that she intended to promise to marry him provided she could get rid of her husband?

And so to the second thing—hinting to her that her husband might have been murdered. That had been a wrong guess, and yet there'd been an immediate reaction. But no tears, no horror, and definitely no fainting. Nothing but that curious smile. It was almost as if she was secretly glad, not so much to know it as because I knew it. The operating word, as they say, was *murdered*. She might have so far forgotten herself as to smile at the knowledge that Black was dead, but to smile—and furthermore, not to press me for details—on hearing that word *murder* was extraordinary to say the least of it. Had she been already aware that it was murder?

And finally there was the morning, twenty-four hours ago almost to the minute, when I'd given her a ride back from

Edenthorpe and had asked her what her plans might be. Again there'd been that enigmatical smile. But a few minutes later, outside her house, another change had come over her. It wasn't yet another flirtation she'd been trying to start, though if it was I'd soon show where I stood. But she'd been far more serious than I'd hitherto known her. She'd wanted to keep in touch with me because, so she said, she might want my help. And she hadn't indicated why, or given me time to ask.

So what did it all amount to? One thing couldn't be dismissed as utterly out of the question. Poisoning, according to all experience, is a woman's kind of crime. Had she been up to the ears in the killing of her husband? Had Ranger been induced to be her ally? And had she managed things so that suspicion should fall entirely on him? I remembered that story of Chaucer's and the treasure seekers at the time of the plague. Three were digging to uncover a treasure. It was hot work and one was sent to the town to buy wine. By the time he returned, the other two had planned to kill him and so share the treasure between just two. So they killed him and then they drank the wine. But he'd had the same idea. That wine was poisoned and both died. And was there in that story the germ of what had happened at Ranger's bungalow? Had Ranger, Lucia Black's dupe, fallen into a trap of their joint devising?

It was a fascinating problem and one that would need a deal of working out: far too much in fact for a hope of a solution for someone driving pretty fast on strange roads with quite a lot of traffic. It was a lovely Sunday of late autumn, and cars were everywhere on the roads. They didn't thin out till I'd left the main road for the side road that would bring me to Tedfold. It was just about midday when I got there.

It was quite a large village with a central green. A pub, the Waggon and Horses, was almost the first building I really saw. It was after opening time, so I drew the car up outside and went into the public bar.

The landlord was behind that bar. I ordered a pint of bitter and asked about lunch. He didn't do lunches but he did find bread and butter and cheese and pickles. While they were coming I asked if he remembered a Doctor Riley. He smiled. I thought what a character Riley must have been. In my experience everyone—even old Doctor Wormgay—had smiled at the mere mention of his name. I said I'd known him many years ago and at once he was asking where Riley was now. I said I'd lost track of him but maybe I could pick up something from the present doctor. His house, I learned, was the white one with the blue paint on the other side of the green.

I don't think I've ever made a meal last so long—that and a second pint. Soon after one o'clock the room had thinned out—Sunday dinner was an event—and a few minutes later there were only the landlord and myself. I asked him about the Cordage boys and if he remembered them. He did, and he remembered the Cordage Case.

"Regular young devils they always was," he said. "And that Indian gentleman that was with them, he wasn't much better."

He gave me his description of Arthur Cordage as he last remembered him, just before he sold the old rectory. It didn't add much to what one could gather from the photograph. He was about five-feet ten or eleven, he thought: on the fat side and dark-haired, and, he thought, dark-eyed. He was very active, he said, and a good rider. There'd always been ponies at the rectory when the boys were younger, and after the rector's death Arthur had kept a couple of hunters. I let him run on and because I wasn't keen on leaving till the doctor had finished his lunch.

The doctor turned out to be a man of about fifty. He raised his eyebrows when I showed him my warrant card.

"Nothing very important," I said, "except that anything you can tell me will be regarded as confidential. I'm really making enquiries about an Arthur Cordage who disappeared after a famous jewel robbery. I expect you heard all about that as soon as you came here."

He had: and about his predecessor, Riley. But he'd never seen Riley. Everything he knew about him was hearsay. I guessed as much, if only because he didn't smile at the first mention of his name.

"Who looked after him while he was here?" I said. "He must have had a daily woman or something."

He did. She was a Mrs. Early, whose cottage I must have passed as I neared the village. He told me just how to identify it, so I thanked him and left. I rounded the green and found the cottage a quarter of a mile on. It was the nearer half of a double-dweller. Mrs. Early was a frail looking woman in the late seventies. An arthritic knee made her walk with a stick but it hadn't somehow affected her house-work. That little cottage looked as spotless as if it had just had a spring-clean.

She was cheerful enough and she must have been remarkably good-looking in her younger days. She seemed pleased when I told her so. Her husband had been killed in 1916 on the Somme. They'd had no children.

"Doctor Leggett asked me to go as his housekeeper," she said. "He was the one before Doctor Riley: he was a bachelor, too, so I didn't have to part with any of my things. I had my own little room with wireless and all that as well as my bedroom."

"You liked Doctor Riley?"

A slow shake of the head accompanied the smile.

"Yes," she said. "He was easy to get on with, but he made an awful lot of work. Used to come in at all hours, and not because of his patients. They tell me he got into trouble where he went later."

"Unfortunately, yes," I said. "But tell me something, Mrs. Early. Did he ever have any people staying with him?"

"Never," she said. "He once told me he hadn't neither chick nor child."

"Another question. It'll probably sound curious to you, but I'd like you to answer it. Suppose he had a friend who'd got into trouble—would it have been possible for him to have hidden that friend in the house without your knowing it?"

"Why, no," she said. "How could he? Every day of my life I was in every room in the house. There were only three bedrooms, and I used the spare as my sitting-room."

"Well, that settles that," I said. "But something else: you knew the late rector's nephews, the Cordage boys?"

"Did I know them!" She smiled. "You couldn't help knowing them. And that young Indian gentleman—the Black Prince as they used to call him here—who used to stay with them."

"Doctor Riley knew them well?"

"He was their doctor." It was like a reminder. "Not that they ever had much wrong with them. But Mr. Arthur, as we called him, he broke his arm one day when he was riding. A rare reckless one, he was. They both were, if it came to that. But that was later. It'd be long after his uncle died. Just before he sold the house: the old Rectory, as we call it now."

"The Doctor didn't have any meals there?"

She frowned in thought.

"I think he did—once or twice. Yes: he went to dinner. Not very often, though. Besides, Mr. Arthur sold the house and went away, as I said. He and his brother, Mr. Hugh, got into trouble, too. I suppose you know that."

The old-fashioned American clock on the mantelpiece said it was three o'clock. She asked if I'd like a cup of tea, but I told her I had a long way to go and I'd like to break the back of it by dark. I'd have liked to give her a tip, but I knew she'd have resented even the offer. She was someone I was going to remember: the natural dignity, the quiet smile and the uncomplaining way of her. When I thanked her she said there was nothing that called for thanks. It was always nice to think and talk about old times.

I drove on for a bit, then pulled up the car and began asking myself if I ought after all, to call on Doctor Wormgay. It would be a pity to have come so far and then to leave and miss even a single word that might throw light on the relationships between his former partner and the Cordages. That, I now knew, was what Jewle and I had done. If, for instance, he had asked Wormgay bluntly if anything had ever happened in the district from which might arise a matter of blackmail, we'd almost certainly have been told about the Cordage Case, and that would have saved a second journey. But for the luck of finding those newspaper cuttings, we could never have tied the Cordage Case up with Ranger.

I thought it well over and then decided to leave things as they were. After all, Tedfold had been a self-contained practice within the partnership, and Wormgay—however much his ears had been kept pricked—could not have known more than he'd told us already. And, as I left the village and began my long drive clean across the Midlands, to Marstead, I knew I was right. I hadn't learned much that day but it seemed to me that I'd learned enough.

It was a question of reorientation: a discarding of previous ideas and unsupported theories that had cluttered up the case. Everything was now more clear and therefore more hopeful. Ranger had known the Cordage boys during all his stay in Tedfold. He'd been on friendly terms and had attended Arthur for a broken arm. Then they had left Tedfold and I doubted if Ranger had as much as thought of them again—at least till he read about the robbery at the Ritz-Plaza.

Then, after the war, he had been appointed to the same prison where Hugh Cordage was serving his sentence. The two must have talked together from time to time, no matter what regulations laid down to the contrary. And Ranger wasn't one to pay too much heed to regulations. What seemed to follow, as the night the day, was that during his fatal illness, or before, Hugh Cordage must have given Ranger some information as to the whereabouts of Arthur and it was after that he'd procured the relevant newspapers and taken the cuttings. Whether it had been arranged by the brothers before the robbery that if one had the bad luck to be arrested and the other escaped, that latter was to adopt a pre-determined course of action, I didn't know. It might have been that, or that Hugh received code messages in the only two letters that reached him in Parkways.

The trouble, as I saw it, was that Ranger received from Hugh insufficient information about Arthur's whereabouts. It seemed the only explanation of why Ranger hadn't found him. Why then he had had the good luck to find him later, and at the very time when he'd been kicked out of his profession and needed a new financial stand-by, was more than I could work out. The only encouraging thing about that was that now it seemed to be the sole missing link. Find out, in other words, why Ranger hadn't been able to locate Arthur Cordage at one moment but had found him at a very convenient other, after what seemed to be a year's search, and the Case should be as good as solved. And why? For the reason that the two things in question—why Cordage couldn't be found and why he was later found—were most certainly to do with Cordage's whereabouts and his manner of life. That meant we would know a whole lot more about him. He was the man about whom we wanted to know things. We had all that was necessary now about Ranger. If we knew half as much about Arthur Cordage, then it shouldn't be hard to identify him.

It was after seven o'clock when I reached Edenthorpe. Henry had been warned about my arrival and dinner had been held up. I'd had to make my report to Jewle and by the time I'd had a bath and a change it was nearer nine than eight. After the meal I felt uncommonly sleepy and soon after ten I was in bed. There was no hurry when I woke in the morning. Unless something urgent turned up, Jewle thought me entitled to an easy day.

Henry thought it would clear away the cobwebs if we played golf and he managed to fix up a foursome that afternoon with Andover and Sterne. Everything was according to pattern. Andover was decked in the usual rainbow hues and Sterne in his natty grey corduroys and grey sweater, and he and Henry gave us the usual hiding. But it was all very enjoyable. Henry wanted the two to take pot luck over tea at Bendacre, but neither could come. Andover had someone coming in and Sterne—it was a bridge night—had preliminary secretarial work to do and had to be at Edenthorpe rather early. So Henry and I had tea alone and it was just when we were drawing up to the fire that the extraordinary thing happened. I should say that we were rather late home from golf—we'd only managed to conclude our game before dusk—and I happened to glance at the bracket clock on the mantel-piece when the telephone went. It was exactly a quarter past five.

Mrs. Slack couldn't have heard the ringing: she was busy washing up. Henry took the call. I heard him say something about someone being here, and then he was calling me. He cupped the receiver and whispered that it was Lucia Black.

"Hal-*lo*, Mrs. Black," I said. "How are you?"

"I think I'm in a jam."

"You mean your car?"

"Car?" she said. "Oh, that. No, I fetched it this morning."

Her voice was quite low and, though it seemed to have an urgency, I could hardly hear it.

"Just a minute," I said. "The line seems pretty bad."

I gave the receiver a good rattle and tried again.

"You there?"

"Yes," she said. "I think it was me, not the receiver. I'm all scared. You've got to come and see me. Not now. Any time after seven o'clock."

"I'll be there."

"Oh, thank you." There seemed an enormous relief in her voice. "I shan't forget this, Mr. Travers. . . . Hold the line, will you?"

There was a silence, or it seemed so: just the little noises that lie in the receiver itself when the line's still live, and then she was speaking again. Her voice had altered.

"Thank you, Mrs. Andover. It was very good of you. See you in the morning then. . . . Yes. Goodbye."

The line was dead. I stood there with the receiver in my hand, wondering what on earth had happened. How had Mrs. Andover got on the line? It was impossible. It was *my* line. Still, all I could do was replace the receiver. Or was it?

I looked up Lucia Black's number, lifted the receiver and dialled. At once I could hear the ring. I waited, receiver at my ear. I decided to let it ring just twenty more times. It did. I replaced the receiver. There was only one answer to that. Lucia Black was no longer there. She must have gone out. I remembered she'd said I wasn't to go round till after seven o'clock.

But the whole thing was very queer. I mentioned it to Henry and he didn't seem to find it odd at all.

"Mrs. Andover had just dropped in for something," he said. "Mrs. Black was talking to her direct and then she forgot herself and hung up on you."

"That's wrong, Henry," I said. "She was talking to Mrs. Andover on the telephone. There isn't a shadow of doubt about that."

He frowned.

"But how could she? The lines couldn't have got crossed, could they? We've all picked up a receiver and overheard someone else's conversation."

"This was different. She didn't replace her receiver. The line was always live. Mrs. Andover couldn't possibly have got on it."

Henry smiled.

"Look, my dear fellow: you'll be seeing her at seven o'clock. She'll explain it all then."

"I don't want to bore you," I said, "but I don't like waiting till seven. There ought to be some perfectly natural explanation. Listen again. She started off in a very agitated voice telling me she was in a jam and wanted my help. That was the first phase. Then she stopped and told me to hold the line. I did, and I'd say four or five seconds elapsed. Then she started talking to Mrs. Andover, and in quite a different tone of voice: all chatty and cheerful. *And*—I insist on this—she was definitely talking to Mrs. Andover on the telephone."

"You couldn't have heard her hang up," he said. "She must have hung up and rung Mrs. Andover."

"No, no," I said. "I had that receiver at my ear. As soon as she lifted hers and began dialling, I'd have heard it." My hands went out bewilderedly. "But let's leave it, as you say. Another hour and a half and I'll be seeing her."

He smiled as he passed me *The Times*.

"Do the crossword," he said. "Otherwise you'll be getting the fidgets."

It was one of the harder variety and kept me busy for quite a time. Then I went upstairs and changed into a quieter suit. I looked through my window at Lucia Black's house but couldn't see it, much less a light, for there was quite a lot of mist. It was almost a fog and I shouldn't have been surprised at it. The warmer a day of late autumn or early winter, the greater likelihood of fog. That's what it would have been in a town. At Marstead it was only a thickish mist.

At five minutes to seven I left the house. Seen in the open that mist wasn't so bad: there was a visibility of quite fifty yards and I had no need of a torch. There's no street lighting in Marstead and the whole village looked deserted except for here and there a chink of light from windows. It wasn't freezing, but it was cold.

I found the bell-push. I heard the bell sound inside the house and I wiped the damp from my stubby moustache while I waited. I pushed the bell again. I put my ear against the door but there was no sound. I picked my way gingerly round by the side of the house and found the back door. I knocked. I knocked again, and listened. I went round again to the front and tried once more from there. After that there was only one thing to conclude: Lucia Black hadn't come home. What I'd do was have my dinner and then return.

That is what I did. At half-past eight I was at Lucia Black's house and once more going through the routine: front door and back, ringing, knocking and listening. Again there wasn't a sound. That house was as if it had never been lived in. But even then I didn't give up. I went back again at ten o'clock that night, and once more it was wasted time. When I got back Henry said that Jewle had rung me. He hadn't said what about. When he'd been told that I was out he'd said it didn't matter and he'd be along to see me in the morning.

"She still wasn't in then?" Henry said.

I shook my head. I said I didn't like it. Then I did something else, and without much hope. I dialled the number again. I could hear the ringing. A minute of it and I hung up.

"What about ringing Mrs. Andover?"

"They're early birds," Henry said. "Why not leave it till the morning? Mrs. Black's bound to be back by then."

16

The Next Day

I SHOULD have had a restless night, but I didn't, though I did wake with Lucia Black very much on my mind. As soon as I'd drunk my early morning tea I went very quietly downstairs and dialled her number. I waited quite a long time with the sound of ringing in my ears and then I reluctantly hung up.

I went back to the bedroom, had a quick shave and wash at the basin, dressed and again went quietly downstairs. It was not much after eight o'clock and there was still a little mist in the air. But the sun was trying already to burst through and I thought the day would be fine.

Now it was a daytime routine, but with a difference. I rang the front bell and noticed that the curtains, upstairs and down, were still drawn. I rang again. Lucia Black, I told myself, must be a sound sleeper and it might take a hammering on the back door to wake her. On the back doorstep was a pint bottle of milk. I gave the door a good rap with my knuckles. I gave it a kick or two with my toe and there still wasn't a sound from inside the house. All the windows, even that of what was probably the kitchen, were closely curtained.

Then I had a sudden idea. I went right round the house and looked through the window of the lean-to garage. The car wasn't there.

For a moment I just couldn't believe it. And then things began almost to explain themselves. Lucia Black had been dressed ready to go out when she had rung me the previous early evening and probably the car had been at the door. She had expected to get back at seven o'clock but something—the mist where she had gone may have developed into a fog—had held her up. Which meant she ought to be back in the course of the morning.

I looked at my watch. Still over ten minutes to go before breakfast, so I crossed the main road and went up the slight slope towards the rectory. Andover, a napkin in his hand, came to the door. He looked surprised to see me, and no wonder.

"Sorry to disturb you at your meal," I said, "but do you think I might have a word with your wife?"

"Of course," he said. "Come in. We're in the kitchen. It saves work. It's something private?"

"Not at all," I said. "It's just a little mystery I'd like to clear up."

More apologies to Mrs. Andover and I was giving an edited version of Lucia Black's telephone call.

"Spoke to me?" Mrs. Andover said. "But I never rang her! And I'm sure she never rang me. I couldn't be mistaken about that. You sure you heard what she was saying?"

"As plainly as I hear you now. What she said was, 'Thank you, Mrs. Andover. It was very good of you. I'll be seeing you in the morning'. Then she rang off."

"Someone must have been playing a trick on you," Andover said. Then he shrugged his broad shoulders. "I still don't see how—or why."

I told them that Lucia Black's car wasn't in her garage and that she'd probably be back in the course of the morning.

Then we'd have an answer to everything. Andover said he'd be glad if I'd give him a ring and tell him what the explanation was. I said I certainly would and that in the meantime I'd be glad if they'd keep the matter confidential. He was getting up from the table to see me out, but his wife stopped him.

"You get on with breakfast, Harry. There's something I want to see Mr. Travers about."

She didn't say a thing till we were well out of earshot and almost at the front gate.

"It's about Mr. Ranger's bungalow," she said. "I don't think Colonel Sterne's been fair. We thought about it for an aunt of mine and Harry went and mentioned it to Colonel Sterne and then the Colonel mentioned his father and Harry went and gave way."

I told her it might be quite a time before it was known who'd inherit the bungalow. My guess was that it would come into the open market and then she or her aunt could bid. She seemed much relieved. She even told me with an exaggerated playfulness that the aunt had money and had to be humoured.

"Just one other thing," she said. "Would it be possible for me to have the loan of the key so that I could look round? Mrs. Gantle hasn't got one now, she tells me."

I told her I'd see what I could do, but as I made my way across the path towards Bendacre, I couldn't help a sudden wonder. It was a preposterous thing to imagine, of course, but could Mrs. Andover or her husband have been the illicit searchers of that bungalow, and, since nothing had been found, was that business of an aunt and the asking for a key an attempt to have another search free from all interference? Then I smiled to myself. The life history of both the Andovers was almost certainly plain for all to read. It couldn't have been they whom Ranger was blackmailing. Or that other person interested in the bungalow—Sterne.

Breakfast was just coming in when I got back to Bendacre.

"You're an early bird," Henry told me. "Didn't I see you going out some time ago?"

I told him what I'd been doing. He seemed relieved to hear about Lucia Black's car. His idea was that she'd been held up somewhere. Maybe the car had broken down again.

"But what about the Andover part of it?" I said.

"Oh, that." He smiled. "If you really heard what you thought you did, she'll give you an explanation when she gets back."

What could I say to that? I insist that I'm a man of mildness but I was never so near to snapping a retort. *If I'd really heard what I thought I did.* Hadn't I assured him that I'd heard every word as clearly—the Andover words—as if I'd been in the room with Lucia Black herself? Did he think I'd been seized for the first time in my life with sudden deafness? And then I think I smiled wryly to myself. Maybe he had some right on his side— at least about the folly of worrying—and with that I got down to my porridge.

Jewle turned up at half-past nine. He and Allman had spent the previous day in tracking down Ranger's friends. It seemed to have been a tricky business: a beginning with the bridge club and an effort to enlarge the circle with that as a centre. He'd brought with him a list of some twenty names and he made no bones about saying there probably wasn't a real friend among them and that some were merely acquaintances.

Henry, pretending—I thought maliciously—not to be listening, was writing something at that knee-hole writing-desk. It was that, and Jewle's list, that suddenly gave me an idea.

"Just a minute, Henry. I've thought of something. It'll need your co-operation."

He laid down his pen and came over.

"What're you smiling at?" he said.

"Just my own enthusiasms," I said. "The scheme doesn't seem all that good now."

"What was it?" Jewle wanted to know.

"Well, this," I said dubiously. "The man we want made two entries into Ranger's bungalow and we know now that he didn't get what he was looking for. We got it, but he doesn't know that. You're with me so far?"

He nodded.

"Then instead of laboriously wading through and trying to check up on this list of Ranger's friends, we might try a short cut, with Sir Henry's help. I think he should throw a cocktail party."

Henry stared.

"The first thing to do is go through the list and see if it overlaps with your friends, Henry: I mean, if you had mutual friends like, say, the Marstead people and possibly some from Edenthorpe and the district, those are the ones you'll invite. And, since the scheme depends on the rooms here being pretty full, you also ask people who're your own friends. Say a grand total of forty or fifty. You could manage that?"

"I don't know," he said. "I'd have to get it worked out. To tell the truth I *had* been thinking of something of the kind. Quite a few people called and I'm afraid I've been rather negligent about hospitality. But what's behind it all?"

"This," I said. "The part about myself is all eyewash. I'm not important in the least, but they're not to know that. You ring everybody and apologise for everything being rather hurried but say it suddenly struck you I'd like to meet them and so on. Say you've put it off rather late but I'm going back to town and mayn't be this way again for quite a time. If the man we want is among them, he'll think the enquiry has fizzled out and that'll give him confidence."

"Confidence for what?" Jewle asked.

"For yet another entry," I said. "Look: there's that walnut writing desk over there with the secret drawers. When the fun's in full swing, Henry must switch the talk with someone to antiques and secret drawers. He'll even start exhibiting that writing-desk, and then I'll pretend to be struck with an idea. I'll say, 'Good Lord! Ranger had a bureau!' I'll be struck all of a heap, and then I'll slip out, taking care to be seen. And what's the odds that our man, if he's there, doesn't try to get to the bungalow before me?"

Jewle rubbed his chin.

"It's an idea. Mind you, it'd take a good deal of working out. Timing, and so on."

"Wait a minute," I said. "After I've said, 'Good Lord! Ranger had a bureau!' I'll say this to Henry: 'Would you excuse me, Henry? I think I'll run out to Edenthorpe and see the Inspector and get the key.'"

"I've got you," Jewle said. "Our friend will think he has a certain amount of time. Say a quarter of an hour at the least. But I and Allman'll be there."

"And I," I said. "I'll go through the motions of taking the car but I'll run it into old Culver's yard."

There was silence for a moment. Jewle gave a queer shake of the head.

"I'm like you," he said. "It sounded a good scheme, but now I don't know. When you let it cool for a minute it seems a bit—well, just one of those things that couldn't possibly come off."

"I don't know," Henry told us mildly. "I rather like it. And what harm would there be in trying?"

I almost shook him by the hand.

"Good for you, Henry," I said. "What about getting to work on a list?"

"Why not?" he said. "But when would the cocktail party be? This is Tuesday. It couldn't be before Thursday."

"Thursday'd be fine," I said. "And I'll be supposed to be leaving on the Friday. If the whole thing turns out to be a flop—well, we can always hatch out some excuse for staying on."

We got to work. There had been something off-hand about the origins of the scheme, but there was nothing off-hand now. We weren't framing some elaborate practical joke or discussing a charade: we were laying a trap to catch a murderer. And we had to believe in it, even if at the back of our minds was the knowledge that the odds against success were enormously large. At any rate, an hour later Henry had worked out his list of guests, and there were just over forty.

"Looks as if I shall be telephoning for the rest of the day," he told us. "And hadn't you better write down just what you think I ought to say?"

That wasn't difficult. For people I knew it would be that I was having to go back to town rather earlier than I'd thought and the party would be a kind of communal chance to say goodbye. For those I didn't know it might be that an old friend who'd been staying with him was going away and, as I might be coming down again in the spring, he thought it a good idea for us to get acquainted. As for the words and music, so to speak, they could be rehearsed on the Thursday morning. I undertook, once numbers were known, to make arrangements with an Edenthorpe firm of caterers. Henry had been to one or two parties which they'd handled, and he said they were good.

We left Henry at the telephone and I went with Jewle to his car and I was telling him about that extraordinary telephone call I'd had the previous afternoon. He was interested. He made me go over it twice.

"Would you like to go there now and see if she's home?"

I went back to the house for my hat and coat.

"Hop in," he said. "I'll drive just round the corner to save time. If she's in, I shall see you go in. If not, I'll come along myself."

She wasn't in. When I came to examine the empty garage from outside, I saw that it was locked. There was a finality about that that I didn't like. And yet she hadn't warned either the milkman or the newsagent. And it was curious that every window in the house should be curtained.

I waved to Jewle and he moved the car on to the house. He saw the newspaper and the milk bottle: the padlock on the garage and the windows with their curtains still drawn.

"I don't like it either," he said. "I think I'll make an entry. There's every justification considering the circumstances. You'd swear, for instance, that she wanted to see you most urgently at seven o'clock. If she *should* come back, I don't see what she could make a complaint about."

He drew the car in till it was almost touching the garage. Then he tackled the front door: the back had an old-fashioned lock and would almost certainly be bolted from the inside. In no more than half a minute he'd slipped back the catch of the Yale lock and we stepped into the house. He let the door close behind us and slipped the bolt with his gloved fingers. He handed me a spare pair of gloves.

"You take down here," he said, "and I'll do upstairs. Don't touch anything more than you can help."

There was nothing unusual in the three downstairs rooms. There was not even a dirty cup or plate in the sink. The ash-tray on the small table in the living-room had quite a few butts in it and all of them had the same colour of lipstick.

"Come up a minute, will you?"

That was Jewle from the landing. I switched off the downstairs light and went up.

"That's the spare bedroom," he said. "All in dust-sheets, as you see. I think the husband slept there and she had this room beyond it in the front. The other bedroom's never been furnished by the look of it. It's her room I want you to see."

At first glance I thought that that room had been searched by some intruder, but it wasn't that. Drawers weren't properly closed and a piece of shelf paper protruded from the bottom of the wardrobe drawer. In spite of the made bed, the room had a curious kind of bareness and when I thought of my wife's room, I knew what it was. The dressing-table was absolutely bare.

"She took her things with her?"

"That's right," he said. "All the toilet stuff and brushes and combs and what-nots—the whole bag of tricks. And from the bathroom. And practically all her clothes. See that mark on the bed where the case was when she was packing it? And this other one that overlaps it? She took two biggish cases of stuff. Just about all she could get in the boot of her car."

He opened a drawer or two to show me. He opened the wardrobe. Only a few summer-looking frocks were hanging there, and on the floor, in their trees, were a couple of pairs of oldish-looking shoes.

"She's gone for good," I said.

"Yes—gone for good. Or till we catch up with her."

"She's got a good start," I said. "She might be anywhere by now. And she'll sell that car."

He stood there, slowly rubbing his chin.

"You can get the car number from the Local Taxation Officer at Edenthorpe."

He nodded but he didn't make a move. Then he gave me a queer sort of look, as if what we'd been saying didn't matter much.

"Look, sir. You'll think I haven't got much of a memory but would you mind going over that telephone conversation again? . . . Wait a minute: try to imitate her various tones of voice. Act as if you were her. Go through the motions with the telephone and so on."

I made as good a hand of it as I could.

"Right," he said. "Let's get downstairs."

He went out by the front door and when he came back he had his finger-print set.

"We needn't try door handles—not yet. If there's an answer it's on that telephone receiver. Draw back the curtains, will you? I'd rather have natural light."

I didn't want to black what light there was, so I didn't stand too close, but I knew that he was using the special powder. It was quite a time before he told me to have a look. "No prints?"

"No prints," he said. "No recent ones, that is. It doesn't matter about bringing up any old ones. Still, we'd better clinch it. Let's get up to her room again."

It was the same thing there. Someone had wiped the prints from every handle and wardrobe.

"It's amazing!" I said. "If she didn't do the packing, who did?"

"Perhaps *she* did. For all we know she may have had a record. If so we ought to be able to find out."

We went down again, this time to the kitchen. Since her husband's death Lucia Black hadn't employed a woman and the prints we found on a glass and a cup should definitely have been hers.

"I'll get 'em to the Yard straight away," Jewle said. "Not that I've got much hope. My own idea is that she went away under compulsion. In fact, I wouldn't be surprised if she was dead."

My fingers went to my glasses. A glimmer of light was beginning to peep.

"Work things out from that telephone call," Jewle said. "She rang you, all agitated-like, and wanted your help to get her out of some sort of jam. Then she asked you to hold the line. And why? Because she heard someone either at the door or else coming in. She didn't replace the receiver, and therefore she didn't go to the door to let that someone in. And therefore, he or she was already in. So what did she do? She couldn't let on that she'd been talking to you, so she made out as if she'd been talking to someone innocuous, like Mrs. Andover."

It was as clear as the light that was now coming through that window.

"But don't let's rush to extremes," he said. "Take X, for example—the one who came in while she was telephoning you. Let's say he was an accomplice of some sort and when she rang you she was trying to double-cross him. That's why she ended with that Mrs. Andover stuff."

"No," I said. "Something's wrong somewhere. Something's badly wrong. I was to see her at seven o'clock and not before. Why not till then?"

Jewle gave a dry smile.

"We can always find answers. The trouble is whether they're right or not. Take this seven o'clock business. Maybe she knew X was coming to see her and she didn't know how long he'd stay. She certainly didn't know he might have changed his mind and would tell her to get away."

"Then what about the fingerprints?"

"It was a hurried job. He helped her pack. And he didn't want anyone to know he'd been in here."

"That means that he had a record."

"Not necessarily. What it means is that if his prints were found here, he was someone whose prints we might be able to check. Someone who might leave his prints on a golf club or a newspaper—or a cocktail glass."

"Maybe," I said. "If so, it's someone I can't think of at the moment. Frank Laving, Sterne and Andover: they're the only ones I know at all well, and every one has a record that makes it ludicrous to connect him with Arthur Cordage. What I can't get away from is the idea that somehow Lucia Black engineered her husband's death, with Ranger's help, and that Ranger made some slip or other and got himself killed in the process. I was thinking about that on my way to Helmsby."

I'd told him some of it before and now I told him again. He didn't see, and neither could I for that matter, where it tied in with the mysterious X. My theory allowed for three people only, and of them, Lucia Black was the only one still alive. Where then did X come in? What had been the need for him?

"We're too close to everything," Jewle said. "Let's get away from it for a bit. It may sort itself out later. I'll rush these prints to the Yard. Soon after they get there they ought to be ringing me up."

He dropped me at Bendacre. Henry had knocked off for lunch and was fortifying himself for the afternoon session with a sherry. After lunch, and before he could begin his telephonic marathon again, I rang the Andovers. A simple explanation, I said. Mrs. Black had gone away for a day or two. As for the use of Mrs. Andover's name, she'd probably been thinking of something else at the time and the mistake had been inadvertent. I managed to hang up rather quickly and so avoided argument.

I was at a loose end that afternoon so I decided to go out to the golf course and practise a few shots. I'd gone about half a mile along the lane when I overtook Colonel Sterne riding a bicycle. I pulled up the car just ahead of him.

"Hallo, Colonel! Where're you off to?"

"Thought I'd go along and get a bit of practice," he said. "My car's out of action. Went phut on me last night."

"Look," I said, "why not park your bicycle behind the hedge there. No one'll see it. I'm going along to the course myself and we can collect it on the way back. That is, if you'd like a game."

He lifted the bicycle over a field gate and parked it and then got in with me. As I drove on I asked him about his car. He'd given a lift the previous night to a fellow member of the bridge club who lived about half a mile the Marstead side of Edenthorpe and they hadn't quite got into the town when the car broke down. Luckily the garage didn't shut down till seven o'clock so it was towed in. The big-end had gone, so the garage had rung him to say that morning.

"I mightn't get it for another week," he said. "It was all right last night because someone took pity on us and drove us home, but you miss a car in the country."

I had only time for nine holes and it was while we were playing that he told me Henry had rung him about the cocktail party.

"I didn't know you were going so soon," he said. "We were all getting accustomed to you being here."

I said I had certain work of my own to do in town, but I hoped to be down for a long stay in the spring. And that was that. He beat me by two and one. He was a good winner.

"Another week or two here and you'd be beating the head off all of us. Besides, I live practically on the course. Whenever I feel like it I put in an hour or two by myself. It makes all the difference, especially to your short game."

We picked up his bicycle on the way back and said we'd be seeing each other on the Thursday night. I felt quite a different man when I got back to Bendacre. The cobwebs had gone and tea was just about to come in. Henry was a bit tired: faint, as he put it, but no longer pursuing. His net bag for the Thursday evening was thirty-one.

"It isn't as many as you'd hoped," he said, "but it might be better. We'll use both here and the dining-room but there'll be fewer to keep an eye on."

Forgive me if I go on ahead a bit and say that the grand total turned out to be thirty-eight. Henry thought of two more couples and some other people rang later to ask if they might bring friends. But about the rest of that Tuesday. Jewle rang me soon after tea.

"No record," he said tersely. "That means we've got to start working things out. What about running along here in the morning?"

I said I'd be along at about ten. The rest of that evening, at least till my brain refused to function, I spent in setting down those theories he and I had sketchily propounded that morning in Lucia Black's house: assessing merits and exposing flaws. I ended up roughly where I began. Or almost so. At the far back of my mind was the feeling that Jewle hadn't been talking sheer nonsense when he'd hinted that Lucia Black might be dead.

17

PARTY NIGHT

I SAW the Edenthorpe firm about the cocktail party next morning and went on to the police station for a talk with Jewle and Allman. It was talk and nothing else, and we didn't see what action there could be till the Thursday evening. As for that worrying business of Lucia Black, it was Allman who wasn't quite convinced about something. Why, he wanted to know, had the telephone receiver been wiped clean of prints since it was Lucia Black herself who'd been using it, and not the mysterious X?

There wasn't a satisfactory answer: plenty of theories, of course, as that X must later have used the telephone himself. And, since the whole system was automatic, there could be no checking. X, of course, could have rung with perfect immunity. He wouldn't have to give a number to an operator and so reveal that he was a man—or woman. We'd got to the state when we didn't even rule that out.

"Talking of telephoning," Jewle said. "I think we ought to find out a bit more about that broken arm that Arthur Cordage had at Helmsby. It might be a means of identification. If we can prove that anyone left Sir Henry's house at the time you do and we don't catch him red-handed, we might have to do some questioning. That's where that arm might come in handy."

I thought it possible that Doctor Wormgay might know something about it. It seemed a chance worth taking, and Jewle thought I might ring. I was supposed to have a more persuasive manner, whatever that might mean. At any rate, after ringing "Enquiries" and getting the number, I had the old doctor on the line in a couple of minutes. Reception was remarkably clear. I recalled to his memory that visit by Jewle and myself.

"That's right," he said. "You were asking about poor Riley."

"Yes," I said, "and now we want some information about someone else at Helmsby. Arthur Cordage. You knew him?"

"Everyone knew the Cordages," he told me. "The uncle—the rector—was an old friend of mine. He died in the late twenties. I think it was '27."

"It was," I said. "Then later, Arthur bought the house from the Ecclesiastical Commissioners. He and his brother had a couple of hunters there. The point is that Arthur broke his arm one day. I think it would be about 1935, just before he sold the house. He'd be just about thirty at the time. You don't happen to know anything about that broken arm?"

I heard his chuckle.

"I ought to. It was I who put it in plaster."

"But wasn't Riley his doctor?"

"That's nothing really to do with it," he said, "except for after-care. Cordage was brought to the hospital here and it happened to be one of my mornings."

"What sort of fracture was it, doctor? Anything one could identify, for example, at the present day?"

"There're always X-rays."

"But suppose one couldn't resort to that: what about sight or feel?"

"His was an impacted fracture," he said. "The ulna. I removed the plaster myself. Quite a good job, but easily identifiable by feel. The left arm, by the way."

I had a sudden idea. I'd be exceeding instructions but it might be worth exploring the ground.

"This Arthur Cordage is still wanted by the police, doctor, for that hotel job in 1938. How do you feel about him yourself?"

"I never liked him or his brother," he said. "A couple of conceited young puppies. They were a bad influence. I wasn't surprised when they ended up as they did."

"Then suppose we had a someone whom we thought was Arthur Cordage. Would you be prepared to co-operate with the police and try to identify him?"

"Most certainly," he said. "I'd only have to look at that arm and I'd know if he were Cordage or not."

"That's fine, doctor," I said. "We may have to take you up on that. I only hope we do."

I thanked him, said what a pleasure it had been hearing his voice again, and rang off. Jewle was pleased at what had happened. When he said that nothing was left but to find some-one for Wormgay to identify, the smiles were just a bit rueful. It was almost like saying that the only thing you had to do to win the Irish Sweep was to buy the right ticket.

After lunch at Bendacre, and just when I was wondering what to do with myself, Jewle rang me. He and Allman would pick me up in about ten minutes' time. I guessed they were going to have a thorough examination of Lucia Black's house. I was wrong.

It was Allman's idea that had started it. He'd had the advantage of not clogging the wheels of thought with all sorts of theories. He'd been the detached observer—if at second hand—and it seemed to him that the only solution of the Lucia Black affair was that she had been murdered. The doors of her house hadn't been locked—why should they be?—and X had called in time to hear her ringing me. He had even heard her say my name before stepping into the room. That was the simple explanation—as Allman had seen it—of why she'd asked me to hold the line and had then pretended to be finishing a conversation with Mrs. Andover.

"All right," Jewle had said. "She's murdered. Her bags are packed and she's put in her car with them. And where's she now?"

"She might be in that gravel pit," Allman said, and Jewle didn't wait for him to go any further. They were finishing a late lunch and immediately he had rung me. He was playing it down, mind you, when he told me about it in the car. That it was something worth trying was as far as he'd go.

We drew the car up at the top of the hill and began an examination of the ground beyond the low, gapped hedge. It wasn't so much a hedge as a few stunted bushes that were left of what had once been a scrubby, continuous hedge, so we found no twigs or small branches that had been pressed down or broken by the weight of a car. As for that arid ground—lichen mostly, and small stones—the dry weather of the last week or two had hardened it and though we found indentations that might have been made by a car, we couldn't be sure. When we came to the rail fence we did find something, even if again we couldn't be sure, for the space between two posts had its only rail—the bottom one—hanging loose at one end. We went through and then we did have some luck. The top edge, above the sheer fall of the pit, had been broken in two places. Allman whipped out his tape measure. The distance between those two surface breaks was exactly that of Lucia Black's car. He knew. He'd checked it at Edenthorpe at the garage just before he and Jewle had left.

We lay at full length and peered over the edge at the water below us, but there was nothing we could see.

"The water oughtn't to be all that cold," Allman said. "What about working our way along here to the bottom?"

We made our way down. I tore my coat, forcing a way through a hedge, but we got to the open meadow with the pool and the sandy rise of the pit in front of us. It didn't look so high when you were facing it from where we stood. Allman suddenly sat down on the grass and began unlacing his boots.

"I wouldn't, Fred," Jewle told him. "What's in there won't run away. By the morning we can have a rubber dinghy here and some grapples."

"Might as well try it now we've come so far," Allman said, and, began wading out. He went a good ten yards before the water came to the turned-up trousers. Jewle whispered to me that he'd been runner-up in the police diving championships.

"Water's not all that cold," Allman was telling us. "Just a couple of quick looks and you'd hardly feel it. What about it, skipper?"

"Why the hurry?" Jewle said. "No point in risking pneumonia when we can do the thing properly in the morning."

"All right," Allman said, and grinned. "You two wander off and come back in about five minutes."

"You'll want someone to pull you out," Jewle told him. "And just a couple of quick dives. You got that? That's an order."

Allman stripped to the raw. He made his way precariously along the side of the pit and then all at once his body went sideways and he was in. He swam like an otter. You could just see the white of his body beneath the water and then, as he came up to get his bearings and to take a deep breath, we saw the hump of his back as he dived. It was a long minute before he reappeared again, and almost by the face of the pit. He spluttered, shook his head and dived again. Another minute and he surfaced once more. The water churned behind him as he crawl-stroked towards us. He got to his feet and the mud and gravel of the bottom spattered his legs as he made the last few yards.

"It's all right," he said, and shook the water from his head again. "There's a car there. All four wheels in the air. I couldn't see inside."

We rubbed him down with his vest, and he dressed. He said he didn't feel all that cold.

"We'll get right back to the hotel in any case," Jewle said. "A hot bath is what you'll have, and a hot toddy."

I suggested stopping at Bendacre.

"The last thing we want," Jewle said as we began making our way up the steep slope to the car. "Not a soul's to be told a word about this, especially Sir Henry. That cocktail party's got to go smoothly. And we can't risk a leakage."

At Edenthorpe we went to the hotel, not to the police station. When Allman came down we had tea and began talking things over.

"What I'll do is go to Ipswich straight away and get their co-operation," Jewle said. "It's a thousand to one it's her car and she's in it, and if she's brought here, then Tagg will know it and Doctor Laving. If he knows it his brother will know it, and then all Marstead'll know it. Handle it the other way and not a soul will know it."

He rang us later. Everything had been arranged. At earliest light in the morning a derrick would be rigged up and they'd hoist the car straight on a lorry and get it away. Allman would be there, but it might be as well if I didn't come.

I woke that next morning with the realisation that it might be Zero Day. I wasn't too hopeful: perhaps I based any hopes on an identification of X more on what might be found in Lucia Black's car than on that rather melodramatic luring to Ranger's bungalow. Soon after breakfast I drove to Edenthorpe. If Jewle had been at work since before seven o'clock I thought he might be back by ten. As it happened he was even a bit earlier.

"She was in that car all right," he told me, "wedged down on the floor in the front. Those two bags were in the boot and she didn't pack 'em. Everything was just rammed in anyhow."

"What killed her?"

"They're going over her now," he said, "but it looks as if she was knocked out with a right to the chin and then strangled. Manual strangulation. No prints anywhere as yet. And I don't think there will be. If they were wiped off in the house he wouldn't have risked leaving any in the car."

There was nothing to keep me at Edenthorpe. Jewle said he had a lot of telephoning to do but he'd be at Bendacre in the early afternoon to rehearse the night's performance. It was curious back there that morning with Henry knowing nothing of the morning's work and even wondering if Lucia Black might possibly be at home again.

The rehearsal went off well and Henry seemed to be looking forward to the evening. Only one thing bothered him—getting the talk round to the question of secret drawers. He thought it might sound a bit too obvious to anyone who might overhear, and that might include the one to whom everything had to seem natural.

"I think I know what you can do," I said. "Button-hole Andover as soon as he arrives and put him up to asking the question. Tell him you'll explain later. Pretend it's some kind of joke or to do with a bet. All he'll have to do at exactly seven o'clock is be near that desk and sort of idly examining it, and then he can call out to you. Just a simple question like, 'Does this desk have any secret drawers?' You can say it certainly has, and then you come over and give a demonstration. Then I come in with my little piece." He thought that would be far more natural.

"And when you go out I just shrug my shoulders to show I don't quite know what you mean about Ranger's bureau?"

"You just be natural, Sir Henry," Jewle said. "Your main job will be to get on with seeing that everyone's got something to drink and you'll be keeping your eyes open to spot anyone who goes out."

Jewle had left Allman at the bungalow. He parked his car well beyond it and he and I went through a gate and across a meadow and got to the bungalow the back way. There was some argument about which way X would come.

I thought he would have to come by the road. It was the shortest route and he'd be working against time.

"We'll take no chances," Jewle said. "You'll nip your car in at Culver's track and then slip round to the back here. I'll take the front and I'll spot you coming in. Fred, you'll be in the actual room, ready to jump him when he goes to the bureau. Behind one of those big chairs seems to be the only spot. We'd better have a look."

At just after half-past six that night people began arriving. It had been an overcast day and by then it was dark—far darker than I'd hoped—and there was a bit of drizzle. Two waiters sent by the firm were handling things and their headquarters was the kitchen. Before seven o'clock everyone seemed to have arrived and I doubt if many more could have been crammed in, for the rooms weren't all that large. I knew practically no one and the people to whom I was introduced had their names forgotten in the effort to remember that of those who came next. Of those I did know there were the two Andovers, Sterne, Frank Laving, and his brother Robert who'd also brought a married niece and her husband from somewhere near Edenthorpe. The noise was almost deafening. My experience of cocktail parties is that noise is one of the vicious spirals. You begin talking louder to make yourself heard and that makes more noise, and you, and everyone else, talks still louder. And people always seem averse to sitting and so making more room.

You don't want to hear again what you know was to happen. It went off superbly. At least three-quarters of the guests wedged themselves round while Henry exposed the secret drawers, and then I said my piece and managed to thread my way out to the front door. I didn't hurry unduly about getting out the car. Well short of the bungalow I shut off the lights and carefully nosed the car in along Culver's track. It was so dark that it took me a good couple of minutes.

I nipped back and across the road and through the bungalow gate. There was never a sound from Jewle. I had a pencil torch and used it just enough to show the back path. I found the clump of lilac bushes just back from the narrow strip of flower garden and about twenty feet from the window of the lounge. As soon as X made his entry, my job was to move quickly to that window and cut off his exit. Jewle would look after the front.

The bushes were so tall that I didn't need to squat and I stood there with eyes trying to pierce the dark. In a minute or two I could just see the bungalow itself and half-way along it to the back path by which I'd come, and behind me was the utter blackness of the wood. There were little noises in that dark: the dripping of water from the trees and a tiny scurrying as of a mouse or rat. An owl hooted from somewhere beyond Culver's Farm and much farther away was the barking of a dog. A car went by on the road. I felt for my wrist-watch which I'd put in my pocket and shielded the dial. Only six minutes had elapsed since I'd left Bendacre and already it seemed more like an hour.

Then I heard the faint sound. It was queer, and I couldn't identify it. Only much later was I to remember it and know what it was—the deep breaths of someone who'd been running and had paused a moment to get back his wind. It seemed to be coming from behind me, and I turned quickly to face that way. A twig cracked beneath my feet and suddenly a light flashed in my face. Then something struck me and I fell backwards. I wasn't out, but I was as near it as could be. And yet my nerves must somehow have been screwed up to some queer intensity or else I'd never have heard that other noise. *It was a curious rustling sound.* It was like the almost inaudible squeaks of a mouse. The light flashed quickly again and then the something struck me a second time and that's all I knew.

I don't know how long it was before I came round, but as we worked it out afterwards, it must have been about ten minutes. The room was a blur, for when I'd fallen I'd lost my glasses. I didn't know what was happening, only that there was a bright light and that Jewle was bending over me. Then Allman came in and I learned afterwards that he'd been looking for my glasses. He cleaned them and put them on me.

"How're you now, sir?"

I went to get up but I couldn't. A rush of blood came to my head but now I knew where I was—in the lounge of the bungalow, lying on the floor, with a cushion under my head. Jewle had a basin of cold water and he began dabbing my head again.

"What's happened? Did you get him?"

"No," Jewle said. "I heard a queer noise—I think you were groaning or something—and when I came along he'd gone. You must have scared him away."

He got his arm under my shoulders till I could sit up.

"That any better?"

"A lot," I said. "But there's a devilish pain in the back of my skull."

"Drink this," he said. "Allman got it from the pub."

The brandy made me splutter and that brought on the pain again. Jewle lowered me down to the cushion.

"Nothing actually broken," he told me, "but you had a narrow squeak. Whatever he hit you with just missed the temple. You be quiet for a bit. I want to have another look outside."

He and Allman went out. I'd managed to get to my feet when they came back, and was in one of the chairs.

"That's better," he said. "What about the rest of the brandy?"

I didn't want it. I felt a bit sick. Then I *was* sick. The blood rushed unbearably to my head and then in a minute or two I felt a bit better. I even felt like talking.

"You didn't have the luck to see him?" Jewle said.

"Not a chance. His torch blinded me and the next thing I knew I was flat on my face."

"No fault of yours," he said. "He came by the wood path and the way we've worked it out, those bushes where you were lay right in his line. Anything at all you can remember?"

I said I seemed to remember him approaching me for that second time, just before he flashed his torch again and knocked me right out. And there'd been that curious noise by my head as I lay on the ground; like a tiny mouse squeaking near my ear.

"But what about the house? Oughtn't we to get along there? What if Henry's spotted someone?"

He smiled.

"Oh, no," he said. "We're staying here till everyone's gone. And you're not fit to go yet in any case. It was Sir Henry's job.

We've got to hope he had some luck. If he has—well, whoever it was won't get far. Once we have a shrewd idea who he was, that'll be the end of it."

An hour later, when Jewle had taken off the cold compress, I was feeling much better. With his arm steadying me I could walk to my car. We halted a short distance away from the house and Jewle got out to reconnoitre. He came back to say that the last guests had gone quite a time ago. We drove in. Henry was on us as soon as the door opened. Jewle didn't give him time to speak.

"What about it, Sir Henry? Who left the house?"

Henry raised his hands and let them fall.

"I don't know. I just couldn't manage it: there were so many people. I assure you I did my best, but I just couldn't keep track. But what about you? Did you—er—get him?"

Jewle let out a breath. He shrugged his shoulders. He gave that wry smile.

"Not this time. But it wasn't a wasted evening. We know that at seven o'clock he was in this room. And now, Sir Henry, I think Mr. Travers ought to get straight away up to bed. And with some sleeping tablets if you have any."

Henry was incredibly shocked. I assured him I'd be as good as new in the morning, but he fussed over me till I was in bed and watched me take the two tablets. And all the time he was full of apologies. It was hard work convincing him that the evening, as Jewel had said, had been lucky after all. The last thing I remembered thinking as I fell into sleep was that I hoped I was right.

A sound at the bedroom door woke me. There was just a sharp twinge as I reached for my glasses and looked at my watch. I thought it was a quarter to eight and that Edith Slack was bringing early tea. It was Edith, but Henry was with her. The time was twenty to nine and what was coming in was my breakfast. There was more fussing. I might be feeling better, Henry said, but I ought to take things easy. Lie on till lunch, perhaps. And he'd bring me a newspaper.

I didn't argue. I had no intention of staying on in bed. A bath and a clean-up, I knew, would put me almost right. So after I'd ruined that tray I had that bath. I came back to the bedroom and drew the curtains. The drizzle had gone. A sun—admittedly a watery one—was trying to break through. Joe Slack, coat off, sleeves rolled up, and corduroys tied in the old-fashioned way below his knees, was manuring an asparagus bed. He made quite a colourful picture against the varied reds of the tall garden wall.

I looked at him again and then there was a tap at the door and Henry came in.

"Brought you the newspaper . . . You're not getting up?"

"I've got to get up," I said. "And you've got to do something for me. Get Jewle on the telephone and tell him to come out here quick. Try the hotel first and then the police station."

By the time I'd shaved, he was back. He'd got Jewle at the hotel and he was probably on his way. Henry gave me an enquiring look but I pretended not to see it. I said I'd be down by the time Jewle arrived.

He beat me to it by a minute. He and Henry were in the sitting room. I told Jewle I was feeling fine. He nodded. Then he wanted to know why I'd asked him to come, and at the double.

"Remember that queer noise I heard last night when our friend was coming up to give me the final knock-out? Like a little mouse squeaking? Know what it was?"

He shook his head.

"Ever wear corduroys—new ones?"

Jewle's eyes popped wide.

"That was it," I said. "The rustling of corduroy trousers. And you know who never wears anything else. And who had on a nicely creased fawn pair last night? . . . Sterne!"

18

THE ACCOLADE

HENRY was horrified. And he just couldn't credit it. Sterne couldn't possibly be the man. And what made it somehow more unbelievable—this would have been amusing in less tragic circumstances—was that only a few minutes ago Sterne had rung him to suggest a game of golf for the Saturday morning.

"Exactly!" I said. "I'd be gone by then. He'd think the case had been shelved. But about Sterne and golf, Henry. Did he ever ride his bicycle to the course?"

"I didn't know he *had* a bicycle," he said. "I've certainly never seen him riding one. But wait a minute. I seem to remember seeing one in his garage one day. It didn't look as if it had been ridden for quite a time."

Jewle and I went to the study to try and fit Sterne into the scheme of things. I don't think Henry would have come if he'd been asked. And the last thing we wanted to disclose was the murder of Lucia Black.

Jewle sprang a surprise even before we'd got ourselves comfortably seated. He was most apologetic about it.

"I know it's easy to be wise after the event, but quite a few days ago I began wondering about Colonel Sterne. The way I saw things was that it had to be a local crime, and that reduced things to Sterne and Andover and Laving. I looked up Andover and he was in the clear. Laving's father was doctor here before him, so that left Sterne. He was the only one whose life history we didn't have in full. We only had it on his own relating—that he'd been fruit farming in British Columbia with his father before the war, and that his father was still there. But there was only Sterne's word for all that, and that's why I got the Yard to make enquiries at the War Office and in Canada. Just before I left this morning I got the first answers. Sterne didn't join up in British Columbia: he joined up in Montreal."

That was important, even if at the moment it wasn't anything like a keystone.

"When he left that hotel he had to go somewhere," I said. "Canada would be a good spot. And claiming British Columbia as his home would be putting any possible enquiries off the track, if he'd never gone further than Montreal."

"Yes," Jewle said. "But the rest of his story is true. He wouldn't need to make it otherwise. He wasn't a fool. He'd know he could be traced through the War Office. But listen to this: the other piece of information that came this morning. Sterne's English regiment was posted to Hong Kong soon after the war. And it was one of the regiments sent straight from there to Korea when the fighting started. You see how that works out?"

I did, with a little help. It was the first tying-in of Sterne and Ranger-Riley. Taking things in order, there is Arthur Cordage, now calling himself Sterne, arriving in England with the first Canadians. He writes to his brother Hugh and manages to convey—by some pre-arranged code—who he now is and what. He writes again when the war is over.

"Just a minute," I said. "He's supposed to have gone to British Columbia on special leave to wind up his fruit farming business. That was just lies, as was the existence of a father. If the Case had petered out, he'd have announced before the spring that his father had suddenly died. And he'd have pretended to go to Canada again to settle the estate."

"That's about it," Jewle said. "But I think he did go to British Columbia that first time, not to sell a business but to buy one. He'd want something as a background and for his brother to go to when he was released. Also, the jewels might have been cached in Canada. Not that it matters. What matters is what happened when he went to Hong Kong and Korea."

That was the tie-in with Ranger-Riley. Hugh Cordage confided in Doctor Riley, and probably in his last conscious moments. But Riley couldn't blackmail Arthur Cordage because Cordage was then in Hong Kong. And, again, when Riley was out of a job, Cordage was in Korea. But then Riley had some luck, and during the eighteen months after Helmsby, Korean prisoners were released and among them a Colonel Sterne. Riley picked up the trail when he came back to England where Sterne spent some time in a convalescent home. Then he lost him again, and our idea was that he found him by trial and error—an examination of all the telephone directories. The Sterne at Marstead seemed the most likely and so, as Ranger, Riley came to Marstead himself, taking care with the house agent that he wouldn't lose any money if that particular Sterne should be the wrong one.

Ranger had to go carefully. Years had passed since he had clapped eyes on Arthur Cordage and what with those facial wounds and the thinness, Sterne must have taken a deal of identifying. And there was the other side of things. Ranger himself would have to take care—till he was sure of Sterne—that Sterne didn't remember Doctor Riley. The whole thing might reasonably have taken the three months on which we'd always worked. After that, Ranger was on top of the world. He first extorted a lump sum in cash and thereafter received—also in cash—a monthly fifty or sixty pounds. There was no point in bleeding Sterne absolutely white: far better keep him as an investment for life.

Sterne certainly fitted in as the poisoner of Ranger. He had only to go out of his back gate and at once he was in the shelter of the wood. After that he had only to keep his eyes open to avoid being seen by any other chance user of that path.

"But what about Mrs. Black?" Jewle said. "Where does she fit in?"

We went over those cryptic remarks she'd made to me about Ranger, and that queer, satisfied smile of hers when I'd hinted that her husband had been murdered, and the same smile when I'd asked what her plans were. To my mind it all added up to this: I dramatized it a bit to bring it more forcibly home to Jewle.

"She had to begin selling things from her house. Let's suppose she offered something to Sterne, saying a dealer had offered only so much and she knew it was worth a whole lot more. Then Sterne thought of something. 'If you really want to make some money, what about doing a little job for me? This man Ranger's a hopeless outsider and the sooner the village is rid of him, the better. I have a private idea he's a crook. You're a bit pally with him, aren't you? So why not get him to talk about himself. Let's see if we can get something on him.' That's the general idea and, if he paid well enough, I think Lucia Black'd have fallen for it. I think that's how he got to know all Ranger's habits: his hours, the back-door key business and so on.

"And that's what Lucia Black was so pleased about. She knew that Sterne must have done that poisoning, and so she tried a little blackmail on her own. It didn't work."

"Sounds all right to me," Jewle said, "but it's something we'll never prove. Sterne would have to own up to it. But what about his alibi? He was at Edenthorpe at half-past six that night?"

"Why not?" I said. "Let's say he'd strangled her, packed the bags and had everything wiped off by half-past five. He went to his garage and got out that old bicycle and saw to the lamp and pumped up the tyres. Another ten minutes? Then he got her into the car, and the bags, and lashed the bicycle on the back. It was a misty night but he could easily have been at that hill ten minutes later. Say six o'clock. Nothing to do then but remove a rail and move the car in. Then he'd cycle back to Marstead and, on account of where he lived, he wouldn't have to go through the village. Say twenty minutes for all that and he still had ten minutes in which to get to Edenthorpe in his own car. He might have had considerably more. All he claimed was that he got there before seven o'clock when the garage would have closed for the night. That's something you could check through the man who was with him.

"And another thing before I forget it. Enquire about something else at the same time. We wondered why Lucia Black's receiver had been wiped. Suppose Sterne tried to make himself an alibi by ringing this man and asking if he was going to be at the bridge club, because, if so he'd pick him up. Sterne might have done that, and have said he was ringing from his own house. And something else—that bicycle. When I over-took Sterne riding it towards the golf-course the other day, I'm pretty sure he hadn't been intending to go to golf. It's a quiet back lane and there're one or two quite deep ponds on the golf course beside the road. I know: I've put balls in 'em. So I think Sterne was going to dump that bicycle. If there should happen to be enquiries he could say he never rode it and then someone stole it one day from his garage but he didn't bother to report it because it wasn't worth the reporting."

"Yes," Jewle said. "Whichever way you look at things, Sterne certainly ties in. You and I are pretty sure he's the one we want." He gave his dry smile. "But you can't arrest a man because he wears trousers that squeak."

"There're other little things," I said. "The man who coshed me had been moving pretty quick. Sterne had had to nip along to his house and get a torch and something to prize open a window, and even a weapon. Then he had to move fast along that back path, and in the dark. He'd been a commando. That wouldn't come so hard to him as to most. It was really commando work."

And yet another thing I remembered. Lucia Black had said I wasn't to come to her house till after seven o'clock. Why that particular time? Wasn't the answer that she knew Sterne would then be playing bridge at Edenthorpe? I admitted that even that wasn't much help, but we still held one trump card— Doctor Wormgay.

"Let Wormgay see him," I said. "Why does Sterne always wear long-sleeved pullovers if there isn't something visible about his left arm?"

"I daren't do it," Jewle said. "I can't bring in Sterne under suspicion and more or less set Wormgay on him without higher authority. No. What I'll do is get back to Edenthorpe and ring the Yard. I'm almost sure to have to report there and I'll arrange for Allman to see that man who was with Sterne when the car broke down. We'll have to think up some good excuse. We don't want the man to mention it to Sterne."

Henry wasn't about when we came out. I walked with Jewle to his car.

"Just one thing," he said. "When I'm at the Yard, do you think I ought to mention Sir Henry? He's been a great help to us in all sorts of ways."

"He's enjoyed it," I said. "Once he's got over the shock of Sterne's being a murderer, he'll be happy as a sandboy. Not that a little official thanks wouldn't help."

"About our friend," he said. "His car's out of order, but I think I'll have him watched. And about you. You're supposed to be leaving tomorrow, so you'd better leave—ostensibly. I suggest Cambridge. Get in touch with me at the Yard as soon as you're fixed up."

I left the next morning soon after nine o'clock. Henry, by the way, was almost his old conspiratorial self again. Even if Sterne was the man—he still held to that *if*—he couldn't help a certain pity. But Henry didn't know about Lucia Black. And, as I'd told him, I could feel a certain pity too, though not much. Sterne might have been a good soldier and, as one put it, made good, but for all that he hadn't returned those jewels or their value. And there are other ways than murder of dealing with a black-mailer—even for a man so up against it as Sterne.

I didn't know what eyes might be on my car, so I took the London Road and then circled round. It wasn't all that distance and before eleven o'clock I was ringing the Yard from a Cambridge hotel. Jewle was in conference but they had my number and just before lunch Jewle rang me. Everything was fixed, he said. Doctor Wormgay would be at Cambridge by the two-fifteen train the next day. I should meet him there with my car and bring him on to Edenthorpe. He himself would be back in Edenthorpe in a few hours.

So the next early afternoon found me at Cambridge station waiting for Doctor Wormgay's train. We met like a couple of very old friends. He was wearing a heavy tweed overcoat and a fisherman's hat, and he looked as untidy and as full of the zest of life as ever. He'd lunched on the train, so all we had to do was take things easily to Edenthorpe. He was looking pretty grim by the time I'd told him all I knew.

And so to the show-down. It ought to have been dramatic, but it wasn't. If it hadn't been for the somewhat overwhelming personality of Wormgay himself, it would have been drab, and even sordid. We were early, and only Jewle was in Tagg's room when we arrived. Sterne was due at two-thirty, he said. Jewle had rung him and said that they'd be grateful for his help in a certain matter that had arisen over Ranger's death, and Sterne had said he'd be glad to help. Jewle also told me that we'd been right about Sterne telephoning to his bridge club friend. He had not spoken to the man but to his wife, and, as far as she remembered, the time of the call was about half-past five.

Tagg and Bestable arrived. The old doctor and I were to be in an adjacent room with the door just ajar. Jewle went down to await the arrival of Sterne. When the buzz came that Sterne had arrived, Wormgay and I went into that other room.

The whole thing was over in five minutes. I couldn't see, but I could hear and visualise.

"Colonel Sterne?" That was Bestable. "Very good of you to come along. Take a seat, will you?"

Jewle was taking it up.

"You know who I am, Colonel. But I ought to warn you that you needn't answer any question that we put to you. If you do answer, it'll be entirely of your own free will."

"This is very mysterious? Just what sort of questions?"

"Well, to begin with, whether your name isn't Sterne at all. Whether it's really Arthur Cordage."

"Arthur who?"

"Arthur Cordage."

"Sorry. No can help. Never heard the name in my life."

"Then I'd like you to meet an old friend . . ."

That was our cue. I didn't follow the doctor in, but I did leave the door open. The doctor went slowly in, peering at Sterne. He halted. He smiled.

"Well," he said. "And after all these years. If it isn't Arthur Cordage!"

"Who *is* this?"

No one spoke.

"I'm Wormgay," the doctor said. "You remember? I'm the one who put that arm of yours in plaster. How is it, by the way?"

"I don't know what sort of a frame-up this is," Sterne told the room, "but I've never seen this man in my life."

"Easy to prove," Jewle said quietly. "Take off your coat, Colonel. Let the doctor have a look at your arm."

Sterne looked slowly round the room. His thin lips clamped together and then he folded his arms.

"All right," Jewle said, and charged him with the murder of Nicholas Riley, *alias* Norman Ranger.

"Take him away," Bestable said. Tagg took him away.

They took Sterne to Ipswich and he still hadn't said another word. We said goodbye to Doctor Wormgay, who was staying the night with Bestable and probably going to Ipswich in the morning for an official confirmation of that arm. Jewle was staying on for a day or two. Sterne would be formally remanded in custody and then Jewle would be busy preparing his case. I said I wouldn't be going back to town till the following Monday and he said he'd be seeing me again.

Before I left the station I used the telephone. I ought to have rung the aerodrome before, but somehow it had slipped my memory. That young officer with whom I'd dealt didn't happen to be in the Provost Marshal's office but I did speak to a staff-sergeant who remembered me. He said that Porelli had had a pretty stiff reprimand from the next higher-ups and had got off with that. He sounded as if he thought Porelli had been lucky.

There isn't much else to tell. When Henry had been told about Lucia Black and we'd been assured officially that Sterne was our man, then he changed his views. He did say that Marstead would never be quite the same place again and he even hinted at a possible change. I knew he wasn't all that serious. And something happened on my last night at Bendacre. One of the Big Bugs—as George Wharton calls them—rang him and proffered preliminary thanks, with official thanks to follow. Henry tried hard to be modest when he told me about it. I said he'd certainly have something to tell his grandchildren.

Just before I left the next morning, when I was thanking him for some superb hospitality and a patience at the way I'd disturbed the suave Bendacre routine, he said he ought really to be thanking me. He said I'd got him out of what was becoming a rut. As for the official thanks of Scotland Yard, that had been practically an accolade.

"Funny you should say that, Henry, but this case has brought me an accolade, too."

"You?" he said.

"Yes, me, Henry." I put my fingers, still not too firmly, on the back of my skull. "A queer sort of an accolade perhaps, but still an accolade."

"I don't follow you," he said. "How do you mean?"

"Look," I said. "This isn't false modesty, but do I look like the ideal detective? Could I trail a criminal? Am not I the sort of person who's once seen and never forgotten? Have I got the patient brain? Am I ruthless?"

"I can see you're not serious," he said. "In any case, I'm not pandering to your ego by any denials, not that I wouldn't like to know just how this is connected with what you called an accolade."

"Easy," I said. "No longer am I the incomplete detective. This case has made me, Henry. You've read plenty of detective novels. Novels about British and American private eyes. You know what's expected of them and what you always get: the real top-notchers, that is. They drink whisky by the quart, their morals are as lax as the clients are beautiful, and they're constantly getting slugged over the head. Well, now I'm in their class. It's taken twenty years to do it, Henry, but I've received the accolade. I too have been slugged."

He laughed.

"That's one way of looking at it." Then his look became roguish. "But you'll pardon one question. Surely you haven't received the complete accolade. What about the whisky? And the women?"

"Don't rush me," I told him. "Give me time, Henry. Give me time."

THE END

Milton Keynes UK
Ingram Content Group UK Ltd.
UKHW030656251124
3091UKWH00017B/38